MURDER IN THE MIST

Persons this *Mystery* is about—

NOLA SPAIN,
a vivid, dramatic personality with features like a cameo—as classical, as finely chiseled and as waxen pale.

GORHAM PARSONS,
a man past seventy-two, his height but five feet one, his weight one hundred five, and not a tooth in his head home-grown.

ESTHER LYNDALL,
a strong woman, decisive, almost masculine. Her weather-browned face has strength and definiteness.

RYON LYNDALL,
an artist with a little pointed beard. He is a timid, ineffectual man who lives like a boy.

TODD AMROE,
a tall, dewy-looking young man. About twenty-two or twenty-three. Golden curly hair, short, freckled, sunburned nose.

RAMONA HEATH,
a gray woman. Her face is thin, harassed, bordered in straggling, gray hair.

ISABEL CHALMERS,
a dwarf in height, a giant in girth, small features and eyes almost lost in shiny layers of fat. Her hair is gray, brushed smooth, rolled into a neat bun.

BABY DOLL,
a very pretty child, with tumbled auburn curls. She hasn't any daddy and she knows it's bad to tell lies so she never does.

MARY CARNER WHITTAKER,
an attractive, youthful, gray-eyed, brown-haired woman with a pleasant voice. She is a detective employed by the department store of J. Blankfort and Company in New York City.

CHRISTOPHER F. WHITTAKER,
a very thin, tall, sharp-featured man, also a detective. He's a sound sleeper. Can sleep like a top on the edge of a nickel.

ALICIA DONATO,
a tall woman with gaunt cheeks, a sallow skin, and a nose which is the muzzle of a thoroughbred collie, narrow, high-bridged.

PAUL DONATO,
an olive-skinned man, black-mustached, black-eyed, black-browed, with an air of good-natured insolence. He is a sculptor.

MURDER IN THE MIST

Things this *Mystery* is about—

A notched narrow ROD . . .

A pearl-set DAGGER PIN . . .

A small green BOTTLE . . .

A heavy MALLET . . .

A WEDDING RING . . .

A pair of FIRE-TONGS . . .

A gray tweed COAT . . .

An oil painting . . .

A LETTER . . .

A *MARY CARNER* DETECTIVE STORY

MURDER
IN THE MIST

By ZELDA POPKIN

Author of "Death Wears a White
Gardenia," "So Much Blood,"
"No Crime for a Lady," etc.

Author's Note—

I have no quarrel with the North Shore. I love its
fogs and foibles, bear no malice toward its dowagers and deacons. And so, lest my friends on Cape
Ann be tempted to identify themselves with charac-
ters and incidents in this book, I hasten to assure
them that each is wholly fictional and Laneport
not one place, but several which may have, at one
time or another, suggested incidents and atmosphere.

Z. P.

DELL PUBLISHING COMPANY

George T. Delacorte, Jr., *President* • Helen Meyer, *Vice-President*

149 Madison Avenue   *Printed in U.S.A.*   New York 16, N. Y.

List of *Exciting* Chapters—

Copyright, 1940, by Zelda Popkin. Reprinted by arrangement with J. B. Lippincott Company.

Murder in the Mist

Chapter One

NOLA SPAIN

MISS TEMPLETON SPREAD the cards for deal and partners. Mr. Parsons drew the highest, the king of diamonds, and Mrs. Lyndall, second high, the ten of spades.

Oh, dear, Mr. Parsons thought drearily, *I've got to play with the battle-ax.* But he changed seats with Miss Hays and faced his partner bravely.

Miss Hays shuffled the deck for him; Miss Templeton cut it.

"By rights," Miss Hays said, "Mrs. Lyndall should be first dealer. She's visiting lady."

"Certainly not," Mrs. Lyndall answered. "High card deals."

"And really,—" Miss Templeton leaned across the table to bring her long jaw level with Mr. Parsons' cheek,— "When you come right down to it, Mrs. Lyndall isn't the visiting lady. She lives in Laneport. Miss Hays and I *actually* are the visiting ladies. So you see, in that case, it would have to be one of us. You understand that, don't you, Mr. Parsons?"

Mr. Parsons sighed. These females always thought they had to explain. *I'm not infant or imbecile,* he told himself with asperity, *but they certainly treat me as if.* That was the only thing wrong with the Rockledge. It was full of garrulous, unattached, unattractive females. They made the evenings horrible.

The days were altogether different and wholly delightful. Mr. Parsons passed the long hours pleasantly in his own company and his chosen pursuits.

Gorham Parsons lived in a world that was half fantasy and half fact, and he skipped nimbly from one half to the other as though they were adjoining rooms. He looked upon the real world with incisive, sometimes devastating, perception but often he saw the things that were imaginary as clearly as the things that were real. He thought up such clever things, such poetic, exciting things, that frequently he amazed himself, but he rarely told these things to people, for he dreaded their blank stares, the polite, toothy parting of their lips. He realized full well that to share a good daydream with the prosaic people about him would be casting pearls before swine.

Few who looked upon his frail person ever guessed at the excitements behind the decorous exterior. At first glance, Gorham Parsons seemed a patchwork of shades of gray—sparse silver hair, slicked down on a small skull, bright gray eyes, parchment skin, mohair summer suit—protective coloration, blending with sand and sky and moors. The tint of living, coursing blood dwelt only in the blue-veined tips of his faun-like ears, in the occasional fever spots of excitement over his cheekbones.

A wisp of moving gray, he merged with the landscape of the wild, windswept moors where 300 years ago there had been the lively first settlement of the village of Lane and today there were only boulders, scrub pines and bayberry bushes. There he spent the rainless mornings, poking his walking stick among the stones of abandoned cellars, hunting—never finding, but always hoping to find—a button, a coin, a scrap of flint, which might link him tangibly to the past. Sometimes he sat amid the tumbled stones which once had been the cellars of Abby Drake and Nancy Loveran, evoking out of what he had read and what he had imagined, the sharp-tongued, strong-willed dames who had been the weird sisters of Lane. Often, when the day was gray as the moors and he was alone, he held convention with these witches, asked them searching questions about the black arts and received their answers.

"*Abigail,*" he would say to the shade of Abby Drake, "*tell me the truth. Did you actually bewitch those oxen? And what is there in that gossip about the wood hopping off the wagon before your door?*"

"*Why, of course, Mr. Parsons,*" Abigail would answer him. "*A witch can do anything she puts her mind to—that is, if people believe she can. Ask Nancy Loveran. She'll tell you.*"

"*You girls!*" Mr. Parsons would chuckle. "*I rather surmise you fancied yourselves, my fine dames, and started the rumors on purpose. However, it's possible you had the power. Everything's possible. I don't deny that you knew what you knew and did what you did.*"

For the rainy days, there were the old sea captains, ill-at-ease in their stuffy parlors, grateful for a listener to their maunderings of courage and of terror at sea, to their scraps of legend, superstition—the lone birds that lighted on the deck, the women in white who came out of the mist to warn when death was near. Or there was the charming library, where pretty young librarians brought him the records of the Cape Historical Society, searched out for him memorabilia of the settlement of Lane. Mr. Parsons told them he was writing a book. But he wasn't. He was merely indulging in the pleasure of acquiring knowledge —one of the few sensual delights that remain to a man who has passed 72, has sound investments, a querulous digestion and has been a widower so long that he remembers only that his wife had pretty hands and violet eyes.

When Mr. Parsons tired of antiquities, there was always the sand and the sea—the white sweep of Hadley's beach, rainbow-splotched by bright umbrellas and gay bathing dresses, and the clouds and the sky and the lazy sails. He lay in the sand, warming his old arteries, bringing charging steeds, combat battalions out of the drifting clouds, racing his doughty sloop across the horizon, rejoicing at his private triumphs, smiling at his witticisms.

Even the piazzas at the Rockledge were not too bad in those hours when the other guests were taking their endless strolls up and down Johnson's Neck, performing their daily pilgrimages from gift shoppe to tea shoppe or setting up their easels on rotting wharves, to paint atrocious impressions of obvious—far too obvious—quaintness. When the porches were empty, it was pleasant to rock slowly back and forth in a well-grooved splint rocker and inquire into the private lives of gulls and sandpipers. One yellowbill stood alone, on one leg, at the very peak of the ledge, nursing a private grievance. *Like me*, Mr. Parsons would tell himself, *he hates crowds; he can't abide that hustle-bustle, that clack-clack-clack, gab-gab-gab, screechscreech-screech of the flock around him.*

Mr. Parsons loved Laneport. He no longer saw or smelled the narrow, winding, ugly streets of the fishing town. Once he had passed the drying sheds of the Laneport Fisheries, he gave himself up whole-heartedly to a world of beauty—azure sea, pounding copper rocks; green lanes, arched by drooping willows; the glorious mountain ash in golden flower, New England gardens riotously blooming; soft, moist air, soothing and stimulating, both at once, tangy with the sea and sweetly scented with the clethra.*

Mr. Parsons had been coming and coming back to Laneport for 15 years, always to the Rockledge, always to the

---

* Clethra, the white alder, a fragrant white-flowered shrub, grows profusely in the moist soil of the Massachusetts North Shore. Its scent, the fishermen insist, is wafted far out to sea, informing them, long before they glimpse the shore, that they are nearing home.

same room in the Annex, to the affectionate offices of Marcus Aurelius Smythe, the ebon chef, and Delia, the hardy perennial of the Rockledge waitresses. Marcus Aurelius kept Mr. Parsons' Postum, his kumquat marmalade, his chutney, on a separate shelf in the pantry, and Delia served them faithfully.

Thus his days were most agreeable. But his evenings were agony, for he was shy and there were too many females at the Rockledge—females like Miss Templeton and Miss Hays, who had rooms above him in the Annex, who taught school three seasons of the year and spattered oil paints at Laneport through the fourth, who talked a great deal about culture and personified it by wearing batik blouses, bouclé suits and hand-loomed scarfs by day, heavy strings of amber beads, Florentine silver chains, and *pince-nez* by night. And because Mr. Parsons was male and un-attached, even though his height was but five foot one, his weight 105, and not a tooth in his head home-grown, they hounded him.

There was no escape for the poor old man. He had never learned to like the movies: they were too definite, putting men and women and events into too rigid a pattern. The teas and private exhibitions in the artists' studios and the lectures at the larger hotels—"My Trip along the Nile," "My Visits to the Homes of the English Poets," illustrated with slides—filled him with horror, in contemplation as much as in attendance.

The Rockledge itself offered no refuge. It was a bar-racks, built during those esthetically arid years when Chester Alan Arthur was President of the United States. It offered in Main and Annex, bed, board and piazza to some 40 ladies and a few gentlemen. Its dining-room was vast and sunny, open to the sea, hung with faded cretonne and the framed masterpieces of departed artist-guests, presented with suitable compliments to the Misses Dow and Moffett who ran the Inn—plump, amiable spinsters, pompadoured, energetic, advertising by their girth the culinary skill of Marcus Aurelius Smythe.

Miss Dow and Miss Moffett ran a good hostelry—unpretentious, but clean and adequate. The bedrooms were bare as ship's cabins and as neat—white-painted iron bedsteads, white-painted dressers, a rocker with a white towel headrest, white tie-back curtains, a solitary, unshaded electric light swinging from the center of the ceiling. Hot and cold water, both tepid, dribbled from the superannuated plumbing.

The public rooms of the hotel consisted of a single large lobby, cluttered with chintz and plush—the harvest of a dozen country auctions—a *mélange* of bad Victorian and overstuffed Calvin Coolidge, touched up with a few odd bits of green-painted wicker and one or two good Colonial pieces—a pie-crust table, a spinet desk. On the mantel shelf over the fireplace, where, on frigid evenings, a coal fire glowed agreeably, a pair of bronze book-ends, reproducing that ubiquitous bit of sculpture "The Fairy Princess," held a dog-eared copy of *Anne of Green Gables,* an Edgar Wallace and a Chamber of Commerce volume of *Trips Around the Cape.* Mr. Parsons had read the *Trips Around the Cape* twice, had taken them once.

The pride and glory of the Rockledge was its view. No other of the sprawling, inflammable hostelries which dotted the Cape could boast a finer. The Rockledge occupied the corner where Central Road met Johnson's Neck—the peninsula of studios and shoppes dividing the inner and outer harbors of the port. Its main entrance was on Central Road and the Annex was around the corner on Johnson's Neck. A wide, covered piazza joined the buildings. One could step from the porch on the ocean side, cross two feet of turf to a low cement wall and over that, drop down to the sea itself. But the Rockledge guests rarely went toward the sea. By day, the ample dowagers and past middle-aged gentlemen rocked sedately, dozing between dialogues.

After dinner, they assembled, the ladies in long, baggy, black and white chiffon dinner dresses, the gentlemen in white flannels and blue suit coats, to watch the setting sun, and they promenaded dutifully from one end of the veranda to the other, their tapping canes punctuating their polite pleasantries.

From one side of the piazza they could see the spires and wharves of Laneport and the massed spars of its fishing fleet; from the other they looked over the limitless expanse of sky and water, past the Coast Guard seaplane hangars on Lane's Island in the outer harbor, past the breakwater, past the Cape Point light. At high tide that view was superb. At low tide, when the sea deserted the wet sands and periwinkle-crusted rocks, the rinds of grapefruit and watermelon, the splintered wreckage of broken crates, twined with the slimy fingers of seaweed; the rotting carcasses of defunct mackerel and pollack, sight and smell were nauseating and the ladies and gentlemen held their noses and fled to the gift shoppes and tearooms.

With nightfall, the air invariably grew chill; the dark, murmuring sea dropped hints of terror. And Mr. Parsons had no place to go, nothing to do. The few men who came to Rockledge were too uxoriously attached. Gorham Parsons was alone and restless and lonely.

Mr. Parsons had struggled long and hard against association with the Rockledge females, but when Miss Templeton had importuned him to make a fourth this Saturday night with her friend, Miss Hays, and her friend, Mrs. Lyndall, he knew that he had no choice. The hours between eight o'clock and half past ten must be filled somehow or sleep would never come. Mr. Parsons slept badly enough, in any case. His mind was too active, and even in sleep, it never ceased its restless weaving of lively fantasies.

He picked up his bridge hand, looked at it without interest, and as he said "by" absently, he wondered whether it had been sheer desperation or a basic weakness in his character that had made him agree to join this game. From the bottom of his heart, he disliked these women—Miss Templeton and Miss Hays for their vapid chatter, Mrs. Lyndall for her overbearing manner. If it were a basic weakness, he must fight harder—resist to the death. . . .

Mrs. Lyndall snapped him out of his self-examination. She said irritably, "I bid one club, partner. Didn't you hear me?" She startled him so that he answered automatically, "One no trump." No one was more amazed than he to find himself playing, at three no trump, a hand which held a king of diamonds, a jack of spades, a jack of clubs, a singleton heart, and all the threes and fours in the deck. He was not the least surprised when, after Miss Templeton led a heart, they were set four.

"You had no right—you simply had no right—to bid a no trump with a singleton," Mrs. Lyndall said coldly. "I thought you understood the game."

A mollifying pleasantry leaped into Mr. Parsons' larynx, but he looked at Mrs. Lyndall and decided not to try it. She was a forbidding female—a massive woman with a granite face. There was a hairy mole on the jutting cliff of her jaw. It reminded Mr. Parsons of a clump of gorse on the moors. It fascinated him to watch it bobbing as she talked.

Miss Templeton nestled to him again. "You see, Mr. Parsons, you shouldn't have bid the no trump unless you had protection in hearts—three times to the queen or the ace or the guarded king, so that if I were to lead hearts, as I actually did, you'd have had a stopper. Mrs. Lyndall is quite right to be resentful. Because she had a very good hand and with your singleton she probably could have made game in clubs. You didn't warn her. The main thing in contract is the bidding—giving your partner correct information."

Mr. Parsons listened with an air of earnest and amiable contemplation. He was trying to decide whether Miss

Templeton's front teeth were 10 years younger than her face—or 20.

Miss Templeton might have gone on explaining indefinitely, bouncing little pebbles of spittle against his face, had not her friend, Miss Hays, felt impelled to rescue Mr. Parsons from excessive instruction. "Possibly," she suggested, "Mr. Parsons had something else on his mind. His work. I'll wager he was thinking about those mysterious researches of his out on the Common."

Mr. Parsons knew then how thoroughly he despised these women. They were the sort, he decided, who are born to wither on the vine. Never to ripen, never to bear fruit. Just to dry up and blow away. And they talked so much. He decided that he liked Mrs. Lyndall better. She didn't clack. Her weather-browned face had strength and definiteness. She moved with an air of competence, not wasting words or gestures. A strong woman, decisive, almost masculine.

But patiently, resenting the intrusion into his private life, he answered Miss Hays, "There's nothing mysterious about my researches. I'm merely interested in the history of the old settlement."

"Ah, yes, the deserted village," Miss Hays breathed asthmatically, closed her eyes. "*Vain transitory splendors! Could not all Reprieve the tottering mansion from its fall?*" She pressed her chest with her palm, rolled her eyes ceilingward.

"That's from Goldsmith," Miss Templeton explained. "*The Deserted Village*. I knew it immediately. Miss Hays and I read poetry to each other." She beamed on Miss Hays. "You spoke it beautifully, dear."

Miss Hays acknowledged the compliment with a deprecatory bob. "I am very fond of the poem," she said. "But Laneport's deserted village isn't the least like Goldsmith's. It's so—so completely empty. Just rocks and ghosts. It's so eerie. Don't you just love to go up there, Mrs. Lyndall?"

Mrs. Lyndall shrugged. "It doesn't excite me. I've known it all my life. Ryon's painting up there today." She frowned, as if she had thought of something. She added, "He hadn't come home when I left."

"Oh, he's too, too wonderful. I think your son's just wonderful," Miss Templeton bubbled.   •

Mrs. Lyndall's face softened. It was plain she, too, thought her son was wonderful.

"Such a true artist!" Miss Hays gushed. "Don't you think Ryon Lyndall is a true artist, Mr. Parsons?"

Mr. Parsons shifted in his seat, trying to evade the eyes of the women. To his mind, Ryon Lyndall was no artist at all. But he kept the peace. He said tactfully, "I think he's very sincere in his work," and added quickly, "But I don't set myself up as an art critic. I fear my appreciation is limited to the works of Mr. Maxfield Parrish."

"Maxfield Parrish!" The ladies moved away from Mr. Parsons. It was as though he had said a naughty word.

Mr. Parsons spoke up quickly: "Shall we play? Miss Templeton deals."

They played four hands in comparative silence. Mr. Parsons kept his mind on the game and redeemed his reputation. He and his partner won the first rubber and the deal came back to Miss Templeton.

Miss Templeton picked up the deck. She dealt a card to each of them and then she stopped, pressed the pack against her diaphragm and hissed to Miss Hays, "There she is."

A woman had come in from the porch by the back door. She had crossed the lobby swiftly to the little counter behind which Miss Moffett, her moon-face etched by silver spectacles, sat among her ledgers and keys, eating peanut brittle out of a paper bag while she totaled up the cash on hand.

From their table near the fireplace, the bridge players had only a back and profile view of the young woman.

Atop a slender, graceful throat she carried a superb mass of copper-colored hair, braided and piled into a coronet. Her dress was an ankle-length gown of India print—reds, blues and browns—tight across her small bosom, flaring over her hips. There were red sandals on her feet.

"Her toes!" Miss Hays gasped. "Painted! She hasn't even stockings on." She blushed for the shamelessness of the red-haired woman.

Miss Templeton breathed, "Imagine! At the Rockledge." She giggled self-consciously. "Miss Moffett must be having fits."

Miss Moffett's face, behind the counter, showed no imminent signs of epilepsy. She was answering a question imperturbably, as though all lodgers were alike to her. They could hear her high, nasal voice: "Cross the street. Take the first turn to the right, up the hill. Mr. Donato's is the third house on the left."

"Thank you." The young woman's voice was husky. "My child—she'll be safe, won't she?"

Miss Moffett answered, "Oh, quite."

The young woman said "Thank you" again and turned around.

Mr. Parsons knew that he had seen her face before. It was a thin face, lost in the shadows of the tower of copper hair. She would look better, Mr. Parsons decided, with her hair unplaited, flowing. Yes, that was the coiffure for her. Then one might see how large her eyes were, how delicately modeled her chin and nose and cheekbones. Her features were like a cameo—as classical, as finely chiseled and as waxen pale. But as it was now, her face seemed all shadow—dark circles under the eyes, hollows in the cheeks and a gash of rouge on her lips. Dangling carnelian earrings fenced her cheeks, seemed to press her face together. She held a lighted cigarette between her fingers. *She looks ill*, Mr. Parsons told himself, *ill or distressed*. It seemed to him that she frowned as she glanced at the foursome around the bridge table and that her lips curled. *Can't say I blame her,* he thought; *she probably knows what they're saying about her.*

The young woman looked away quickly, walked across the lobby, opened the front door and went out. Mr. Parsons thought he had never seen anything more beautiful than the fluid movement of her body. *She walks,* he told himself, *like a young tree swaying.*

When the door had closed behind her, Miss Templeton said, "She has the room under mine. In the Annex. On the ground floor. The front room of the A suite. There's a child with her."

"Is there really?" Mr. Parsons was deeply interested. "A pleasant diversion indeed to have a child at Rockledge."

"No treat for me," Miss Hays said sourly. "I've thirty-five from September to June. That's quite enough for a whole year."

"I saw *it* in the dining-room," Miss Templeton added. "Impertinent little thing. Gave itself grown-up airs."

"How old was the child?" Mrs. Lyndall asked.

"About four or five."

"Oh! Any father in sight?"

Miss Templeton smirked. "You wouldn't expect *that,* would you?"

"She asked the way to Donato's," Miss Hays put in. "Do you think she's a friend of Mrs. Donato?"

"More likely of Mister," Miss Templeton suggested. "That sort of woman usually is."

Mr. Parsons cleared his throat. "You really don't know what sort of woman she is," he protested.

Mrs. Lyndall answered sharply, "You can guess."

"Oh, Miss Moffett," Miss Templeton called to the inn-keeper, "that woman who just went out. What's her name?"

"Some queer name," Miss Moffett gulped her peanut **brittle.** "I'll look at the register. . . . A very odd name. Spain.

Nola Spain."

"Where's she from, Miss Moffett?" Miss Hays asked.

"New York."

"Oh, New York!" The spinsters exchanged glances, as if the mention of the metropolis affirmed their suspicions of the character of Nola Spain. "Is she staying long?"

"I've no idea. She's on a day rate." Miss Moffett's aloofness indicated a commendable disinclination to discuss her guests.

"Who is she? Do you know?" Miss Templeton persisted.

"A model, I believe."

The ladies exclaimed "oh" and Mr. Parsons thought "*oh*," but with a vastly different intonation. So she was a model. Oh, yes, so she was, so she was. Mr. Parsons realized, with sudden glee, why her face had seemed so familiar. He had seen it at least a hundred times, in plaster, in *papier-mâché*, in chocolate bronze and green bronze—in advertisements, on Christmas cards. Except that wherever he had seen it, it had worn a swirl of drapery, a diadem on flowing hair, had carried a wand, and the arms were upstretched and eager, the face smiling and the name of "Fairy Princess" was engraved on her pedestal. There she was on the mantelpiece—two of her in bronze. He squirmed around to look at the book-ends. Ah, yes, it was she. So it was.

Now she had come, in the flesh, to stay at the Rockledge. The "Fairy Princess," looking sad and ill, as, Mr. Parsons reflected somberly, fairy princesses probably would look if they had to live with mortals. But he smiled with delight over the pleasant surprise that had come into all their lives.

The ladies saw his smile, misunderstood it, brought him promptly out of his daydream. "Shall we play?" Miss Templeton asked.

"Oh, certainly," Mr. Parsons answered with an alacrity he did not feel. He was relieved and grateful when his partner ventured, "Would you all mind too much if we stopped now?"

"Why, Mrs. Lyndall?" Miss Hays asked. "Are you tired?"

Mrs. Lyndall nodded as if articulation was too wearing.

Miss Templeton swept the cards together. "I'd rather just chat myself," she said. "That's what we seem to be doing anyway. We've done a lot more talking than card-playing."

Mrs. Lyndall pushed back her chair. "I wonder if you'll excuse me," she said. "Ryon. He hadn't got home yet when I left to come here. I'd like to make sure he's had his dinner."

"These artists!" Miss Hays simpered. "Never thinking about mundane things. How would genius ever survive if there weren't conscientious people like dear Mrs. Lyndall to look after them?"

"It's a pleasure to look after Ryon," Mrs. Lyndall said.

Mr. Parsons helped Mrs. Lyndall with her wrap. She picked up her cane. Mr. Parsons took his own cane. "I shall be happy to escort you home," he said.

Mrs. Lyndall shook her head emphatically. "Good heavens, no. I wouldn't think of it. . . . Good night, all. It has been a pleasant evening."

"In spite of my unfortunate three no trump?" Mr. Parsons ventured.

Mrs. Lyndall gave him her hand to show that she had forgiven. She said briskly, "Good night, Miss Moffett."

Miss Moffett answered, "Good night, Mrs. Lyndall, do come and see us again soon. Always glad to have you."

Mr. Parsons walked her to the door, followed her out on the porch. The night was clammy with the insweeping fog. The street lights at the corner wore fuzzy feather boas of mist.

"You're certain you'll be all right?" Mr. Parsons asked anxiously. He was relieved when she answered, "Quite. I was raised on these fogs. It's perfectly safe in Laneport, day or night. Safe as a church."

Mr. Parsons closed the front door of the Inn behind him. He leaned over the porch rail, watching Mrs. Lyndall as she rounded the corner and was gulped by the mist on Johnson's Neck. He shivered in the chill air and he remembered Nola Spain. *She's out in this, without a wrap,* he thought; *she'll catch her death of cold.*

He went down the steps and peered into the darkness as if he were looking for her. He shook his head fretfully and turned back. He stared at the entrance to the Rockledge.

The lobby lamps glowed warmly behind the frosted, etched-glass door pane and the curtained front windows. A gilt-painted sign flapped under a lighted reflector above the steps. On the porch columns, flanking the sign, hung two ship lanterns, one red, one green. Mr. Parsons cherished the lanterns. Whenever he looked at them steadily enough, the Rockledge turned into a ship. He watched them now and listened to the swish of the tide. The rhythm of the waves caressed his brain and addled it a little, until he began to see the sprawling white hostelry swaying, rolling, like a vessel with the waves beneath it and the fog swirling around it. So potent was his hallucination that he gripped the balustrade and pulled himself, lurching, up the steps, as though he were climbing a gangway.

The piazza was a deck and he leaned across the rail, spying into the dark. *"I am a captain—I am the captain of my soul—I am the master of my fate,"* he declaimed to himself, *"adrift on a dark sea, a fearful sea."* The fog-shrouded street lamps were the beckoning lights of a distant shore; the passing automobiles hissed like waves parted by the prow. The moo of the foghorn on the Point came faintly to his ears. His heart thumped. *It is a dangerous night,* he said to himself; *we are drifting in a fog. Drifting, drifting on a storm-tossed sea. . . . We are in deadly peril.*

He shuddered. He clung desperately to the rail. And then he heard a slap-slap-slapping sound and he thought, shaken with distress, *Oh, dear, oh, dear, there's a man over-*

board. Swimming for dear life in the heavy seas. What shall I do? How shall I save him?

He was spared an answer. A tall, young, good-looking man, in slacks and sweater, emerged from the haze, looked up at the Rockledge sign, ran up the steps, saw Mr. Parsons at the rail, lifted a yachtsman's cap, asked breathlessly, "Where can I get some information?"

Mr. Parsons touched his sleeve, "Why, you're not even wet," he cackled. "A miracle!"

The young man stared at him and Mr. Parsons recognized the familiar, uncomprehending look of the alien, thrust abruptly into his secret world. He sighed and he said, "I didn't see you coming."

The young man shrugged. "Is the office inside?" he asked impatiently.

Mr. Parsons opened the door for him, indicated Miss Moffett. He followed the young man into the lobby and closed the door upon the fog-filled night.

Chapter Two

THE SILVER HAMMERS

Miss TEMPLETON AND Miss Hays had put away the card table and were seated side by side upon a sofa. Miss Templeton patted the armchair next to her. Her head bobbed a peremptory invitation to Mr. Parsons to sit down. Mr. Parsons looked around for succor, saw none, sank into the chair. He cocked his ear toward the young man at the lobby counter. He heard the young man ask Miss Moffett:

"Is Nola Spain stopping here?"

When Miss Moffett answered "Yes," the young man demanded eagerly, "Is she in, do you know?"

"She's gone out," Miss Moffett replied. "A short while ago."

"Oh." The young man's jaw fell. He prodded the carpet with his toe. Then he said, "Will you give her a message? . . . Just tell her the *Cynisca's* in. She'll understand."

"The *Cynisca's* in," Miss Moffett repeated impassively. She wrote the message on a slip of paper, stuck it into a mail cubicle.

"You'll give her that message?" The young man seemed very anxious and a shade distressed.

Miss Moffett melted. "I believe she's gone up to Donato's. Know where that is?"

The young man said, "No," and, "How do I get there?"

Miss Moffett told him. He seemed grateful. He fairly ran out of the lobby.

Miss Templeton sniffed and said loudly, "Well!"

Mr. Parsons felt in no mood to argue. He relaxed in his chair, thinking how right it was that Prince Charming had come to seek the Fairy Princess, had come on the *Cynisca*. Cynisca—cygnet—a swan—the swan boat—Lohengrin. . . . Come to rescue Elsa. How interesting the world was if one had the gift of fantasy!

Miss Hays barged right into his daydream, pushed it out of her way. "Did you walk Mrs. Lyndall home?" she asked.

He shook his head.

Miss Templeton said, "It was too bad Mrs. Lyndall had to leave. We could have played another rubber."

"She's so marvelous, so devoted to her son, always doing things for him," Miss Hays jabbered.

"Even though it's so hard for her to get around. She's a bit lame, have you noticed?"

"Lame?" Miss Hays said acidly. "She's not lame. It's bunions."

Mr. Parsons shrank into his coat collar. How could women be so crass?

The outside door opened just then and a middle-aged woman came in with a younger one shuffling behind her. The elder woman wore a tight, pinched expression and a tight, pinched permanent wave, corrugated like the beards of the Assyrians; a printed chiffon dinner gown dragging under a white sports coat and glittering *pince-nez* over small, hard eyes. The younger would look like her mother one day, Mr. Parsons realized, looked like her already, although she was trying her best not to. She had the older woman's absurd, small nose, the pouting mouth, the sallow, unattractive skin, the little, myopic eyes. Her chest was concave. Yet, with all that handicap, she strove for the casual grace of youth. Her mouse-colored hair was done in a long sleek bob, curled just above her shoulders. She wore saddle oxfords, a white sports dress, bloused over her inadequate bust, a blue jacket to hide her spindly hips. Her lips and nails were scarlet and she slouched. Mr. Parsons thought of her name—Lorna Doone Bean—and groaned,

"Oh, dear, oh, dear, how can people be so cruel to their children?"

Mrs. Bean and Miss Bean crossed to the corner where Mr. Parsons sat with the spinsters. He got up gallantly to offer his chair. Mrs. Bean sank into it and rewarded him with what she fancied was a gracious smile. "Pull up a chair, Lorna-dear," she said.

Lorna-dear tilted her chin and crouched on the arm of the sofa.

Miss Templeton smiled at her. "Did you have a nice walk, Miss Bean?"

Miss Bean glared. "Oh, yes," she answered. "Simply thrilling." She rolled the *r*.

Mr. Parsons drifted away, moving, one step at a time, softly, like a cat, so that they might not notice his departure and summon him back. Miss Bean's voice floated with him: "So exciting. . . . Mother wanted to go down to the Bonnie Blue Bell. They have such pretty Christmas cards. She always buys her Christmas cards in July. . . ."

"Just like Mrs. Roosevelt," Miss Templeton smirked.

"Don't mention her!"

Mr. Parsons stopped in his tracks, halted by the passion in Mrs. Bean's voice. He swung around. The lady's face was purple; the cords of her throat were taut.

Miss Bean hunched her narrow shoulders. "Mother can't even bear the name. She blames That Man for all my poor dead father's troubles."

"Miss Templeton didn't know. She had no idea." Miss Hays defended her companion loyally. "But you did have a nice walk, didn't you?"

"The walk was quite pleasant." Mrs. Bean recovered her poise. "Even though Lorna grumbled every single minute. I really don't know what ails the child. She certainly can't expect me to let her run around with all those wild—"

Miss Bean got off the arm of the sofa, strolled toward the windows where Mr. Parsons stood moodily staring out into the thick night. Her mother's voice pierced his mastoid bones: "We walked all the way down the Neck and we went into the Copper Kettle. Their vanilla ice cream, with the ginger, is simply delicious."

"Very thrilling," Miss Bean muttered into Mr. Parsons' ear.

He smiled at her consolingly. "Older people appreciate small pleasures," he said.

"Older people. Older people. Only older people. . . . Buried alive in this tomb!"

"Why, Miss Bean!" Her fervor startled him and pleased him, too. The child had more spirit than he had imagined —very commendable, very promising.

"—then we walked over to the Marine Railways and there was the most magnificent yacht in. Lorna wanted to stay and look at it but the fog was getting bad. . . ."

"The *Cynisca*," Miss Bean breathed dreamily. "The most beautiful thing I ever saw. The *Cynisca*. Isn't it a glorious name?"

Mr. Parsons hesitated. *Shall I tell her?* he asked himself. *Dare I?* Tentatively, he began, "Probably a derivation of the word 'cygnet'—a swan—a swan boat—the boat in which Lohengrin came for Elsa. There's a young man on that boat—a tall young man with curly golden hair . . ."

"A young man!" The words leaped from Lorna Bean's lips and eyes.

"He came to find Nola Spain."

"Nola Spain? That exotic creature—with the child? The one who has the room opposite us?"

"So you've seen her too. She's beautiful."

"Oh, yes, she is," Miss Bean answered darkly. "Too beautiful for a place like this."

He braced himself to try to tell her that beauty was a necessary thing—for this place—for any place—but Mrs. Bean forestalled him. "Lorna," she shrilled. "Come, dear. We've got to get to bed. You're very tired."

"Ten o'clock." Miss Bean spoke through clenched teeth. "Ten o'clock. Saturday night. Go to bed, Lorna."

That girl will crack, Mr. Parsons thought; *she'll do something desperate*. But he touched her sleeve, said gently, "Good night, my dear. You can see the swan boat tomorrow."

"Tomorrow. Tomorrow. She'll never let me see anything —do anything. . . . All right, I'm coming, mother, I'm coming."

Again, Mr. Parsons stood alone at the window, his eyes looking out into darkness, his mind picking up the bright threads of his fancies. He barely turned his head when Miss Fern Godwin, the artist-in-residence at Rockledge, swept in with her party and filled the room with stale sachet and chatter. He did not move from the window until the door had opened once more and he heard the voice of his friend, Dr. McAlistir. Then he came away, gladly, and strolled over to the doctor. His head came to Dr. McAlistir's shoulder. He looked like an impertinent gnome, cocking his head over one shoulder and peering up into the taller man's face. "Well, Alpheus, gadding again?"

Dr. McAlistir twirled the end of his white mustache, straightened his shoulders, drew his stomach in. Then he exhaled sharply and chuckled. "It's no use, Gorham. Let's sit down. There's a limit to what flesh and blood—"

They found a sagging sofa beside the front door, away from the jabbering women. Dr. McAlistir stretched his flannel-clad legs. "Now I can have some peace. Lucy's gone to bed. She's got to get up early for church. Gad, how that woman can gad! Came up here for a rest and discovered culture. Culture! At her age! If it isn't art class, it's shopping. If it isn't shopping, it's an exhibition or a studio tea. Or a lecture. And church too! I shall rebel, Gorham. I warn you, I shall rebel. . . ."

Mr. Parsons smiled sympathetically.

"This shindig tonight. Lucy kept talking and talking about that wonderful artist, that great sculptor, Donato. Donato. Donato. For two whole weeks the woman's been angling for an invitation."

"I could have told her how to get one," Mr. Parsons said. "Make a noise like a prospective customer. It's one sound that can be heard from the Point to the Common."

Dr. McAlistir slapped his thigh. "Excellent, Gorham, excellent. I'll remember that. Tell it to Lucy in the morning. But the joke's on us. We were invited to Donato's and he wasn't there. His wife made some lame excuse about his being called away suddenly. That's an obnoxious female, Gorham."

"Most of them are," Mr. Parsons assisted. "All but a very few."

Dr. McAlistir raised his furry brows. "That one's the worst," he said. "All tongue and bones. Cut yourself on her clavicle."

"Many people there?" Mr. Parsons asked.

"Many? It was the Union Station! I don't like a sculptor's studio, Gorham. Reminds me of a dissection lab. Cadavers. Winding sheets. But the women loved it." He shook his head. "Longer I live, the more women amaze me. They're born ghouls. Nothing scared 'em; everything pleased 'em."

"Was there a red-haired woman there? A very beautiful young woman?"

"Ah, Gorham!" Dr. McAlistir winked. "Nothing wrong with your eyes!"

"Well, was there?" Mr. Parsons persisted.

"Come to think of it, there was. An arty creature. Smoked constantly. Looked tubercular. Just stayed a little while. A young man called for her."

So Prince Charming had found the Fairy Princess, had taken her away. His mind relieved, Mr. Parsons leaned against the sofa back, watching the ladies swish back and forth, shrilling good-nights, and hobbling off to bed. The lobby at last was empty. Miss Moffett clicked off the bridge lamp, looked inquiringly at the two old men. They understood the hint. They stretched their legs, commenced to get up. Then the front door opened and two strangers came in. The old men dropped back on the sofa.

A pretty, youngish woman and a very thin, tall, sharp-featured man had entered. The strangers wore city clothes, dark and wrinkled. On the lapel of the woman's blue silk suit, a listless white orchid drooped in a nest of amber lilies-of-the-valley. The brown hair under her pert, small hat was wind-blown, her nose shiny. A heavy tweed sport coat hung, cape-fashion, across her shoulders.

The man took off his fedora politely. A few grains of rice dribbled from it. He looked from them to the young woman and grinned.

"Bride and groom, Gorham," Dr. McAlistir whispered. "Gad, sir, it stirs the blood!"

"Alpheus!" Mr. Parsons seemed shocked. "At your age!"

The doctor leered. The two old men bent forward, cocked their best ears toward Miss Moffett's counter. They heard the man say, "Policeman at the Information Booth sent us. Said you had accommodations for transients. We'll have a double with bath."

Miss Moffett answered, "The best I can do tonight is a double in a suite. Out in the Annex. It's a large room, quite comfortable, but you'll have to share the bath with the other party."

The young woman pouted and the man shook his head negatively at Miss Moffett.

"I'm sorry," the innkeeper said. "There isn't another vacant double in the house. I've two nice singles, with bath." She looked at them dubiously. "On the same floor, in Main."

"No sale," the man said quickly. "The lady's my wife. Married today."

"Oh!" Miss Moffett's expression wavered between sympathy and embarrassment. "If you'd made a reservation—"

"We did," the man replied. "At Kennebunkport. Didn't expect to stop here at all. Missed a turn and lost time on the road out of Salem. That road's a terror, ma'am. Narrow, winding macadam. Slippery as hell. And fog so thick you can spread it on bread."

Miss Moffett bristled. "The North Shore road is very beautiful," she said coldly. "Our guests don't usually arrive as late as this."

The young woman spoke up. "Let's take whatever there is, darling." Her voice was pleasant but very tired. "And be glad to get it." She slipped her sport coat from her shoulders, folded it over her arm. "I'm dead tired."

"Right you are, ma'am. Whatever you say, ma'am. . . . Any port in a storm."

Miss Moffett swung the register around and thrust it toward the couple. The man tried the desk pen, groaned. He took a fountain pen from his pocket. He said, "How'll I write it—Mr. and Mrs. Mary Carner—or—"

The young woman laughed. "Goose! There isn't any Mary Carner any more. The name's Whittaker. Mr. and Mrs. Christopher F."

He answered, "O.K., beautiful, O.K.—no harm in asking."

"They're going into the Annex, with us," Dr. McAlistir whispered to Mr. Parsons. But before Mr. Parsons could tell his friend how pleased he was that there would be so many attractive new people in the Annex—the "Fairy Princess" and her little girl and this lively young couple— the strangers wounded him to the heart. While Miss Moffett was sorting her keys, the young woman murmured to her husband, "This isn't a hotel, Chris. It's a museum."

Her husband answered, "You bet. We're in the Egyptian room. Don't look now, but there are a couple of mummies on the sofa."

The woman's eyes flickered over Mr. Parsons and Dr. McAlistir. She dimpled. "You're a hound, Chris. They look like darlings."

Mr. Parsons felt a little better. He watched the couple go out the back way to the porch which led to the Annex, heard the man ask Miss Moffett, "What *is* that weird noise?" and Miss Moffett answer, "The foghorn at Cape Point," and the man say, flippantly, "Ah, yes, pity the poor sailors on a night like this."

Dr. McAlistir shook his head reprovingly. "City slicker," he muttered. When the door had closed, the men got up together, arching their backs. They went over to the register and read the names written in a careless, sprawling hand: *Mary C. Whittaker and Christopher F. Whittaker, New York City.*

"Wonder what business he's in," Dr. McAlistir said. "Looks like a crook to me. . . Mummies! Gad!"

Mr. Parsons took out his watch. "Turning in, Alpheus?"

"Nothing else to do, Gorham."

They went out of the lobby to the piazza.

The porch floor was damp. Its boards echoed their footsteps hollowly. The surf pounded and hissed on the rocks beyond the sea-wall and the foghorn mooed.

In the rectangular open space between the Annex and the Main building, parked automobiles, dripping with mist, glistened in the frail glimmer of the porch lights. They stopped before the parking space, watching the newly arrived Mr. Whittaker drive a small sedan up behind the massed cars, take out a pair of traveling bags, carry them into the Annex entrance. "Machine guns!" Dr. McAlistir whispered. "Better look out for that—" He broke off, clutched Mr. Parsons' arm, drew away from the rail, into deeper shadow. "Stay back here. They don't like to be seen."

Mr. Parsons said, "Who?" and he saw and said, "Of course, poor things!"

The porch light dropped on two figures, sliding along the wall of the Annex, toward the entrance, keeping close to the building, as if the night and its shrouding mist were not concealment enough. They were women. One of them seemed wider than she was tall.

For an instant, as the women went up the steps, the light lay full on their faces. One face was thin, harassed, bordered in straggling, gray hair, but the other was a lump of dough, with a gash for a mouth, two pin-pricks for eyes—pasty, white dough—a pie, rather than a human countenance.

"Sad, isn't it?" Mr. Parsons said.

"Glandular," the doctor answered. "Mrs. Heath says her sister's so sensitive about her appearance she won't leave her room. Has her meals brought up. They slip out at night for air, after everybody's gone to bed."

"Sad for both of them," Mr. Parsons said. "It can't be very pleasant for Mrs. Heath either."

"She's quite devoted to her sister. A very unfortunate case. I hear Miss Chalmers weeping in her room sometimes. Surprising the Rockledge takes them. Depressing to the other guests."

"The poor things must go somewhere." Mr. Parsons shivered. "Let's go in. Bit too chilly tonight to stand gabbing. . . . Good night, Alpheus. See you at breakfast, I presume."

"Good night, Gorham." Dr. McAlistir climbed the steps.

Mr. Parsons waited with his hand on his doorknob, listening to the closing of the door of Mrs. Heath's room on the second floor, to Dr. McAlistir's receding footsteps on the stairs. He felt like a father—the head of a household—seeing his children safely off to bed.

As he stood there, the door opposite his own opened. He caught a swift glimpse of the lighted bathroom of the A suite—of a little clothesline strung above the tub, hung with a child's socks and panties, a woman's pink undergarment and dangling tan silk hose. He heard Miss Moffett saying crisply, "I hope you'll find everything comfortable."

Suddenly a child wailed. "Mommy—Mommy. Are you here, Mommy?" Miss Moffett stepped to the door of the other bedroom of the suite, called through the panels, "Your mother's out. She'll be back soon. Go to sleep, dear."

The baby's voice did not answer.

"I hope you don't mind children," Miss Moffett said. "There's a little girl in there. . . . Your key's on the inside of your door. You'll have to keep the suite door open. Mrs. Spain is still out."

Mr. Whittaker fiddled with the key in his lock. "I'm afraid it doesn't work," he complained.

Miss Moffett tried it, half-heartedly. It did not turn. She sighed. "I know. Sometimes these old locks get rusty. Dampness. But it doesn't really matter. Most of our guests never bother locking their doors at all. Perfectly safe." Then she said "Good night" and closed the door of the suite. She saw Mr. Parsons watching and listening and her voice went half an octave higher: "Oh, Mr. Parsons. Well! You've plenty of company tonight. The Annex is full. Good night."

He said "Good night" and closed his door. He did not even touch his key. Years before, he had given up the futile struggle with the Rockledge hardware.

He jerked his light on, pulled down his window shades. He went to his dresser and took out his diary, sat down in the rocker, nibbling the top of his fountain pen. Then, under Saturday, July 27th, he wrote:

This has been a full day. In some respects a promising one. Things are changing greatly here. In one day we have seen the arrival of a child and a honeymoon couple. And the Fairy Princess is here—just across the hall from me. But Prince Charming has come for her in his swan boat. She may have to leave.

He closed the book, put it back into his bureau. He undressed languidly, put on his flannel nightshirt, crawled between the clammy sheets. He realized with annoyance that he was not sleepy. At first he fretted about the "Fairy Princess," out in the cold fog without a coat. Did she know that Miss Moffett turned out the porch lights and locked all the outside doors at midnight and that it was hard to rouse anyone to open them? Then he worried about the child, alone and wakeful, wishing its mother would come back.

Just before midnight he heard the tenuous threads of voices—a man's and a woman's—on the porch. Then the door of the A suite opened and there was a thump as of someone stumbling in the dark, before the shutting door sound came through to him and the click of departing heels on Johnson's Neck. The "Fairy Princess" had come home. She was safe in her room. Mr. Parsons relaxed. A few minutes later, he heard Miss Moffett's brisk tread, the snap of the spring lock. He rolled over, tried to sleep. He was cold. The Rockledge blankets, he decided, had grown much thinner since he had first covered himself with them. The blankets—or his blood. He lay shivering, debating with himself whether he would feel very much colder if he got up to close his windows. Finally, he crawled from his sheets, spread his flannel robe atop his covers. Then he dozed off.

Two hours later, a drunken voice woke him—a voice out on Johnson's neck, singing gaily at the top of a lusty pair of lungs: *"Nya, nya, said the little fox. Nya, nya, you can't catch me."*

Mr. Parsons sat up. The radium dial of the traveling clock beside his bed was at quarter past two.

"Nya, nya, said the little fox." That was a silly song. An ungentlemanly song to be singing on Johnson's Neck in Laneport. On a Sabbath morning . . . Sabbath . . . Witches Sabbath . . . *"Nya, nya, you can't catch me."* An imperti-

nent song. An impertinent fellow, disturbing a sleeping
community with his roistering. But as he thought about it,
Mr. Parsons warmed to the image the song evoked. There
was something oddly comforting in the thought of the
hunted little beast, jeering at the red-coated men on the
towering horses, at their packs of baying hounds. Sassy
little creature, thumbing its nose. Mr. Parsons saw the fox
under a tree, waving its white plume, tossing its white
head. A white fox. But that was wrong. A fox wasn't white.
It was the foxhounds that were white. Not the fox. But the
image he had seen was definitely, plainly, unmistakably, a
white fox. A fox as white as a ghost and tall and graceful,
like a woman—a white woman.

"Pshaw." Mr. Parsons complained. "I'm all mixed up."
He listened for the drunken voice again. Out of the night
came only the growl of the foghorn and the beat of the
surf.

Sleep had left him. He tossed and turned now and his
teeth chattered; his shanks quivered with the cold. Once,
he thought that he heard soft, cat-like footsteps and a
vague, indefinable sound as of a window moving. He tiptoed to his door, listened but heard nothing. He padded to
his window, raised a shade, peered out. He removed the
screen, closed the window, went back to bed. Someone
else was moving about upstairs. The house was wakeful.

But he dozed off and he woke again to a sound of tapping. Tap, tap—tap, tap, tap. Silver hammers tapping on
the forehead of the Pope to make certain that he is dead.
Tap, tap, softly. Tap, tap, tap. . . . *But I'm not the Pope.
. . . Of course not . . . And I'm not dead. But somebody is,
or the silver hammers would not tap, tap, tap. . . . But if
I'm not dead, then who is dead?*

Chapter Three

A Big Bad Witch

THE BRIDE SLEPT. Beneath the windows of her bridal chamber, surf pounded the rocks and spume hissed against the sea-wall. Through the screens drifted the eerie hoot of the foghorn and the clammy ribbons of fog.

At ten o'clock on that Saturday morning, Miss Mary Carner and Mr. Christopher Whittaker, detectives both, employed by the department store of J. Blankfort and Company in New York City, had stepped into the Little Church Around the Corner and she had said, "I, Mary, take thee, Christopher Frederick," and he, "I, Christopher Frederick, take thee, Mary." There had been a wedding breakfast at the Tavern-on-the-Green and after that they had stowed their bags into a borrowed sedan, pretending not to see white ribbons trailing and a *Just Married* sign on the spare tire. Detective John Reese of the Homicide Division of the New York Police Department had tossed them the keys to the car, had said, "So long, kids. Don't do anything I wouldn't do," and then had led them, in a police squad car, with siren screaming, up the West Side Highway to the city line.

The broiling afternoon had been a nightmare: streams of honking cars, dovetailing like zippers, buses spewing monoxide, sun beating down on the steel roof of the sedan, turning it into a fiery furnace—Connecticut, Rhode Island, Massachusetts—parched landscape under a brassy sun—miles of inferno between the humid city and the cool forests and surf of Maine.

The bridegroom, with sublime confidence in his ability

to take punishment, had been certain they could make Kennebunkport by midnight. But after dinner and dark, the fog had rolled in from the sea on the North Shore of Massachusetts—waves and walls of icy mist—blinding, paralyzing.

It was disconcerting to find oneself thrust into the intimacies of other people's lives—the wash-line over the bathtub: a strange woman's panties and stockings, a baby's socks, and the alien washcloths and toothbrushes. "It's like visiting the family," the bride complained. "You don't mind *too much,* do you, Chris?"

"If you don't, I don't, Mary. It's that goddam racket that gets me. Noisiest ocean I ever met. . . . Listen to that horn."

She had listened to the sea and the foghorn and she had shivered with chill and with some nameless dread. But her heart had leaped from terror to joy in the knowledge that Chris was here—to share whatever perils might be, to cherish, to protect.

Fear was new to Mary Carner, and unseemly. She felt a twinge of shame whenever she acknowledged it. Yet danger and death, once met face to face, had taught her to respect it. *I am afraid* was a warning to eyes and ears and nerves. *Be vigilant,* it said. *Take care.*

She pulled the window shades down to the low sills to shut out the sea and the mist and she came to her husband's arms.

He said, "Darling, you're shivering. Are you cold? Are you afraid of anything? Mary, sweet, you're not afraid?"

She answered, "As long as you are with me, I shall never be afraid. The two of us, together. That's the way it is; that's the way it will be, forever and ever."

Emotion filled his throat. He said, gruffly, fiercely, "Cut that out! Get sentimental and I'll bust you in the snoot," and he kissed her hair, her throat, her lips.

The room was black and cold when she awoke. She lay tense, with heart pounding, and wondered what had waked her. Then she felt the flutter of light fingers on her arm. She cried out, "Who's there?"

A child answered her—a reedy voice, hiccoughing with tears. "Can I come in your bed?"

She sat up. Her sleep-clouded eyes could barely make out a small figure beside her bed. The room was full of confusing noises: the beating surf, the foghorn and a persistent staccato tapping. "Who's there?" she repeated.

"It's me. I'm cold. Please let me in your bed." Little hands clawed her blanket.

"Of course not," she answered sharply. "Go back to your own room. Ask your mother to take you into her bed."

The child drew back reluctantly. Then she came forward, pushed against the bed. "I asked Mommy and I asked her," she whimpered. "But she didn't answer me. She won't wake up."

"We'll see about that." Mary threw back her blankets, groped for the cord of the light, blinked in the sudden, garish illumination. Her husband in the adjoining bed lay on his side, his chest rising and falling in the rhythm of deep sleep. She put her finger to her lips to warn the child to quiet. *That hammering!* She told herself. *It's enough to wake the dead.*

She pulled on her negligee, thrust her feet into slippers. "Come on, sister," she whispered. "I'll take you back. I'll tuck you in."

The little girl put her small, soft fingers trustingly into Mary's. She was a very pretty child, with tumbled auburn curls, blue eyes matching the ground of her scottie-sprigged pajamas, round, dimpled, sleep-flushed cheeks.

The light behind them stretched a pathway across the little foyer which separated the two rooms of the suite. The tapping sound seemed louder as they crossed the threshold. The child gripped Mary's hand. "I don't like that funny noise," she wailed. "Why doesn't it wake Mommy up?"

On the nearest bed, in a chamber that was chill and damp as a tomb, lay the nude form of a woman—white and still as marble—sleeping, oblivious to cold and shame, with open eyes.

The child's fingers dug into Mary's palm. "That's my mommy. She won't wake up."

Mary said, very quickly, "Sister, go back to my room. Right away. Hurry up. Stay there till I call you." She gave the child a little push, closed the door behind her.

Then she went into the bedroom where the marble woman lay. She pulled on the overhead light. As she looked down on the bed, she felt an odd sense of recognition—of the tapering thighs, the slender, graceful arms, the delicately rounded shoulders over which two long plaits of copper hair lay like golden serpents, coiling down to the firm, small, pointed breasts. She came closer. She saw that below the open, sightless eyes, the mouth was twisted as if with pain, and that under the left breast, a slim, black pencil leaned, its tip embedded in the flesh, like a pointer marking the spot where a heart had beat.

A fat mosquito nuzzled against the quiet forehead.

Mary knelt beside the bed. She sniffed the stale fumes of alcohol and tobacco. She felt for the pulse and could not find it. Yet the inert hand seemed warmer than her own. *This has just happened,* she thought; *someone's just done this.*

The impact of the realization stunned her. Murder had been done under this roof, a few feet away from the room in which she and Chris were soundly sleeping. Here— somewhere in this house or somewhere near it—within the sound of her voice, perhaps, an assassin skulked.

Her knees turned to rubber. She stood beside the bed, shivering in her thin silk garments, her brain crying "help, help," her tongue and feet paralyzed with horror. Then her senses, goaded by fear, sharpened, began to take note of sight and sound. Her ears strained for the patter of retreating footsteps. But the house had grown abruptly silent as if it too were listening. The tapping had ceased. Even the sea was quieter, the foghorn more remote.

Her eyes raced around the room, found the windows. Over two of them, the shades were drawn. The third gaped like the woman's eyes, wide open but blind, revealing nothing. A window screen leaned against the wall. A woman's printed cotton dress sprawled on the rocker; a pair of scarlet sandals rested on the floor. An open suitcase lay in a far corner; earrings, a comb, a brush, a purse, an ash tray heaped with red-smudged butts, were on the dresser top—things for living people which had no connection any longer with the figure on the bed.

She stared again at the black pointer over the heart. It resembled a slate pencil but it was thicker, longer. A glitter at the exposed end made evident that it was metal. Mary knew that she had never seen its like before.

She tugged at a sheet, pulled it up, all the way, until it covered the body and the face and the eyes of the woman on the bed. Her hand touched the flesh again, felt its reminiscent warmth. She pulled the sheet down to the throat so that the face might draw breath if it could.

She threw open the door of the suite and ran out into the hall.

The hall was quiet and deserted. A night-lamp burned dimly on a table in a corner behind the stairs. She stood for a second, irresolute, her hand on the knob. A door across the passage creaked. A gnome-like figure, with pointed ears and nightshirt flapping around skinny shanks, stood in the doorway. "Who is dead?" the figure asked.

She was aware, through the haze of her own confusion, of the singular pertinence of the question and the assurance with which it was asked. She pointed at a door behind her, but she said only, "Where's a telephone?"

"Why do you need a telephone?"

"To call a doctor," she answered impatiently.

The figure shook its head. "Too late," it said. "When they tap with the silver hammers, it's too late for doctors."

"Please," she begged. "This is no time for jokes. We've got to get a doctor. Quick!"

"A doctor? Oh, certainly. Doctor McAlistir's right up-stairs. I'll call him for you." The little man turned back to his room, mumbling something about his dressing gown.

She did not wait for him. She ran up the steps, screaming as she ran, "Dr. McAlistir . . . Doctor . . . Doctor. . . ."

An apparition rose before her on the landing of the second floor—a round, white shape, floating mistily in the dark hall. Human sounds seemed to come from it. "Oh—I," the shape said plainly. A door opened. A woman's arm emerged. It clutched the white figure, pulled it back. An angry voice scolded, "Isabel, what are you doing out there? Get in here and go to bed." The figure vanished through a doorway. A door slammed.

Soft footsteps padded up the steps behind her. The old man's voice said, below her shoulder, "I'll wake him. I know his room." The little figure, wrapped discreetly now in a flannel bathrobe, swished past her, paused before Dr. McAlistir's door, turned to her again. "Tell me the truth," it begged. "I can stand the worst. Is it the 'Fairy Princess'?"

"Don't ask silly questions," she snapped. "Get the doctor."

The old man hammered on the door, called, "Alpheus, Alpheus."

The doctor's door opened, and doors upstairs and down, until the corridor swarmed with disheveled women in bathrobes and curling pins, jabbering, "What's happened? . . . Is anybody sick?"

Mr. Parsons shuffled among them on tiptoe, the heels of his slippers slapping. "We don't know yet, Miss Hays." "The Doctor will tell us, Miss Templeton." "I don't know, Mrs. Bean, I don't know. Someone is dead. That's all I know. She—" He glared at Mary, leaning against the closed door to the A suite. "She knows. But she won't tell me whether it's the 'Fairy Princess.'"

"Mister," Mary asked sharply, "why are you so sure someone's dead? I never told you that."

"But I know it," the old man answered simply. "The white woman appeared. Anyone in Laneport will tell you that that means death. The white woman appeared and they tapped with the silver hammers."

Dr. McAlistir came out of the A suite, his shoulders and mustache drooping. "There is nothing for me to do," he said somberly. "We must send for the police."

Mr. Parsons dropped down on the bottom step of the staircase. "Then it is the 'Fairy Princess.'" His words seemed swathed in crepe.

Mary said heavily, "This isn't just death. It's murder. It has just happened. And the murderer may still be in this building."

There was a second of stricken silence. Miss Templeton gasped, "A murderer! Oh, my!" and Mrs. Bean made a little gurgling noise and staggered back against Miss Hays. The faces in the hall looked expectantly toward Dr. McAlistir, moved aside to let him through to the unsteady Mrs. Bean.

"How dare you say such things?" Miss Templeton turned on Mary. "How dare you frighten Mrs. Bean?"

Mrs. Bean's daughter laughed shrilly. "Mother'll be all right. She simply doesn't know the facts of life. It's never occurred to her that murder's one of them." Her little eyes were shining.

"Take your mother to her room, Lorna," Dr. McAlistir said brusquely. "Make her lie down."

Miss Bean pouted. "I always have to be out of everything," she grumbled. She took her mother's elbow. "Come now. Go to bed, mother dear."

Dr. McAlistir came over to Mary. "Young lady, how did you chance to go into that room?" His voice and manner were unmistakably challenging. The little group in the hall swung, as one person, toward Mary, probing her with accusing eyes.

Oh, dear Lord, the man suspects me! Mary thought. But she answered, "Her child woke me up."

"Her child! Her child saw that!"

"I don't know what the child saw or didn't see," Mary replied cautiously. "Please, let's leave the questioning for the authorities. Please, one of you gentlemen, please telephone them."

"Where is your husband, young lady?" Dr. McAlistir's tone had deepened with suspicion. "Why isn't he out here too?"

She answered, "Please get the police, somebody," and then she opened the suite door and slipped back into her room.

The light glittered in the ceiling but Chris still lay on his side, snoring unconcernedly. In Mary's bed sat the child, hunched up in the blankets, wide awake, her eyes big with tears and terror. She cried out when she saw Mary, "Won't my mommy wake up for you, either?"

Mary put her arms around the youngster. "Darling," she said. "Your mommy had to go away, far, far away. You'll have to stay here with me till we find your folks." She wondered as she said it how on earth they could take care of the child.

The little girl stared at her. "My mommy won't ever come back? Never? Not even to kiss me good-night?" The blue eyes were glass marbles. Tears spilled over, ran down the child's cheeks. "She can't go away from me. Mommy can't," she sobbed. "She told me she never, never would."

Mary held her tightly, stroking her curls, mopping her tears. The little girl turned in her arms, trembling violently, gripping her hands, clinging to her with a desperation eloquent of loneliness and fear of loneliness.

"Darling," Mary's soft voice caressed the frightened

child. "You're not alone. You're with Chris and me. Don't be afraid. We'll take care of you. . . . Don't cry so, dear. . . . You've got to be a big girl now, a big, brave girl. . . . That's what Mommy'd want you to be. A big, brave girl who doesn't cry." She repeated the words as if she were teaching a lesson. "Only babies cry. A big, brave girl never cries." Eventually her words and her solace had their way and the child groped for Mary's handkerchief, blew her nose in it, gulped, "I'm a big, brave girl . . . Mommy's big, brave girl. . . . I won't cry any more. . . ." The tears started again but she blinked them back and parted her lips in a pathetic imitation of a smile. "See, I'm not crying any more."

Mary said, "You're swell, darling. . . . You'll do." She released the child and went around to the other bed and shook Chris lightly.

He grunted, snorted, popped up like a jack-in-the-box. He saw his bride, smiled drowsily and stretched his sleep-drugged arms for her. "Fancy meeting you here," he said.

"Chris. Wake up. Wake up. Hurry."

"What's doing?" He yawned, stretched. He saw the little girl. "Well—company! Who the hell's that?"

"Sweetheart." She spoke directly into Chris's ear. "Her mother's dead. Murdered. Next door."

Christopher Whittaker yelled "God damn" and leaped out of bed.

When Mary had told it to him once more and had added what she had seen in the room across the hall, Chris looked again at the child, curiously, this time, and pulled his wife's head down to his and whispered, "The kid. She must have seen whatever it was."

Together they approached the other bed. Mary asked, "Baby, what was it that woke you up?"

The child's lips trembled. "I was cold," she answered.

"But when you were cold and you woke up, did you see anybody, anything, in the room?"

The child's eyes dilated with remembered fear. "I saw something in the room." She clung to Mary, buried her face in Mary's sleeve. Her body was torn by long shuddering gasps. "I saw something awful."

"Was it a man or a woman?" Chris asked.

The child looked up. "It wasn't neither," she replied.

"Little girl," Mary stroked the child's hair. "You must tell us what you saw. You don't need to be frightened."

"What did you see, baby?" Chris persisted.

The child sucked her breath in, held herself taut. Then she let the wind out of her tight little chest. She gripped Mary's fingers. "I saw a witch." She panted. "A great big, big witch. On a broomstick. A witch as big as the whole, whole room."

Chris said "God damn" again and strolled over to the window.

The child looked after him, shocked. She said primly, "You mustn't say words like that. My mommy says you mustn't say them unless you're very, very mad at somebody. Are you mad at somebody?"

"You bet," Chris growled. He came back. "Excuse me, baby."

Mary said, "Darling, this is very important. You must tell me everything you saw, exactly what you saw and heard after you woke up. Do you know what a lie is?"

"Of course I do," the child answered. "A lie is when somebody calls up and says he has work for Mommy and he just wants to have a date with Mommy." Her voice seemed a dozen years older than her face.

"I *will* be god-damned," said Chris. "Even if the little lady doesn't like it."

"Darling," Mary ignored him. "If you know what a lie is, then you know what truth is. Tell me the positive, absolute truth of what you saw and heard in that room."

The little girl looked at Mary; she looked at Chris. Then she folded her hands, said determinedly, as if she had memorized the words, "I was cold and I woked up and I saw a great big witch coming right in through the window. I knew it was a witch because I saw her broomstick. And the fire all around her. And she flew around the room, just as quiet as anything, and she leaned over my bed and I was so scared, so awful scared, I closed my eyes up tight so I wouldn't see her. And when I opened them up she was next to Mommy's bed and then she flew right out of the window, right on her broomstick. And I cried to Mommy and Mommy wouldn't wake up."

Chris played a tattoo on the bedstead. "Well, that's just dandy," he observed. "That makes everything perfectly clear." He turned to his wife. "That's what Walt Disney's done to them. The Snow White influence. Baby, you didn't see Dopey and Sneezy, too, did you?"

The child began to cry.

"O.K. . . . O.K." Chris patted her shoulder clumsily. "O.K., I believe you. Lovely stuff to hand a jury. Where do we go from here?" Then he cocked his head, listening to a putt-putt-putt, faint at first, and growing louder. "The law! Paul Revere rides again." He grinned. There was no mirth in his grin.

A motorcycle stopped with a crash at the parking space beside the house. Heavy feet tramped the porch outside the windows, lighter footsteps pattering alongside. The tread came into the Annex, into the room across the little foyer and out again. The door knob rattled; the panels shook under heavy rapping: "Officer Dolliver. Open up. In the name of the law."

Chris reached for his bathrobe, tied it around his middle. He said, "O.K. Open it yourself."

A chunky, sunburned youth in police blue stood in the doorway, twirling his cap. Behind him, in the tiny passageway, were the heads of the Misses Dow and Moffett and their guests.

Mr. Whittaker bowed ceremoniously. "Come right on

in. Everybody. The Whittakers are receiving. Pardon my informal attire."

The policeman scowled. He waved a traffic-signaling hand at the crowd behind him. "Wait in the hall, all of you. I'd rather talk to the person who found the body—alone."

The policeman swaggered into the room, weaving a little as though he had learned to walk on the rolling deck of a ship. He said, "Now, which of you found the body?"

Mary touched her finger to her lips and bobbed her head in the direction of the wide-eyed child.

"Who's that?" Officer Dolliver asked.

"Make him go away," the baby wailed. "I don't like him."

Officer Dolliver frowned deeply. "Your little girl?" he asked.

Mr. Whittaker made a fine show of indignation. "The lady and I were just married this morning—yesterday morning. Give us time." Mrs. Whittaker blushed. The bridegroom crooked his finger, beckoned the officer over to the window. "It's *her* child, the dead woman's. My wife found the body."

Officer Dolliver took out a black notebook. "Name?" he began.

Chris reached under his pillow for his wallet. He spread a handful of cards fan-wise before the policeman. "Here's the dope," he said. "Cree-dentials. Store's Mutual Protective. New York City Police Department. J. Blankfort and Company, Fifth Avenue, New York. The little lady has the same."

Officer Dolliver put his hat on, tipped it, took it off, extended his hand. "Always glad to welcome a visiting fireman," he said. Then he added, "Mighty strange, you being in here, next door to that."

"Yep." Chris shrugged. "Crime follows us around. Started out to be a vacation. Turns out to be the same old grisly grind."

"Tough luck." Officer Dolliver was suitably sympathetic.

Then he said, "Might turn out to be good luck for us. You people right on the scene like this."

"I doubt it." Chris answered. "I'm a sound sleeper. Sleep like a top on the edge of a nickel. Besides, larceny's my racket, petty mostly. Not homicide. But Mary—in case you read the papers up in this neck of the woods, you'll be pleased to know you're in the same room with the famous Mary Carner. Don't tell me you never heard of the McAndrew case? The Phyllis Knight case?"

Officer Dolliver glanced at Mr. Whittaker's wife. He saw an attractive, youthful, gray-eyed, brown-haired woman in a rose-colored negligee and rose satin slippers. "Detective, eh?" he said. "Looks more like one of them glamour girls to me. . . . Nope, never heard of her." He cleared his throat apologetically. "Y'see, we're kinda busy up here. Big fire in the glue factory last winter. Lot of trouble this spring with boys breaking into the summer cottages. And there's been some pin-ball machine robberies in some saloons in town. And bingo parties giving us a headache. And we had a county Legion Convention this spring took up a lot of time. Don't get much chance to read the papers."

"No hard feelings," Chris answered. "Let's see, what time's it now? Three-thirty, eh? Well, sir, between this minute and eight o'clock in the morning—or maybe nine —when we pull out for Kennebunkport (How far is it, officer? Road pretty good?) you're going to have some of the finest detecting assistance Laneport ever saw."

Officer Dolliver shook his head. He said, "Take it easy. Won't be an inquest before Monday, the earliest. Chief won't let you leave before."

Mr. Whittaker snorted. "Like to see *your* Chief spoil *my* honeymoon. He ain't God, is he?"

Officer Dolliver sighed. "I wouldn't be surprised if he thinks he is."

Mr. Whittaker said, "Mary, time's awasting. Come here and solve this man's crime for him right away. We gotta get going in a couple of hours."

Mary came over. In quick, clipped tones, she said, "Statement of Mary C. Whittaker of New York City. (Write it down, officer. I'll dictate it straight.) I was awakened at approximately three o'clock by a child who had apparently entered through the unlocked door of my room (the keys don't work, officer). The child said she was unable to awaken her mother. I went into the adjoining room and found the body of the woman upon a bed. I could detect no signs of life. The body was still warm. The eyes were wide open. I noted that a thin metal rod was imbedded in the flesh over the heart. I did not touch it. I noted that the bedroom door and one of the windows was open. I saw no signs of a struggle. I did not disturb the position of the body or touch anything in the room except the doorknob and the sheet with which I covered the body. I immediately summoned a doctor who is a guest in the hotel and advised that the police be notified."

"You know your stuff," Officer Dolliver said admiringly. "Question anybody?"

"Only the child," she said.

"Sure," Mr. Whittaker interrupted. "She was a big help. Told us a lovely bedtime story about seeing a big bad witch, riding on a broomstick."

"I did too," the child cried out. "I saw a witch. I did, with my own eyes."

"There y'are," Officer Dolliver shook his head. "That's what happens when you get into the history books. People can't think of anything but witches when they get up this way." He went over to the little girl. "Did you see a man or a woman in your mother's room?" he demanded.

"I saw a witch," the child answered promptly.

"All right, all right, you saw a witch. Man or lady witch?"

"There's only one kind of a witch. A big bad witch. Big as anything. With fire all around her."

The policeman sighed. "When they get to telling stories

like that up around here, we give them sulphur and molasses. What's your name, sister?"

"Baby Doll," the child replied.

The policeman spread his hands helplessly.

Mary said, "Your real name, dear?"

"Baby Doll," the child repeated.

"Is that what Mommy always called you?"

The child nodded.

"But what do other people call you?"

"Baby Doll."

"What's your mommy's name?"

"Nola."

"Nola what?"

"Nola."

"Doesn't anybody call her anything else?"

"Sometimes they call her Princess."

"Princess Nola?"

"No, just Princess."

"What's your daddy's name?"

The child's lower lip came forward. "I haven't any daddy." The marbles rolled from her blue eyes again. "I haven't any daddy. And now I haven't any mommy."

Officer Dolliver grunted. "Hard luck." He moved away from the bed. "Baby Doll's not going to be any help," he said to Mr. Whittaker.

"Have you searched the premises yet, officer?" Mary asked.

"That's next."

"I'll go with you."

"You will not," her husband said. "You're not going to be running around with strange policemen."

She patted his shoulder, rolled her hair into a bun, stuck hairpins into it, slipped her coat over her negligee.

"If you go, I go," her husband said.

She shook her head, positively. "No, indeed. Somebody has to stay with the baby."

Mr. Whittaker's wrists went back to his hips. "Chris, you're a dope," he told himself. "With all the females in the world, you had to pick a career woman. Married one day and she leaves you home with the baby and goes out to work."

Chapter Four

Like a Cloven Hoof

OFFICER DOLLIVER flung open the bedroom door. He said to Mrs. Whittaker, "Come right with me, ma'am." He was grim, the lady somber.

A whisper raced through the huddle in the hall: "He got *her*. *She* did it."

Officer Dolliver paid his respects to the whisper. He said "Just you keep an eye on these folks, Miss Moffett—nobody's to go into that room. Stay right here till I get back."

The raw night air slapped Mary's cheek as she stepped out on the piazza. The porch lights had been turned on, glimmering feebly through shrouds of mist. The main building of the Rockledge, at the far end of the connecting shed, seemed disembodied, cut off from land or sea. Yellow eyes winked in the lobby windows but above the first story the building was dark, the guests slumbering, unaware behind their rattling window shades. The surf seemed quieter, its restless surge more remote, but out on the Point the foghorn marked the minutes with its weird, pervasive growl.

They walked in silence until they were well out of ear-shot. Then Officer Dolliver asked, "What's your opinion, ma'am? Is it an inside job?"

"I'm a stranger here," Mary answered. "Don't know anything about anybody in this place or in this town. How could I have an opinion?"

He said, "It's awful funny—you coming along at a time like this."

"Not so funny. Even detectives have to sleep somewhere."

They came into the deserted lobby and Officer Dolliver jiggled the phone hook, tapped the desk with his knuckles. "Betsey's taking her beauty nap," he complained. "She hasn't had a call at this hour since the glue factory burned down. . . . Oh, hello. Betsey? Sam Dolliver. Get me the Chief. No, he's home. Step on it, Betsey. . . . Hello. Oh, Chief, Sam Dolliver. I'm out at the Rockledge. It's a homicide. . . . That's right. That's what I said. A murder. Woman. . . . No, nobody you know. Summer visitor. Woman named Spain. Nola Spain . . . N as in Nantasket, O as in Ocean, L as in Laneport, A as in Annisquam. *Nola.* Got it? . . S as in Salem, P as in Peabody, A as in Annisquam again, I as in Ipswich, N as in Nantasket again. *Spain.* Got it? A Princess or something. From New York. . . . No. . . . No. . . . No. . . . No, sir. . . . Stabbing. Some kind of a steel spike. . . . O.K., Chief. . . . Sure, Chief. . . . Oh, Chief, there's a woman here. A couple. From New York. They say they're detectives. Ever hear of a woman detective named Carner? First name's Mary. (That right, ma'am?) Mary Carner. She's supposed to be well-known . . . No, I never heard of her, either. She found the body. Says she wants to help us out. . . . O.K., whatever you say, Chief. I'll tell her that. . . O.K."

He turned from the telephone. He said, "No, thanks. The Chief said 'No, thanks.' Between the force and the District Attorney's Office and the State Police he says we got all the good detectives we need."

"That's fine," Mary said. "I'll catch a few winks and we'll be on our way."

"Oh, no, ma'am. You discovered the crime. They'll need you for the inquest." He grimaced, half-humorously. "Let that be a lesson to you, ma'am. Don't you go around finding corpses."

Mary dug her fists into her coat pockets, hunched her shoulders as if she was cold. "They find me. It's a curse," she said. "See here, it'll be a while before your Chief get his pants on and brings in his bloodhounds. This murder' fresh. Just let me carry on till he gets here, will you? T make certain nothing gets away."

Sam Dolliver pondered the suggestion. "Well, all right, he mumbled, finally. "Just till the Chief comes." Sudde shyness crept up on him. "See here, ma'am," he said, with stammering humility, "would you, could you, if we found out anything, could you sort of let it be in my name?"

She laughed. "Anything you say. All I want is to see the murderer found and caught and punished. But I don' care who makes the catch—you or I or anyone else. Just s long as the job is done. I don't like murder." She was vei definite about that last.

Mr. Parsons sat on the bottom step of the staircase, his head in his hands, his heart leaden. Mrs. McAlistir, two steps above him, bent down, from time to time, to pat his shoulder blades consolingly.

Miss Dow and Miss Moffett's other guests were mutter ing because at first too much had happened and now too little. Running and shouting had dragged them out of sleep and bed, had sent them tumbling into public view without time to do essential things about hair and dental plates Then the cry of Murder had chilled them to the marrow and Officer Dolliver had come out of the mist on his motor cycle, striding into one room and another of the A suite emerging with the stranger, walking away. Nobody had asked *them* anything, nobody had told *them* anything; just left them standing around. It was, Miss Hays protested definitely unfair. "Are we children to be treated this way —or criminals?"

"Madam," Dr. McAlistir reproved her, "no one is keep ing you here. You may go to your room and wait until you're sent for."

"All very well for you to say, Doctor," Miss Hays retorted. "You've been in there. You *know* what's happened."

"What I cannot understand," Miss Templeton said, "is how the Rockledge takes in people like that."

"People like what, Miss Templeton?" Miss Moffett asked.

Miss Dow, a soft, squashy woman, whose warm black eyes were close set and upper lip darkly hairy, like the anile face of a pansy, edged alongside her partner and chirped, "Yes, Miss Templeton, like what?" The top of Miss Dow's head came only to Miss Moffett's chin but her belligerent positiveness gave her stature.

"Like women who are unfortunate enough to get themselves killed, I suppose," Miss Moffett suggested.

"She was a very low type," Miss Templeton said acidly. "I saw her myself."

"She came well recommended." Miss Dow's throat shook with outrage. "You have to take someone's word for something."

"She really isn't to blame for getting herself killed. If someone else killed her, then we certainly can't blame *her* for it," Dr. McAlistir's wife ventured.

"We definitely can," Miss Templeton's rebuke was sharp. "Only certain types of people get themselves murdered. People who have done something which makes other people want to kill them. People like ourselves, for instance, our sort of people never gets murdered."

"An unfortunate oversight," Dr. McAlistir growled into his mustache.

Gorham Parsons, squatting behind him, reached up to squeeze his wrist. "The more I know you, Alpheus, the better I like you."

Miss Templeton shuffled up to Mr. Parsons, bent over him. "I didn't catch what you said, Mr. Parsons."

Mr. Parsons edged away.

"But I want to explain what I mean." She sprayed her words over his face. "I've always had a deep conviction that murder is just retribution. Somebody has done something vile and somebody else takes it on himself to be the avenging instrument. The sword of fate, if you see what I mean."

Mr. Parsons took his hands away from his face. "You didn't like that young woman," he said through tight lips. "You were against her the minute you saw her. Did you conceive yourself as the instrument of destiny?"

Miss Templeton bridled, her face purpling. "Well, I never! . . . I had nothing against her personally. Why, you don't, any one of you, for a minute, think that I—" She began to sputter and then to cry. "I recognized her type," she blubbered. "I just knew her for what she was—an adventuress." Tears choked her. She pulled a handkerchief from her bathrobe pocket, doused her nose in it.

Miss Hays put a consoling arm around her friend's shoulders. "There, there, dear. You didn't want to be under the same roof as an adventuress, that's what you mean isn't it? We understand, dear. We see now how right you were. Now that this has happened."

Mrs. Bean tottered from her bedroom door. "Lorna. Lorna. Where are you, dear? Where's Lorna?"

"Shh." Miss Dow silenced her. "Here comes Sam with that woman."

"Where's he taking her now?" Mrs. McAlistir asked.

"To the scene of the crime, undoubtedly," Miss Hays declared. "To get her confession."

The police officer poked his head in at the door. "Everybody all right? Stay where you are. The Chief's on his way up." Then he and the lady went past the door and down the porch.

They heard the lady say, "Have you a light?", saw Sam Dolliver take a flash from his pocket, switch it on, hand it to her. They craned their necks through the portal, watched the policeman and the lady moving cautiously along the edge of the piazza, the beam dropping white pools on the floor and the walls of the building.

Mary said, "Here's the room." She played the light over the sill and window frame, dropped it to the floor again. "It's too bad we've wasted time. This damp floor takes prints beautifully. But mist blots them out like rain." She caught the policeman's arm: "Look!" A parallel row of footprints ran down the center of the wet porch floor, went, as though they were sure of their way, around the corner. They ended in a pair of sport shoes and a lean rump, doubled over the sill of the open window which framed the lighted bedroom where marble death lay in little hillocks under a white sheet.

A girl backed away from the window. Officer Dolliver grunted. "What do *you* think you're doing here?"

A frightened face blinked into the flashlight in Mary's hand. The girl squirmed in the policeman's grip. "Let me go. You're hurting me." She whined, "I wasn't doing anything."

"Who're you?" Mary asked.

The girl bit her lip. "Who are *you?*" she answered defiantly.

Officer Dolliver said sternly, "Who are you and what are you doing here?"

The girl looked down at the floor. "I'm Lorna Bean," she mumbled. "I'm not doing anything—just looking."

"Window shopping, eh?" Mary's tone was caustic. "See anything you wanted to get?"

A shudder rippled from Miss Bean's fingertips to her toes.

Mary said curtly, "Keep the little fool out of the way. If there were any prints on this window she's taken care of them."

She played the flashbeam steadily on the sill, turned it on Miss Beam, ran it over her blue skirt and white sweater, her blue jacket. Then she said, "Dolliver, there's a shred of

wool—two shreds, three. Gray. Caught on this window sill
See them? There. There. There. You saw them first, Dolliver."

She stepped carefully away from the window, went beyond it, down the porch, hugging the wall, playing the
beam along the floor. She came to a little flight of stairs.
She went down the steps, found herself on a strip of grass
before the sea wall. The lawn was close-clipped. Under the
spotlight it had the artificial verdancy of stage grass and
the dew sparkled like rhinestones. Mary crouched over it,
holding her garments tightly around her cold, bare ankles.
At the foot of the steps she saw a pock-mark in the turf—a
small round hole, and 12 inches farther on, another. It was
a trail—two trails, for the pock-marks ran in parallel rows
outlining a sort of path—a swath of grass, flattened, less
moist, as though something had blotted out the glittering
globules of the dew. She followed it for a few paces and
then it was lost to her in the fog-walled night.

She turned back, came up the steps, her hair mist-
spangled, her slippers soaked. She went past the drawn
shades of her own bedroom. Her husband's voice floated
through the open windows: "And the big bear said: 'Who's
been eating my porridge?'"

"That's a *baby* story, Chris." The child's voice interrupted him. "Don't you know any real stories?"

"You're too fussy, Baby Doll. That story was good
enough for me and it was good enough for my father—say,
what's your idea of a real story, anyway."

"The ones Mommy used to tell me. *The Birthday of the
Infanta* or—well, even *Pinocchio's* better than *that!*"

"You're a humdinger, Baby Doll." His voice had a lilt of
proud, proprietary affection.

Mary went to the end of the piazza, turned another corner, walked around until she came again to the entrance.
Then she returned, slowly playing the light across the
width of the porch. Her eyes narrowed in concentration

upon the damp boards of the floor. She bent lower until her eyes were a foot away from the moist boards. She began, then, to see vague markings in the center of the porch, beginning a bit to the left of the steps. Not footprints—merely their fast-melting residue—a dot, a curved line—but no clear prints that might tell that some other human creature had passed that way. She followed them until she was back at the open window again. Miss Bean's footprints were still there—plain, identifiable but fuzzing with the moisture gathering swiftly on them. And there was something else. She sang out, "Officer, come here."

Sam Dolliver let go of Miss Bean. He crouched on his haunches beside Mary, stared where her flashbeam pointed. He saw in front of the small, neat marks of Miss Bean's sport shoes, directly under the low window sill of Nola Spain's room, a dimming print which was like the spoor of a cloven hoof.

He scratched his head; he pulled at his jaw; his mouth dropped open; his lower lip came forward in a puzzled grimace. "We never sent a cow to the chair yet in this county," he said.

Tires slithered on the damp road; brakes squealed in the parking rectangle; a car door slammed; heavy feet thumped the steps of the Annex porch.

Sam Dolliver took back his flashlight. "That's all for now," he said. "The Chief's here."

Miss Dow and Mrs. Whittaker met the Chief at the same moment. Miss Dow had scurried from the portals of the Annex to greet Jacob Haskell, the squat, grizzled man who was head of Laneport's six-man police department. She sighed with the relief of a bewildered child finding its long-lost parent, "Oh, Jacob, I'm so glad you're here. We don't know what to do," at the very moment when Officer Dolliver presented the informally clad Mrs. Whittaker and said, "Here, Chief. Here's the lady found the body. The one I was telling you about. Mary Carner. . . . It's a very queer case, Chief."

Chief Haskell took off his hat, simultaneously nodded brusquely at Mary, shook hands with Miss Dow and asked Officer Dolliver, "Made any arrests yet, Sam?"

"Arrests, Chief? Hell, no."

"Why not? You been here half an hour."

A second car stopped in the parking space. A tall, gaunt man came up the porch steps. The Chief said, "Hi, Doc. Go right in. Be with you in a minute."

The huddle in the hall parted to let Dr. Nathaniel Sulloway, the Medical Examiner, through.

"O.K., Sam," the Chief said. "What's so queer?"

Sam Dolliver crooked his finger. "Come with me, Chief. Wait here, will you, Miss Dow." He led his superior officer around the side of the house. "I wanted you to see it first thing." He flashed his light on the floor under the sill. The wet boards winked at him maliciously. He drove his light back and forth. He rubbed his cheek; he flushed under his Chief's rebuking stare. He said, "I'll be a son-of-a-gun. It was here a minute ago."

"What was?"

"The funniest goshdanged footprint you ever saw. A print like a hoof—if you get what I mean, Chief."

Chief Haskell raised his eyebrows. "You ain't been talking to these summer people, have you, Sam?"

"We both saw it." Mary came forward. "A print that looked like a cloven hoof. Under this window."

Chief Haskell's salt and pepper eyebrows rose again. "So you're the famous lady detective!" His inflection left nothing more to be said.

Sam Dolliver's jaw, in the glow of his flashlight, was a deep maroon. "Anyway, Chief," he stammered, "these are still here." He flashed the lamp on the shreds of gray wool.

The Chief bent over the sill. He picked the clinging fibers from the soft, splintery wood. He held them on his fingertips for a second. He crinkled his nose. And then he flicked them off into the mist. He grunted, "Who's been showing you how to be a detective, Sam?" He scowled at Mary, spread both palms on the window frame and vaulted into the room. "Now," he said to the detective and his policeman, "*I'll* find out what this is all about."

Mary stared, dumbfounded. Under her breath she said to Sam Dolliver, "I thought that technique went out with the whipping post."

Sam Dolliver shifted from one foot to the other. "Chief's all right," he said. "Just likes to do things his way." He lowered his voice. "Don't say a word, ma'am. His brother-in-law's the Mayor."

Within the lighted bedroom, startled ecru moths fluttered around the Medical Examiner's bald head. Dr. Sulloway flung back the sheet, surveyed his cadaver, commented, "Lady slept raw, Jake."

The Chief grunted amiably. "Summer people! Whaddya expect? What's the thing in her side, Doc? A spike."

Doctor Sulloway raised one shoulder blade. "Danged if I know," he said. "Never saw one like that before." He yanked at the metal pointer under the breast. It came away easily—a notched narrow rod, some eight inches long and a quarter inch wide—trailing a scarlet ribbon of blood and tissue. He examined its point. He passed it to Mr. Haskell.

The Chief hefted it. "Weighs something," he said with accents of surprise. "Steel, I reckon. Sharp point too." He grasped the blunt end of the metal rod. "Get a good grip on this," he murmured approvingly, "and it handles neat as a stiletto." He studied it with a child-like curiosity. "Never saw a thing like that before. Where you think they got it, Doc?" He put it down on the dresser.

"Search me. These summer people bring in the dangdest things. Went in about an inch and a half. Wonder she didn't holler." Doctor Sulloway prodded the slender larynx; he flashed a pencil light into the staring pupils; he flexed the white fingers. "Not much *rigor mortis* yet," he added. "But plenty of nicotine." He wiped his bony hands on the bed sheet. "That's all, Jake. Send it around for autopsy. Do it for you Monday."

"Say—," the Chief protested.

"I have never done an autopsy on the Sabbath. I have no intention of commencing now."

Chief Haskell shrugged. He slapped his wrist, scowled at a blood smudge. "Danged mosquitoes," he snarled. "Must be starved to death if they're willing to work on my tough hide."

"The room's full of bugs," Doctor Sulloway complained. "Whyn't you put the screen in, Jake? There 'tis, over against the wall. Some danged fool took it out."

Chief Haskell picked up the window screen, swung it around in his hands, set it clumsily in the window frame, scowling as he did so at his policeman and the visiting detective, outside, looking in. He said, "These summer people must of never heard of the Laneport mosquitoes."

"We haven't exactly advertised 'em," Doctor Sulloway smiled sourly. "I told your brother-in-law to get some of the WPA money to clean out the breeding places. But no, he was set on putting up that monument on the Square."

"Hell, Doc, Ed knows what he's doing. No sense wasting money. The town folks are used to them. And the summer people'll stand for anything." Mr. Haskell pulled a pipe from his coat pocket, shook tobacco into it from a tin, tamped it thoroughly, struck a match on the seat of his trousers, sucked the stem until the smoke made a nimbus around his bullet-shaped head. "O.K. All set," he said.

"Sherlock Holmes stuff, eh?"

"You know me, Doc. Old Sherlock Haskell. Got to hunt for clues now."

He hunted. He attacked the job with the finesse of a tornado. He pulled back the covers of the bed in which the child had slept. He threw them on the floor. He shuffled back and forth between the beds, around the room. He hurled clothes out of suitcases, dumped them on the floor beside the tumbled sheets and blankets, pulled open dresser drawers, churned their contents, slammed them shut. "I don't see a thing, Doc," he complained.

Mary, on the other side of the window, thought she was going to have a stroke. It was sheer vandalism. It was more than flesh and blood and a well-trained detective could bear.

At last the Chief came back to the window. "Hey, Sam," he barked through the screen. "Call up Judkins. Tell him to send the wagon. Call up the State Police and the District Attorney and tell them what's happened. Tell them I've got everything well in hand. . . . Come in here, ma'am. I want to question you."

Mary went around the porch and through the hall and came into the death chamber by its proper door. Chief Haskell greeted her from the rocker, where his blue-clad haunches were pressing fresh creases into Nola Spain's discarded dress. "Now see here, Miss," he began. "I want you to tell me how you come to crash this party."

Ten minutes later, browbeaten and chastened, Mary followed the Chief out of the door and sat down on the hall steps. Mr. Parsons inched over to make room for her.

"All right, now." Chief Haskell took a stance in the center of the hall, addressed himself to the Misses Dow and Moffett. "You two girls tell me what you know about that woman in there."

Miss Dow spoke up first. "We don't know very much about her, Jacob. You see, she only came this afternoon. I mean yesterday afternoon. This is Sunday, isn't it? That would be Saturday she came. Around two o'clock. With a little girl and two suitcases. Lonzo Carter drove her up from the station in his taxi."

"She have a reservation?"

"Oh, yes. It was made for her by—" Miss Dow caught herself, looked about dubiously. She lowered her voice.

"I'll tell you that privately, Jacob." She raised it again. "All our guests have reservations."

"Except," Miss Moffett interrupted, "the transients that came tonight. That lady on the steps and her husband."

Everyone looked at Mary then, and Mary tried to look as though she weren't aware of their notice. The Chief coughed to bring their attention back to himself. "What was her right name, Phoebe? That woman inside."

"Mrs. Spain. Nola Spain."

"Darned funny name. What's all this talk about her being a princess?"

"The 'Fairy Princess,' " Mr. Parsons murmured from the stairs.

"You sure have a prize collection," Mr. Haskell said. "Witches and princesses and what nots. Driving me dizzy. Go ahead, Phoebe. . . ."

"Well, I don't know much more than I've told you, Jacob. She came up by the two o'clock train and registered and went to her room, and I saw her afterward coming out with her baby in a bathing suit and walking down to the beach, and then I saw her at dinner with the little girl and then I went off duty. It was Olive's night on."

Miss Moffett took up the tale. "About nine o'clock, she came into the lobby and mentioned to me that she was going out and asked the way to Donato's."

"The fellow that makes statues?"

"The sculptor," Miss Moffett answered. "The one who did those book-ends we have over the fireplace."

"She was his model for them." It was Mr. Parsons again. "The model for the 'Fairy Princess.' "

So that was it, Mary realized. That was why the nude body had seemed so familiar. A dozen likenesses of Nola Spain in bronze and plaster stood on the counters of Blankfort's store. Housewives gobbled them. The statue was so popular that it was almost impossible to keep it in stock.

Miss Moffett went on. "I told her how to get to Donato's.

And then, a little after nine, a young man came in and asked for her. Left a message. Something about—"

"The *Cynisca's* in. The swan boat," Mr. Parsons prompted.

Miss Moffett glanced at him reproachfully. "I was about to tell it, Mr. Parsons. He said, 'Tell her the *Cynisca's* in.' You can find the message in her mailbox. I wrote it down. I said she had gone to Donato's and told him how to get there."

"He met her there," Dr. McAlistir supplemented. "I saw her meet him. She seemed quite glad to see him. They went out together."

"He didn't kill her," Mr. Parsons said firmly and quite unexpectedly.

The Chief swung toward him. "Is that so? Is that so? How come you know so much about it?"

Mr. Parsons sighed. It was no use, he realized, telling these people that no Prince Charming ever killed his Fairy Princess. And so he said, "Why, I heard her come in just before Miss Moffett locked the door."

Mary watched him with deepening interest. She recalled his macabre certainty, when she had met him first, that someone was dead. It was clear that he knew more than he had yet told. She asked, "How did you know that that was Mrs. Spain coming in?"

"Everyone else was in," he answered simply.

"You didn't hear her go out again—or anybody else come in?" the Chief demanded.

"Why, no." Mr. Parsons picked his words with care and forethought. "I heard Miss Moffett, locking up, right after the 'Fairy Princess' came in. The porch lights went off then."

"Did you hear anything else?"

Mr. Parsons hesitated. It seemed such a silly thing to talk about. "I must have fallen asleep," he began, "till about two o'clock. . . ."

"And what woke you up then?"

"Somebody was singing. Out on the Neck. Singing a song about a fox." Mr. Parsons shivered and wondered why he did.

Mrs. McAlistir said from the upper steps, "I heard it too. Disgraceful. On a Sabbath morning."

The Chief scowled. "I'll find out who was selling the stuff after midnight." He turned to Miss Moffett once more. "What kind of a lock do you have on this door, Olive?"

"A spring lock," Miss Moffett answered. "See for yourself. It snaps shut. You can open it from the inside, with this knob, but you have to have a key for outside. We put it on this year. It's the only door in this building that really locks. Most of the guests don't bother about locking their rooms. You see, we've never had any trouble before. You know that, Jacob. Phoebe and I have been here twenty years and we've never had so much as a handkerchief stolen."

"Who's got the keys to this door?" the Chief demanded.

"Why, we have, Phoebe and I. Nobody else." Miss Moffett pulled a clanking bunch from her bathrobe pocket. "Here's mine. Do you have yours, Phoebe?"

Miss Dow's bunch jingled in her hand. "Here's mine, Jacob." She carried the keys to him eagerly. "Nobody else has a key, Jacob, and I'm sure mine wasn't out of my room."

"Has it occurred to any of you," Miss Templeton spoke up, "that she might have brought someone in with her? That young man of the yacht?"

Miss Dow shuddered. "How disgusting! I'd have you know that our guests—"

The Chief stopped the argument. "It looks to me like an inside job," he stated, with heavy finality. "If that door was locked from the outside and the doors of all these rooms were unlocked, anybody in this building could have come into that room." His accusing glance swung around the hall. "Is everybody who sleeps in this building here **now?**"

Miss Moffett said, "I think so—oh, no, Mrs. Heath isn't here or her sister, Mrs. Chalmers."

"Get them," the Chief commanded.

Miss Moffett drew back. "I can't, Jacob. You see, Jacob —oh, I know them very well. There's nothing suspicious about them. They've been coming here for years. But you see, they don't like to be seen. Not Mrs. Heath. She comes down to meals, but Miss Chalmers—you see, she's sort of— deformed." She ran her hands over her hips and bosom, suggesting elephantine contours.

The Chief snickered. "Aunt Eppie Hogg?"

Miss Moffett blushed. "I wouldn't want to say that. She's a very nice woman. Never gives any trouble. But she doesn't like to be seen. I could get Mrs. Heath but I promised that Miss Chalmers wouldn't ever—"

The Chief interrupted her. "Get Mrs. Heath then. Right away."

Miss Moffett started reluctantly up the steps. When she came alongside Mary, she paused. "Your husband's not here either," she said, portentously.

"He's taking care of the baby. Nola Spain's little girl."

"What about this little girl?" The Chief turned toward Mary.

"Speak to her yourself," she answered. "In your own inimitable, kindly way."

The hall lapsed into embarrassed silence. Faces turned upward, staring to see what went on on the upper landing, listening to the murmur of Miss Moffett's voice, to another voice—high-pitched, tremulous—answering hers.

A gray woman, kimono askew over a flannel nightgown, bedraggled hair framing a frightened face, trailed Miss Moffett down the steps. "I've got Mrs. Heath," Miss Moffett announced, triumphantly.

The Chief took his pipe out of his mouth, touched the brim of his hat. "How do, ma'am. I've got to question you. Same as the others."

"Why?" The woman raised a trembling hand to a twitching mouth. "What's happened?"

"What's happened? Oh, nothing. Nothing at all." The Chief waved his pipe airily. "Only a murder." His tone was jovial.

"A murder!"

Mary wondered how one spoken word could possibly contain such volumes of incredulity, horror and anguish. A second of silence on tiptoe. Mrs. Heath swayed, toppled.

Doctor McAlistir sprang forward. He raised the woman's shoulders. The Chief lifted her heels. Mary opened the door of the A suite. Her husband met them in the doorway, his forefinger on his lips.

"Can't you all be a little quieter out here?" he complained querulously. "I've just got the baby off to sleep."

For a minute, it looked as though Mrs. Heath would be torn in two. Mr. Whittaker declined emphatically to move away from the door.

Mr. Haskell, holding the lady's heels, was all for carrying her into the chamber where the corpse lay. "That's the way to get a confession out of her when she comes to," he insisted.

But Dr. McAlistir, supporting Mrs. Heath's shoulders, said, "Of course not. Barbarous," and urged the lady toward the other side of the hall.

Dr. McAlistir won the tug-of-war. The unconscious Mrs. Heath was spread at last on Lorna Bean's bed. Mrs. Bean darted around the room like a distracted moth. "Oh, dear —oh, dear, the room's a mess." She jerked a brassière off a chair, thrust it into a bureau drawer. "Oh, dear, please don't mind the appearance of the room." She rolled her undergarments into a towel.

"Don't worry about that, Mrs. Bean." Dr. McAlistir held Mrs. Heath's wrist. "Have you any aromatics—smelling salts?"

Mrs. Bean's hands fluttered helplessly: "Somewhere,

Doctor—I hope I can find it." She riffled a bureau drawer. "Oh, where's Lorna? Lorna could find it."

Mary said, "My husband has a pint of Scotch. I'll get that." She crossed the deserted hall.

Chris whispered, "What's up, darling?"

She answered, "I never saw anything like it and I hope I never do again. That Chief of Police is an idiot!"

"Darling, it's his murder. Not yours. Don't feel so personally responsible. What happens to the kid now?"

Baby Doll was asleep, her lips puckered into a bud, her creamy cheeks flushed. Conversation passed over her unheeded.

"She looks like a little angel," Mary said.

"And smart, Mary. Smart as a whip. . . . Think we could ever get ourselves one like that?"

"I'll do my best. But I've got to have co-operation." She opened a suitcase, took out a bottle of liquor. "There's a swooning lady. Needs a drink. . . . Know who the kid's mother was? The model for the 'Fairy Princess.'"

For a moment, Chris seemed puzzled, then his face brightened and he said with a sort of incredulous delight, "Not the book-ends?"

"You bet."

"I'll be damned. First time I ever heard of a book-end being bumped off. Who killed her?"

"If the Chief hangs around much longer, they'll never know."

They closed the door quietly behind them. In the foyer between the bedrooms, they halted. A metallic tapping filled the corridor.

Chris said gruffly, "Stop that noise. It'll wake the kid."

Mary puckered her brows. "I've heard that before," she said. "When I first woke up."

Chris shrugged. "Antique water pipes," he decided. "Defective pump somewhere."

Mrs. Bean had found her smelling salts and Mrs. Heath's

spare frame was shuddering under the stimulant of the aromatic vapors. Her eyelids fluttered, opened to reveal blank pupils and rolling white eyeballs. They shut again. Mary gave the Doctor the bottle and Miss Dow dashed into the bathroom for a toothbrush glass. The Doctor raised the woman's head, separated her lips, poured the acrid liquor between her clenched teeth. Mrs. Heath choked, gasped, struggled to sit up. She stared wildly at the curious faces ringing the bed. Her mouth writhed. She pushed the glass away, covered her face with her hands and commenced to sob.

Dr. McAlistir said, "I think she'll be all right now. These middle-aged hearts can't stand surprises."

Mr. Haskell came over to the bed. Mary slipped her hand into her husband's, whispered, "Watch the subtle approach."

The Chief pointed his cold pipe. "Now, then, ma'am, now you're feeling better, tell me exactly what you saw and heard last night."

Mrs. Heath moaned through her muffling fingers. "I didn't see anything."

"Didn't you wake up during the night? I understand there was a racket out on the Neck. Didn't it wake you up?"

Mrs. Heath's shoulders twitched. "I didn't hear anything," she moaned.

"Didn't hear anybody come in or go out during the night eh? . . . Didn't hear any noise after this—over there—happened?"

"No." The monosyllable trembled.

"Ain't hard of hearing, are you? Everybody else in the house woke up and came out."

Mrs. Heath took her hands away from a gray, flabby mask of sorrow and despair. "My sister and I have nothing to do with what goes on in the house," she said.

"Your sister, eh? Did *she* wake up?"

Naked terror filled the woman's eyes. Her lips trembled,

barely parted, as she whispered, "My sister slept soundly all night. I left her asleep, now." She started up out of the bed, swinging her skinny, naked, blue-veined legs over the edge. "I must go back to her. I can't leave her alone."

A question trembled on the tip of Mary's tongue. She pushed it back, deciding, *Not while the genius is in charge.* She wondered, despairingly, whether some intelligent authority would eventually appear, with whom one might, at last, begin a serious homicide investigation.

"All right, everybody," Jake Haskell said. "Get back to your rooms. And stay there. The troopers'll be all along any minute. Everybody got to be searched."

Mrs. Heath gripped the bedstead, braced herself, looked despairingly from the Chief to Miss Moffett and Miss Dow. "Not Isabel," her lips and eyes pleaded. "Not Isabel."

Miss Dow patted her shoulder. "Don't worry, dear," she said. "I'll explain everything to him."

Chapter Five

BABY DOLL

MORNING FILLED THE window panes with white cushions
of fog. Judkins' black coach glistened in the driveway between Main and Annex. Two men slid a narrow wicker
basket into it, drove away.

After the mortuary wagon had gone, a horde of troopers
swung off their motorcycles, swarmed over the piazzas and
lawns. Sergeant Patrick Sargent of the State Police saluted
Jake Haskell. "Morning, Chief, hear you've got a little
trouble."

"Uh-huh." The Chief hitched his pants buckle. "Stabbing. Woman. From out of town. We got to take it easy,
Pat. The girls. Olive Moffett and Phoebe Dow. (You know
'em, don't you, Pat? I went to school with Phoebe.) Fine
girls. Run a nice, respectable business. They feel awful
bad. Keep it under, see. No publicity—yet. . . . Now listen.
I got it all sized up. It's an inside job. No doubt about it. No
doubt about that at all. But you know the District Attorney. *He* got to have evidence. *He* got to have a case. So we
got to search everybody. Print everybody. Them in the
Annex anyway. Where it happened. Wouldn't bother you
boys but I'm short handed. Tommy's on vacation. Down
New York for the Fair. Mike Silva's laid up. Got a fish hook
in his thumb. Thought nothing of it. And now Doc's treat-
ing him for blood poison. Shows how you got to be careful."

Sergeant Sargent asked, "Made any arrests?"

Chief Haskell raised a protesting palm. "Don't rush me.
Don't rush me. Listen, Pat, my boy, this is how we work it.

You get busy on that couple on the first floor in the Annex. Man and wife. Them first. I'm *very* much interested in them. Don't let 'em talk you out of anything. They're great talkers, they are. They'll try to tell you they're detectives." He tapped his forehead. "Cuckoo. Get the idea? I'll be with you in a couple of minutes. Got to make a phone call."

Sergeant Sargent rapped loudly on the Whittakers' door. Mr. and Mrs. Whittaker, dressed for travel, had at that moment pressed down the lid of their overnight case. Chris scuttled to the sleeping child, stood over her protectively. Mary opened the door.

Sergeant Sargent touched his hat brim.

Mary said with relief and welcome, "State Police? Glad to see you." She looked over her shoulder. "Child sleeping. Can't we go somewhere else to talk?"

The trooper shook his head. "No, ma'am." He strode into the bedchamber. His demeanor staked a claim. He said, "You sit right over there, lady. And don't make things harder, if you know what's good for you."

Chris raised his eyebrows. "What's doing, trooper?"

"This your luggage?" the trooper answered.

"Help yourself," Mary told him. "You won't find a thing but you're welcome to it."

The little girl stirred, awakening. She whimpered, "Mommy."

Chris patted her shoulder. "Take it easy, baby, take it easy."

Sergeant Sargent glanced casually at the child. "Your little girl?"

Chris shook his head. "Belongs to the late lamented."

The trooper looked at Baby Doll, again. Then he flipped up the lid of the overnight case. "Getting ready to leave?" he asked.

"Immediately," Chris replied.

"Relax. No rush. Weren't planning to take the little girl, were you?"

Mary spoke up this time. "We haven't decided what to do about her."

The child's russet head popped up from the pillow. She wound her arms around Mr. Whittaker's neck.

"She likes me," Chris said, giving a most unconvincing imitation of helplessness. "I've got a fatal fascination for women. All ages, all sizes. It looks as if we're elected if no papa or grandma turns up."

"You needn't bother," Sergeant Sargent assured him. "County authorities'll take care of her."

Chris answered, "That's what I was afraid of." His sharp profile took on a pinkish coat. "You see, we like the kid. We're crazy about her. Wouldn't mind taking her home. But—this is embarrassing as all hell—my reputation don't matter—but Mary here, if she came home from a two weeks' honeymoon with a five-year-old kid—"

Sergeant Sargent grimaced sympathetically. "Better five-year-old than five-day," he ventured. He regretted his lapse immediately. His face froze up again. "Don't make a move. Stay where you are." He tapped his holster. He turned to the suitcase again. He worked swiftly, efficiently.

While Mary and Chris, perched beside Baby Doll, watched him with interested amusement, he lifted each neatly folded garment from the bag, shook it, turned it inside out, inspecting as diligently as a dry cleaner's spotter, dropped it, when he was done, on the floor. He removed Mary's toilet case, Chris's military brushes, held them to the light, put them on the dresser, grunting as he did so. "Ought to be plenty prints on these."

Chris said, "There's a .32 in there, too. Want to see the permit?"

Sergeant Sargent churned the bag, found the revolver, scowled at it, laid it beside the brushes.

Chris got off the bed. "You can't take that. I need it in my business."

"Your business, hey? . . . Sit down." Sergeant Sargent

touched his holster again. "Three medals," he added, significantly. "For hitting the bull's-eye. Keep your shirt on."

Mary giggled. The giggle became hysterical laughter.

The trooper gripped her shoulder. "Cut that out," he growled. "Or you'll be laughing out of the other side of your mouth."

Chris bellowed, "Take your hands off my wife." He snapped out his wallet. "Credentials. We're New York detectives."

Sergeant Sargent waved away the proffered cards. "Get a new line," he said frigidly. "Last fellow pulled that one on me is up in State's prison. Extortion. Impersonating an officer."

Then, the door opened without a warning knock and Jacob Haskell came in. He had a revolver in his hand. He waved it at Mary and Chris. "Don't make a move," he said. "I got you covered." He glowered at them. "Show's over. Don't try any funny work." He smiled benignly at Sergeant Sargent. "Find anything, Pat?" He did not wait for an answer. He took a pair of handcuffs from his pocket. "Exactly what I thought, Pat," he crowed. "Pair of phonies in a stolen car. I got New York on the wire. And guess what? The little sedan they came in belongs to Detective Reese of the New York Police. Talked to him myself. Says it was taken from him yesterday."

Mary looked at Chris with blank amazement. Chris looked at her. Anger pushed his lower lip forward, tightened his jaw. He said, "If that's Johnny Reese's idea of a gag, I'll cut his throat."

"You will, hey?" The Chief twirled his gun from his hip. "You will, will you?" He leered. His chest swelled like a pouter pigeon's. "Gettin' somewheres, eh, Pat?"

The Sergeant agreed. "I got their gun," he supplemented.

The Chief inspected Mr. Whittaker's .32. "Neat little gadget." He chuckled. "All the fixin's. Liquor. Gun. Stolen car. Say, that's a Federal offense, ain't it, Pat? Taking a stolen car across the state line?"

"It is."

"O.K., boys," Chris grinned sardonically. "Call in the FBI. See if we care."

"That'll be enough out of you," Jake Haskell snapped. "Thought you were smart, you two. Come last night in a stolen car. Got yourselves fixed up in the room next to hers. (They must of studied the layout before, Pat.) He done it and she made out she discovered a crime. They told Sam Dolliver they were detectives. Showed him some papers."

"Printing's cheap," said Sergeant Sargent. "Mail order house sells these fake detective cards. Somebody gave me the address once."

"Didn't fool Jake Haskell. Not for a minute. I got wise to them right away when this woman tried to tell Sam how to run the case. Sam's new to this business, see. Been catching codfish all his life. No experience with crooks. The stuff she told him, Pat!" He hunched his shoulders. His belly shook with mirth. "Hoofs! Witches! Funniest damn stuff you ever heard. Trying to get him off the track, see, till this guy gets all the evidence cleaned up and makes up to the kid. They won't let anybody in their room, see. (Baby's sleeping. Sure, the baby's sleeping. Probably drugged her. That's what they come for. That's what I figure.) That's what you came for, you two—to get that kid?"

"Why, certainly," said Chris. "How'd you guess?"

"Hah!" The Chief tipped his chin. "How'd I guess? Got to get up early in the morning to outsmart Jake Haskell. She must be an heiress or something. It's murder and kidnapping, both. (Think I really ought to call the FBI, Pat? ... Naw, I don't think I will. They got enough publicity without this. We'll keep this one for us). Might have got away with it at that if they hadn't used a stolen car. These smart crooks. Always make just one slip. And then they find out crime don't pay."

"It pays," Chris said. "You don't get rich at it, but you eat regular." He smiled at his wife, as if to reassure her by his levity.

But Mrs. Whittaker, definitely, was not amused. She spoke up tartly: "Of course that's Detective Reese's car, officer. He's our friend. He loaned us the car."

Mr. Haskell winked at the state trooper. He said, "O.K., lady, let's see the owner's registration."

Chris fumbled in his wallet. As he searched, his chin dropped. He asked finally, "Didn't Johnny give it to you, Mary?"

Mary shook her head.

The Chief grinned broadly. "We-ll. And all packed up for a getaway." He chuckled, slapped his thigh. "Right on the nose, Pat. Not a second to spare." He jangled the handcuffs, moved toward Mr. Whittaker's wrist.

Chris caught at his sleeve. "Listen, you jackass—" he began.

The Chief cut him short with a decisive left to the jaw. That was the hand in which he held the bracelets. The metal slashed Mr. Whittaker's mouth.

Chris staggered back against the bed, clapped his hands over his jaw. "Well, I'll be a—" he muttered, through bloody fingers.

Baby Doll screamed.

Mary got up and came forward, her eyes glittering. "That's all, officer," she said. "You've had your fun." Her voice deepened with fury. "Your brother-in-law's the Mayor, isn't he? This'll look lovely in print. Appointing his halfwit relative Chief of Police. Halfwit, did I say? Pardon my exaggeration."

Chris Whittaker's hands came down slowly. In all the years he had known Mary, he had never seen her look as beautiful as she did now, with cheeks bright pink and eyes glowing. The Chief of Police and the state trooper were staring at her too, staring and gaping, not at her charms, but at her temerity.

"You!" She took up the matter of the state trooper next. "When you came in, I was glad to see you. Yes, actually glad. After this genius, I welcomed anybody who looked reasonably bright. We didn't mind you searching our things. We don't mind giving you our fingerprints. Heaven knows we have no reason to object to sensible police routine. But no bullying. No hitting an innocent man. (If he hurt you, Chris, I'll have him locked up for a hundred years, so help me. I'll send him to the electric chair and good riddance to bad rubbish.) Come on, genius, take me to the nearest telephone. Put cuffs on if you want to. We'll get this cleared up, right away, once and for all."

She flung the door open and marched out. The Chief of Police had no choice but to tag after her. Chris smirked at the trooper. "Did I or did I not marry a wonderful woman?" He hugged the wide-eyed child on the bed. "Our Mary's a honey, Baby Doll. She's not afraid of anything. Cops or anything. Stick around with us, baby. You'll see some fun."

Behind the windows, yellow sunlight tinted the thick down pillows of the fog. Mary's heels clattered across the porch. She strode into the lobby.

Miss Dow, back of the counter, ducked her neck into the white collar of her dress. "Oh, Jacob," she began. "Did she confess?" No one paid any attention to her.

Mary said, "You make the call, genius. Just to be sure that I don't try to put anything over. Call Spring 7-3100. That's the number of the New York Police. Ask for Chief Inspector Heinsheimer. If he's not at headquarters, the switchboard will locate him and connect you. . . . Step on it."

Miss Dow's back teeth and tonsils came up for air.

The Chief's voice quivered as he called "New York, Spring 7-3100" and asked for the Chief Inspector. He held the wire until a voice at the other end said, "Heinsheimer speaking," and then he gave the receiver to Mary. His hand shook.

"Hello, Inspector," she said. "This is Mary. Mary Carner. . . . Thanks. . . . Oh, Chris is just fine. Having a little trouble with his jaw. Nothing serious. . . . Yes, we're having a lovely time. Wonderful. Been up all night with a murder. . . . That's what I said. . . . I can't help it, Inspector. Homicide follows me around. . . . Artist's model. Nola Spain. Ever hear of her? If the boys can pick up a line on her background, her connections, I'm sure the local Chief of Police will appreciate it. He needs help. Plenty, if you ask me. . . . Where are we? Place called Laneport. Massachusetts. Hotel's the Rockledge. And say, if you should see Johnny Reese this morning, tell him Chris is going to cut his throat. If it's his idea of a good gag to say we stole his car. . . . Well, for a minute it wasn't funny. . . . No, we're not in any trouble. Nothing we can't get out of with a phone call. . . . Here. talk to a brilliant gentleman and tell him what you know about the Whittakers. Talk slow. Words of one syllable. He's at the foot of the class. 'Bye, Inspector, see you soon. . . . Take it away, genius."

She gave the receiver to the Chief. He said diffidently, "Haskell. Chief of Laneport police."

Inspector Heinsheimer's hearty voice boomed through the receiver into the Chief's maroon right ear: "Smartest detective in New York. Doesn't miss a trick. I've known her for years. Her and her husband. You'll be in luck, if you can talk her into working for you."

The Chief said "Thanks" and hung up the receiver. His face was deep purple. He looked at the floor, twisted his cap in his hand. His embarrassment was so abject that Mary almost felt sorry for him.

But she shrugged off the impulse to be generous. She said cruelly, "There, there, little boy, mama'll wipe your nose so the big boys won't laugh. Mama'll help you find your murderer. . . . Now get moving. You've wasted enough time. First you go back to the Annex and get down on your knees to my husband and pray he doesn't take you apart, limb from limb. And then you rope off that porch and post a guard at that door and get down to business. If the army hasn't trampled up the lawn you may find something there. . . . You'll roast in hell for what you've done this morning. A double-hot hell for stupid, arrogant cops. Handling that window screen! Never occurred to you that somebody might have taken it out for any other reason but to give the mosquitoes a snack. Sending down a cadaver without taking photographs! Handling the weapon! Scuffing up a room before footprints were checked! Cooking up a theory before you even made a reasonable examination. Where'd you learn to be a dectective? Whose whodunits have you been reading? Chief of Police!" She stopped only because she had run out of breath.

The Chief was strangling. He muttered, "Aw . . . We . . . I . . . Aw . . ."

Mrs. Whittaker caught her second wind. "What's the population of this town?" she asked.

Mr. Haskell looked up, startled. "Thirty-five hundred winter, five thousand summer," he stammered, grateful for what seemed to be a sudden shift of the angry lady's interest.

"That's a break for you. The homicide rate's only eight in a hundred thousand. You'll be safe in a home for feeble-minded before another one comes this way."

Mr. Haskell fled. Mary watched his retreating back. She brushed off the palms of her hands. "That's that and a good day's work, Mrs. W.," she said to herself and to the room.

A Chinese gong bonged softly. Miss Dow's mouth snapped shut. She pressed her heaving bosom. "Breakfast is served, Mrs. Whittaker," she gasped.

"Oh, I didn't realize there was anyone here." Mary seemed momentarily dismayed. Then she said, "You won't say anything about this? We'll leave it between you and me and Mr. Haskell, shall we?"

"I never gossip," Miss Dow answered.

Mrs. Whittaker smiled. She turned to go. At the door she changed her mind and came back to Miss Dow. "I've just remembered," she said. "Out in the hall you said there was more about the reservation for Nola Spain than you could mention publicly. What was it?"

Miss Dow glanced furtively around the lobby. Breakfast-bound guests were dribbling down the staircase. "I was going to tell Jacob." Miss Dow's voice was a whisper. "I suppose now—after this—you might as well know. (Good morning, Mrs. Merrill. No, I think it'll clear before noon. The wind's shifting.) Paul Donato was the one who made the reservation for Nola Spain. Donato, the sculptor. A week ago Monday. He said I was not to mention it to Alicia. That's his wife. (Oh, good morning, Miss Godwin. Have a nice time last night? . . . Yes, I'd like very much to hear about it. But not right now, dear. . . . Miss Godwin, this is Mrs. Whittaker. One of our new guests. We're talking over a little private matter. You don't mind, do you, Miss Godwin?) Miss Godwin's our artist. She was at Donato's last night. Well, Paul Donato said, 'Nola Spain's coming up to work for me but I'd rather Alicia didn't know I sent for her. I'd rather Alicia thought she just happened to be in Laneport. I'll guarantee her board bill.' Those were his exact words. . . . Why, you don't believe," Miss Dow blinked. "You don't believe Alicia Donato could have—"

Mary answered, "I never name suspects till I have all the facts. That's where the Chief and I differ."

She hurried back to the Annex. She found a trooper in the corridor of the A suite, guarding the chamber where Nola Spain had met her death. Locking the barn, she thought, after the horse is stolen. She opened the door to her own room. Sergeant Sargent had gone. Baby Doll sat astride on the foot rail, watching Chris, his lower lip neatly mended with a strip of plaster, re-pack a suitcase.

"Everything all fixed?" Chris asked.

"Perfectly. The Inspector sent his love."

"Did you tell him about that rat, Reese?"

"I gave him all the news. How's your jaw?"

"Flea bite. Forget it. The Chief offered me everything but his undershirt to say no more. You certainly gave him the works."

"How about breakfast?"

"I figured we'd check out and pick it up on the way. Had all I want of this place."

Mary glanced at the little girl. She said, "I'm ashamed of you, Christopher. Would you walk out on Baby Doll?"

He dropped the lid of the suitcase. "But, Mary," he pleaded. "This is our honeymoon. We can't get cluttered up with kids and crimes."

She answered, "Baby Doll, you poor chick, you must be famished. I'll get your clothes and dress you."

The state trooper barred Nola Spain's room. "No, ma'am, nobody goes in. Sergeant Sargent's orders."

"I can't take a child in to breakfast in pajamas," Mary protested.

He shrugged. "That's not my business. Can't let you in here."

"Where's the Sergeant?" He pointed up. Sergeant Sargent stood before Mrs. Heath's door. The entrance was open a hand's-breadth and the Sergeant had his shoe in the crack. Through the opening Mary saw the tip of a nose, a bloodshot left eye, a wisp of straggling hair, heard Mrs. Heath's voice, frightened, unconvincing: "We have nothing to hide. Nothing. But Miss Moffett promised us privacy."

"I hate to interrupt this pleasant tête-à-tête," Mary said. "But the little girl needs her clothes. Tell your gendarme to let me in, Sergeant."

Sergeant Sargent took his foot reluctantly out of the

crack, growled, "I'll be right back," to Mrs. Heath, followed Mary down the steps, said, "This one's O.K., Bud,"
to his subordinate, tramped upstairs again. By the time he
came back Mrs. Heath had pushed a chair and two suitcases against her door. The Sergeant pounded the panels.
"Open up. Open up." His shouts and banging echoed
through the house.

In the chamber where Nola Spain had met her death, the
light still burned in the center of the ceiling, its glass globe
plastered with the singed bodies of defunct gnats, moths
and mosquitoes. The room was a shambles. When Mary
had come into it first it had been peaceful—a quiet tomb.
Death had been neat, precise, but those who had come
after it had left the impact of violence.

The marble form was gone but the bed still traced its
outlines; marked the brutality of its earthly end in a smear
of blood on tumbled sheets. On the dresser, where the
vandal hand of Jacob Haskell had tossed it, lay the lethal
weapon. It resembled a pencil; it resembled a spike, a
chisel, yet it was none of these. Neither as tool or weapon
had Mary seen its like before.

Overhead, the banging on Mrs. Heath's door had
stopped abruptly. Falling furniture clattered on the ceiling. Sergeant Sargent yelled, "Oh, no, you don't." Running
feet pattered. There were sounds of scuffle, the thud of a
body, a mingling of sobs and little strangled screams and
at last no sounds at all save the heavy tread of the trooper's
boots.

For a moment Mary stood under the echoing ceiling
with fists clenched, thinking how brutal it was to treat a
pair of frightened women so. And then she remembered
a white form in the upstairs hall and a hand and a voice
through an open door, and she thought how strange the behavior of these women was: "If one or both of them did
this thing, they're fools to make that fuss. The innocent
never mind questioning. The guilty try to act as if they

don't—if they've any sense."

She tiptoed around the room, avoiding the middle of the floor, the spaces nearest the open window and between the beds. She gathered up the child's apparel—dresses, playsuits, undergarments, sweaters, shoes and socks. They were fashionable clothes, she saw, expensive, new. On the shelves of Blankfort's store such things as these wore high-price tags, were bought by its wealthiest clientele.

When she had assembled the child's wardrobe, had piled it into an empty suitcase, she was surprised to see how little remained: two cotton dresses, a pair of slacks, a wool sweater, the long print gown, an old sport coat, two pair of slippers, a housecoat, a scarf-turban, a few undergarments.

In the top dresser drawer lay a thin red handbag. Mary opened it. She found a lipstick, worn down, runny, a powder compact, a stub of lead pencil, a clump of amber hairpins and a coin purse. The purse held a dollar bill and 40 odd cents in change. There was no checkbook. There were no papers. Nothing to indicate that Nola Spain had more in the world than the few things in this room. The woman had come to an expensive inn without the funds to pay for a night's lodging. Had her money been stolen? Was robbery the motive for this murder? But that couldn't have been. Paul Donato had told Miss Dow that he guaranteed her board bill. He must have known she was without means. Yet the child's wardrobe was luxurious. At that moment, the life of Nola Spain seemed no less a puzzle than her death.

Mary closed the handbag and went back to her own room. "Such pretty dresses, Baby Doll," she said. "Mother buy them for you?"

"Oh, no," the child answered promptly. "Mommy didn't have any money. She couldn't buy me dresses."

Chris Whittaker, department-store detective, looked at his wife, Mary Carner, department-store detective. Silently, they took inventory. Each nodded at the other to affirm the findings. Chris said, "Mommy just brought them back from the stores, without money?"

The little girl giggled. "You're funny, Chris. Nobody gets dresses from stores without money."

"You'd be surprised," said Chris.

"Then, where did you get them?" Mary asked.

"The Agency gave them to me."

"What Agency?" Chris demanded. "Don't tell me Home Relief's handing out Paris imports and Mary Lewis cottons."

For an instant Baby Doll seemed bewildered. Then she patted Chris Whittaker's cheek. "You're a goosie, Chris. Don't you know anything at all? The Agency that takes my pictures gave them to me."

"All right, chick," Mary said. "Our mistake. Which dress do you want to wear today?"

"The blue one. With the val collar. Mommy said to wear that one today. She said little girls who stay at hotels have to look nice on Sundays."

Mommy said this. Mommy said that. Mommy, still and cold in death, instructed them. How queerly intimate they had become with a woman whom they had never known until death had struck her down.

Nola Spain's dead, Mary thought, as she waited for the tub to fill for the child's bath. *To us who never knew her living, she has come alive through death. Who she was. What she did. Whom she knew. We'll have to learn all that for we have her child on our hands, her death on our minds. We've got a responsibility now. We've got to stay with it. For the little girl's sake. To protect her. And for simple justice's sake. Nola Spain was murdered. Why? By whom? What person? A person. Not a witch. Of course, not a witch. That's baby talk.*

How about that cloven hoof under the window? That was nothing—the residue of a human footprint, distorted by the mist. If that damn fool Haskell hadn't messed the room, there might have been prints worth something. Those pock-marks on the lawn? They might mean something. They might mean nothing. If that room only hadn't been messed up. As it was there were no clues—none at all, except the hysteria of a frightened child. One mustn't take her words too seriously. Or must one? Even hysterical impressions spring from something. From something which seems like something else.

But there are leads more tangible than the impression of a witch. Isabel Chalmers in the upstairs hall. She had been out of her room. She could have come down the steps, have gone into the hall, into any room. Why were they all so determined to hide Miss Chalmers? Any of the people in this house might have gone through the hall and in and out of any room they pleased, through these unlocked doors. That weird little man with the pointed ears, for instance. He who was so sure it was death before death was mentioned. His babble about the swan boat and Prince Charming. And who was it—the doctor, the one with the white mustache—who had mentioned a meeting with a young man last night? That was important. Perhaps she brought him home with her. A jealous lover or a madman who stabbed her with a sliver of steel. Where Nola Spain went, what she did in her last living hours. Those were the things to find out. A motive led to a murderer as surely as any footprints in the fog. And where did that steel pencil come from? Now, there were these Donatos—the man had sent for Nola Spain and didn't want his wife to know. . . .

Baby Doll hopped into the bathroom. "Chris says hurry up. He says he's as hungry as a big, bad wolf. He says he'll eat me all, all up if he doesn't get his breakfast." She stepped out of her pajamas, hung them on a doorknob.

Mary lifted her into the tub, soaped a washcloth.

"You don't need to bathe me, Mary," Baby Doll protested. She swished a froth of soap across her chest. "I'm Mommy's helper," she said proudly. "I work."

"You work, dear? At what?"

"Modeling." Baby Doll scoured her face. Its babyish softness contrasted strangely with the grown-up gravity of her speech. "They put pretty dresses on me and they take my picture." Her breath made a bubble of the soapsuds. She blew it away. "It gets so hot with the big, big lights and I get so tired. Then Mommy says: 'Be good, Baby Doll. Just a little while longer. Please, Baby Doll.' And I keep quiet as a mouse for Mommy." She scrubbed her arms. "I have to do that for Mommy," she explained. "Mommy always needs the money awful bad."

Mary lifted the child from the tub, set her on the bathstool, patted her body with a towel. "Tell me all about you and Mommy," she said gently. "Where you lived. What you did. Everything you remember. Where was your apartment in New York, Baby Doll?"

The child wrinkled her nose. "It wasn't a 'partment, Mary. It was a room. A teeny-weeny room. Not a nice big room like that one here. Mommy and me used to sleep on the couch together and Mommy used to say, 'Lie still, Baby Doll. Don't move. Let's pretend we're statues.' Only it was so hot before we came up here. It isn't nice to sleep so tight with Mommy when it's hot."

Mary slipped a tiny shirt over the child's head, pulled on her panties, unrolled a pair of socks.

The child said, "I don't know why you dress me, Mary. I can dress myself. I'm a big girl. I work, I told you. The man gives me five dollars every time he takes my picture."

"Didn't your mommy ever work?"

"Oh, no." The child's bright curls bobbed. "Mommy was too sick. She used to lie on the couch all day long, 'cepting when she had to take me to the Agency or when Todd came up to take her out at night."

"Who's Todd?" Mary asked sharply.

The child folded her lips. "Mommy said never to discuss him." She buckled her slippers in silence. She jumped off the bathstool. "I'm ready for my dress now. Isn't it pretty, Mary? Mommy picked it for me to wear today. Oh, Mary," she buried her head in Mary's shoulder. "I want Mommy to see how pretty it looks. Oh, Mary, why did Mommy go away? She loved it here. She said, 'I'm so glad Paul sent for me.'" Baby Doll rubbed her eyes with her wrist.

"Paul? Paul Donato?" Mary asked.

Baby Doll nodded. "Do you know him, Mary?"

Mary answered, "No. Do you?"

The child shook her curls. "He was a friend of Mommy's. But I never met him. Mommy worked for him a long, long time ago, before she got sick. When he made the 'Fairy Princess.' Did you ever see Mommy's 'Fairy Princess,' Mary?"

"Often. I think it's lovely. You'll always have that to remember her by."

The child's lips quivered. Her eyes filled. "I love Mommy." She burrowed in Mary's shoulder again. "Oh, why did the wicked witch take my pretty mommy away?"

Mary held her tightly until the sobs had ceased. Then she commenced to comb out the auburn curls. She said, "Do you like Chris and me, Baby Doll?"

The curly head wagged.

"Do you want to be our little girl for a while?"

The child answered with a tear-choked gurgle.

"Then you'll stay with us, dear, till we find your folks."

"I haven't any, 'cept Mommy."

"You've a grandma, or an aunt. Everybody has an aunt."

"I haven't anybody," Baby Doll said firmly. "'Cept Mommy and you and Chris."

Chapter Six

SECOND SIGHT?

THE ROCKLEDGE dining room was in a dither. It began when Miss Hays and Miss Templeton took their seats at the round table for six over which Miss Fern Godwin presided like a batik Buddha.

"You look rather pale, dear." Miss Godwin appraised Miss Templeton with condescending solicitude. "Didn't you sleep well?"

"Sleep well? .... Oh, my dear? Don't you know?"

"*Glamis hath murdered sleep,*" Miss Hayes explained. "*Therefore Cawdor shall sleep no more.*"

Miss Godwin protested crossly, "I don't know what you're talking about."

"She's told you." Miss Templeton waved a listless hand. "Exactly what happened. There's been murder in the Annex."

The dither bubbled. It became a jabber most unseemly for Sunday morning in a New England inn.

"I wondered about those troopers," Fern Godwin said. "I passed Jake Haskell. He barely said 'Good morning' . . . Why, Mrs. Bean, you look so distressed! What is it, dear?"

Miss Templeton whispered, "She had a very bad night. She practically swooned."

"Oh, my poor darling!" Miss Godwin pressed a plump, warm hand on Mrs. Bean's arm. "Sit down, dear. Do. With us. And have your breakfast."

"I can't." Mrs. Bean hovered between sitting and standing. "Till I find Lorna. The child's disappeared."

"Sit down, dear," Miss Godwin coaxed. "She's probably

just out for a walk. A little constitutional before her breakfast."

"In this awful fog!"

"Why not, dear? It's so good for the complexion. Don't fret, dear. Do sit down with us."

Mrs. Bean sank into a chair. "I won't have a thing. I really can't eat. That child worries me so. . . . Well, just a cup of hot water."

"Take a little lemon in it, dear," Miss Godwin urged. "Clear your system."

The dither took on a cackle of sour amusement when Delia, the waitress, placed the typewritten menu before Mr. Parsons, fidgeting at his table for one near the window, and asked, as if she did not know his invariable order (hot water, prune juice, one two-minute egg, one piece of whole wheat toast, unbuttered, kumquat marmalade and a cup of Postum), "What'll it be this morning, Mr. Parsons? . . . You look awful tired. I bet you didn't get a wink of sleep, with that business over in the Annex and Ryon Lyndall waking up the whole town."

Mr. Parsons exclaimed, "Ryon Lyndall!" and Miss Templeton, at the adjoining table, perked up: "Did you say Ryon Lyndall, Delia?"

Delia wheeled, faced both tables at once. "Ryon Lyndall," she repeated, beaming with awareness of her sensation. "Drunk as a lord. Singing all the way up Central Road and down Johnson's Neck."

"I'll be a kitten's uncle!" Dr. McAlistir exploded.

"Ed Swinson found him," Delia went on. "Ed was coming home from a date. Ed saw him reeling down the road, singing at the top of his lungs. Ed said to himself, 'That can't be Ryon Lyndall. Not Ryon Lyndall, the artist.' But when he got up close, he saw it was. You could have knocked Ed over with a mackerel fin. When Mr. Lyndall saw Ed, he said, 'Hi, boy,' or something like that to Ed. 'Some fun.' 'Hi, boy. Some fun!' " Delia snickered. "Ed took him home. His mother was waiting up for him, Ed said. There was a light in the window anyway. And a good thing, Ed said, because you could hardly see your hand in front of your face. Ed said it was a mercy Ryon Lyndall wasn't run over in the fog."

"A mother's instinct," Miss Templeton declared sententiously. "Remember how worried Mrs. Lyndall was because he hadn't come home for his dinner. She just knew something was wrong."

Dr. McAlistir wiped his mustache. "Nothing's wrong," he snorted. "A man has a right to let off steam once in a while."

So Ryon Lyndall was the fox. The white fox. The image came back to Mr. Parsons clearly, stood before his water goblet. The white fox which he had thought was the white woman, facing the hunters defiantly but quaking a little, as if aware of the awfulness of its defiance. But if Ryon was the fox, who could the hunters be? *Pshaw,* Mr. Parsons concluded, *I'll have to keep things straighter than this. Ryon wasn't pretending to be a fox. He merely sang about a fox.*

Miss Dow came into the dining-room. She said "Good morning" with a measured smile—cordial but not exuberant. She clapped her hands for attention, raised one for silence. "May I say a few words. Now that you're all together. Miss Moffett and I have talked things over. Perhaps some of you already know. We felt you should hear about it first from one of us, before you learn about it from strangers. There's been some unpleasantness. One of the guests over in the Annex—I've always been particular about my clientele. You know that."

Her eyes beseeched Miss Templeton and Miss Hays. "That unfortunate young woman came well recommended. And we mustn't speak ill of the—departed—must we? Now," her manner became brisk, business-like, "I'm afraid some of you may be questioned by the police. Of course Miss Moffett and I will try to spare you all we can. Jacob

Haskell's an old friend of ours. You won't have to worry about *him*. But there's a young woman. A Mrs. Whittaker. She and her husband arrived last night. She's a well-known detective, I understand. Mary Carner. You may have read about her. Her husband's one too, but not as famous as she is. (Are they coming, Delia?)" She peered around her shoulder. "If she wishes to interview any of you, I'd personally appreciate it if you gave her every co-operation. It'll save trouble." Her voice trembled on *trouble*. "She seems to be taking care of the little girl of the—" Her cough permitted her listeners to complete the sentence. "Just one thing more. It would be a great favor to Miss Moffett and me if you just didn't—well, talk about this unfortunate affair—to outsiders."

Mrs. McAlistir pushed back her chair, picked up her gloves and handbag. "I am going to church," she announced. "Would you mind, Miss Dow, if I said a prayer— a little, quiet, private prayer—for the repose of her soul?"

"Oh, my dear! But softly, softly. You understand our position. Here they come." Miss Dow scurried to and fro like a chicken in the road before an approaching automobile. "They have the little girl with them. I think I can depend on you all to be tactful. . . . Where'll we seat them? Oh, no, Delia, not *there*. That's where *she* sat. We'll leave that vacant for a day or so. We'll give them this table. Mrs. Prentiss won't mind. I'll speak to her. . . . Good morning, Mrs. Whittaker." She pulled out Mary's chair herself, bowed over it deferentially. "Good morning, Mr. Whittaker. Don't you think the fog's lifting a little?" She asked the question as though hers was personal responsibility for the Laneport weather.

She brought them the menu. "The melon may be out. I'll go and see." She intercepted Delia at the pantry door. "Delia," she said, "I'll serve Mr. and Mrs. Whittaker. You'll have to run over to the Annex with the tray. Service for two this morning. Mrs. Heath isn't coming down. She's too upset. They searched her room. Pat Sargent did. Forced his way in—I'm sick over it, Delia, absolutely heartsick."

Chris asked, "What do we order for Baby Doll, Mary?" But the child spoke up for herself. "Mommy said I could have two poached eggs this morning," she announced.

"Think it's good for her, Mary?" Mr. Whittaker gave an excellent exhibition of paternal anxiety.

"Mommy said so," Baby Doll reproached him. "Mommy said I could eat everything I wanted. She said for me to get strong and big in the country."

Miss Hays bent across her wheat cakes and sausage. "The child said 'Mommy,'" she whispered. "She's not afraid to mention the dead."

Miss Templeton answered, "You'd think they'd have dressed her in black. Not that blue party dress." Her critical stare pivoted from Baby Doll to Mr. Whittaker. "He's perfect," she announced after 60 seconds of study. "The Sherlock Holmes type. Isn't he, dear?"

Miss Hays appraised Mr. Whittaker's aquiline profile. "William Gillette's Sherlock Holmes or Basil Rathbone's?" she asked.

Miss Templeton unveiled her front teeth. "You must be older than I, dear," she replied sweetly. "Mr. Gillette's Sherlock Holmes was before *my* time."

Mr. Parsons dawdled over the crumbs of his toast and the cold dregs of his Postum. When Mary and Chris and Baby Doll had put down their napkins at last, had pushed back their chairs, he got up, too, with sudden alacrity. He followed them to the porch, almost treading on Mr. Whittaker's heels. Timidly, he plucked Mary's sleeve. "Excuse me, ma'am," he said. "I'd like to speak with you." He saw Miss Templeton hovering, added quickly, "In private, if your husband doesn't mind."

Chris said, "Don't worry about me. Baby Doll and I were just going to take a walk."

Mr. Parsons touched the lady's elbow. "If you please,

ma'am, off the porch. Where no one can hear us."

"Good enough," Mary agreed.

They walked silently through the damp grass beside the sea-wall until they came to the corner where a bean pole fence made a right angle with the wall, cutting off the Rockledge grounds from the rest of Johnson's Neck. Mr. Parsons said, "I don't think they can hear us now."

Mary hoisted herself up on the stone ledge. Mr. Parsons scrambled stiffly up beside her. She smiled at him encouragingly, waiting for him to start the conversation, but he sat without speaking, probing her face with his bright gray eyes. His stare was disconcerting. She looked away from him toward the sea.

The fog and tide were ebbing. From the top of the wall, Mary looked down on wet sands, on rocks, dull brown and gray, crusted with periwinkles, splotched with dark, sullen pools of sea water. Sandpipers scuttled, like giant daddy-long-legs, across the refuse-strewn beach. A vagrant sunbeam caught the flashing squirt of clams buried deep in the sand. Beyond the rocks, the opaque curtain of the fog hung down to the sea. The rusty-hinge creak of invisible gulls made a weird cacophony with the moo of the foghorn on the Point.

Mr. Parsons cleared his throat and Mary turned expectantly. "Do you believe in clairvoyance, ma'am?" he began.

Mary's heart sank but she replied politely, "I haven't ever given it much thought."

"Oh." Mr. Parsons seemed taken aback. "But you have no prejudice against it?"

"Hardly. How can one be prejudiced against things one doesn't know anything about?"

"Ah, ma'am," he shook his head sadly. "That's what prejudice is. Ignorance hating what it knows nothing about. Ignorance hating itself for being ignorant, you might almost say."

She was annoyed. She nudged the conversation. "Was

that all you wished to talk to me about—clairvoyance? This is hardly the place or time—"

He got off the sea-wall. He bowed stiffly. He said, "I beg your pardon, ma'am, for wasting your time."

She saw that she had offended, had pushed him back within himself. Whatever he might have been able to tell about the death of Nola Spain might now remain untold. And so she tugged his retreating coat sleeve and said, "Please, Mr. Parsons, I'm sorry. I'm really very much interested. Truly I am. Please go on with what you planned to say."

He answered coldly, "I have followed a life-long rule never to discuss with strangers subjects to which I felt they were unresponsive."

She apologized, "I was too abrupt. My life, my activities, you see, have been concerned with the actual senses—the things you can see and hear and touch."

"That's just it." A reluctant note of triumph crept into his voice. "Few people realize that there's an additional sense. Some call it clairvoyance; some call it telepathy; some call it second sight."

"And you feel," Mary asked, "that you have that sense? You knew before it happened that Nola Spain was about to die?"

"Of course," he answered blandly. "I saw the white woman. Any person in Laneport will tell you that the vision of the white woman means impending death. I saw the white woman when Ryon Lyndall sang that song about the fox."

She thought sourly, *Every little bit helps. Baby Doll's witch and this lad's spooks*, but her voice was still patient as she persisted, "Were you acquainted with Nola Spain?"

He shook his head again. "We never exchanged a single word." His voice held a poignant note of regret. "I saw her enter the lobby last night. I was engaged in a game of cards. Miss Hays, Miss Templeton, Mrs. Lyndall—the

mother of the intoxicated man who sang about the fox—and
I. The 'Fairy Princess' came in alone. She looked distressed
and ill but she was very beautiful. She walked like a
young tree swaying. . . . The ladies made some invidious
criticism. We may disregard it."

"No," Mary said quickly. "We can't disregard anything
that anyone said or did before Nola Spain was killed."

He sighed. "I am loath to repeat it. I can understand
quite well how those women in whom youth and beauty
died still-born might resent a different sort of female. Let
me go on. Nola Spain went out into the night and then the
young man came to look for her. A fine-looking, golden-
haired young man. Prince Charming. The young man
from the *Cynisca*. The swan boat. It is a yacht, I have been
told, a beautiful vessel at anchor at the end of Johnson's
Neck. We can go and find it if you wish. It can't run away
in this—" He gestured toward the fog-masked sea. "Doctor
McAlistir informs me that the young man met her at Paul
Donato's. The sculptor's. Mr. Donato was not at home. His
wife received the guests alone. The young man went there
and found his Fairy Princess. But I know of my own knowledge that she came home before midnight. She spoke with
someone on the porch and she came in alone. I believe she
came alone." He spoke less surely now. "It seemed to me I
heard her stumbling but I am certain that I heard his footsteps, hurrying away, just as he had run when he came to
meet her. I had a strange sensation when he first came to
find her," his tone grew dreamy, vague, "that he was a man
overboard in a fog-bound, stormy sea."

His words were weaving a fuzz in Mary's brain, his
gentle droning voice mixing up observation, hearsay, pre-
sentiment.

"I must have fallen asleep," he went on ruefully. "I must
have been asleep until Ryon Lyndall's singing woke me up.
I didn't know it was Ryon until this morning. It was past
two o'clock then. It was a song about a fox. An impudent

little song. But it was then that I saw the white woman. And I knew that death was near. I looked for it, I listened for it. I heard its steps. Yes, I heard its footsteps quite distinctly."

"In the hall, Mr. Parsons?" she asked eagerly.

"Oh, no. They came from the sea. Soft footsteps, padding quietly, but surely, as if they knew their way."

"How long after you heard the singer did you hear the footsteps?"

"About an hour. Oh, it wasn't Ryon Lyndall. He had nothing to do with this." His head bobbed emphatically. "Oh, no. It wasn't Ryon."

"Your sixth sense told you that?"

His lips curled impishly. "No, Delia told me that. The waitress. Her friend Ed Swinson took Ryon Lyndall home and saw him into his house."

"Where does Ryon Lyndall live?"

"Down the Neck." Mr. Parsons pointed. "If you've sharp eyes you can see the house. A white house. Trimmed with blue."

She looked down Johnson's Neck. The edges of the mist trailed like smoke away from a small white house with cobalt shutters.

"His mother has a lovely garden," Mr. Parsons said irrelevantly. "One of the most beautiful in Laneport. It is a pity Ryon feels that he must put it on canvas."

She said impatiently, "After the drunken artist passed the Rockledge, you heard no sound until you heard the footsteps an hour later. Is that correct?"

"It is."

"And then what did you see or hear?"

"Why, nothing. Except a window moving. Not till the silver hammers tapped. And then you opened the door and I knew that she was dead."

"That's all." Disappointment curdled her voice—10 precious minutes had gone by, sitting on a damp sea-wall, listening to the drool of a garrulous old man.

He seemed to sense her disappointment. "I don't presume to be a detective, ma'am," he said humbly. "I don't presume to any knowledge of the techniques of criminal investigation. (Oh, I could read up on it, if you thought it might be helpful.)" He was fumbling for words to frame his eagerness. "If my abilities might have any practical value—I know there are matters of taking fingerprints and measuring distances and examining materials left upon the scene. I am not concerned with those. I should like to be a— a collaborator—to supplement the visual and auricular observations of the authorities by using my mind and my own special sense. There are, you know, things the eyes see and other things the mind alone sees."

She smiled. She said, "Of course. Bertillon measurements and ballistics tests aren't all there is to crime detection, by any means. The best detectives I know—those who work on homicide cases all the time—hunt with their minds as well as their eyes. But they call it playing hunches. A hunch by any other name—psychological insight or even clairvoyance—is just a hunch. But I'm not in that class. I'm no homicide investigator. I'm only a thief spotter. My trade needs sharp eyes chiefly. You see," she warmed to her thesis, "when I look out on this vista, I note not only that the fog is lifting but the way it lifts. I see that the roof from which the fog has lifted is a deeper green than the tree beside it, that on that big rock out there in the harbor where the low white buildings are—"

"Lane's Island," Mr. Parsons murmured helpfully. "Coast Guard hangars."

"—are hundreds of gulls. But one single gull is standing alone at the tip of the rock."

"He's stood there alone all summer," Mr. Parsons added. "He can't abide crowds."

She ignored his assistance. She was peering into the mist. She said, "I see a ship, out there, now, beyond the Island.

White. Moving out to sea. Almost like a ghost ship."

Mr. Parsons' gaze followed hers. He shook his head. "I doubt it. No master would take a vessel out in a fog like this."

She turned away from the seascape. "It doesn't matter," she said. "I was just showing off. . . . I'm certain the police will appreciate any help you can give them."

"The police!" His tongue dripped disgust. "I have no wish to collaborate with the police. If I might work with you—"

She said, "I'm flattered. But I'm not in this for the duration. My husband and I mean to be on our way to Maine as soon as the inquest is over. We really haven't time to investigate the dark deeds of the Laneport witches."

"The Laneport witches!" His back stiffened. His eyes lit up. "Abby Drake and Nancy Loveran?"

She shook her head. "I've never met these ladies. And I haven't the least notion of what that's all about."

"Oh!" He seemed profoundly disappointed. "I had believed for an instant, for a single instant, that you shared my interests. Abby Drake and Nancy Loveran were the witches of Lane. You'll find them in the history books. This entire coast, you know, succumbed to the witchcraft delusion and those two ladies of Lane were believed to be possessed of occult powers."

"You and Baby Doll ought to get together." Her tone was derisive. "Possibly one of those two was the witch she claims she saw in her mother's room."

Red headlights of excitement flashed in Mr. Parsons' cheeks. "She says she saw a witch! Does she indeed!"

Mrs. Whittaker slid off the sea-wall. She said tartly, "Really, Mr. Parsons, I didn't expect you to take that seriously, too."

He caught her wrist. "Don't go away, ma'am. You can't understand what this means or you wouldn't talk that way."

She said, "I understand perfectly. I understand that a witch is a creature of myth and legend, and no grown-up intelligent person gives any credence whatever to tales of witches or witchcraft. I understand that a good many years ago some misguided fanatics on this coast cruelly put to death a number of harmless old crones under the fantastic delusion that they were witches."

"Ma'am." Mr. Parsons was pleading now. "Listen to me, ma'am. This is something I really know about. A witch is not a harmless old woman. A witch is the personification of the unknown evil men dread. Those women who were hanged as witches weren't just doddering crones. They were powerful women. They were women who knew more than their neighbors—more secrets of the woods or skies —or of human hearts. Women who had strong wills, violent tempers, bitter tongues—some source of power over their neighbors. Something that made them feared. Something that set them apart from the nice, conforming, pious women of their villages."

Mary shrugged her shoulders wearily. "Very educational," she said. "Would you, by any chance, consider Miss Chalmers a witch?"

"Miss Chalmers?" Mr. Parsons' eyes grew puzzled. "Why, of course not. No, of course not. Why do you ask that? . . . Oh, I know. She was awake last night. She was out of her room."

"You saw her too? Mr. Parsons, what is the secret of Isabel Chalmers?"

Mr. Parsons shook his head sadly. "There is no secret save the vanity of woman—I haven't thought about her. But I will. I will, of course, if you think for a moment that she—"

"Could she ride a broomstick? Fly through a window in a circle of fire?" Mary laughed. "I'm sorry. This has been entertaining. But not particularly helpful." The old man had led her to expect far more than he had told her. He was just a starry-eyed meddler—the sort of excitement-hunting crank who turned up at every homicide, the amateur who always knew more than the police. Anyone could be clairvoyant after the fact.

Mr. Parsons seemed let down, too. He stood beside the sea-wall, digging the turf with his cane, looking thoroughly crestfallen. Mary could not know how hard it had been for him to bring himself to this conversation. This woman had seemed keen, alert, understanding. But, like all the rest, Mrs. Whittaker hadn't the remotest understanding of what he was talking about. In the core of his disappointment lay, like a leaden weight, the heaviness of his grief over the death of the Fairy Princess and his deep concern that her murderer be found. *I must find someone else,* he told himself, *someone who'll know the meaning of a witch.* His eyes followed Mary as she hurried away from him. They came to rest on the auburn hair of Baby Doll, who was swinging like a monkey, with Chris Whittaker's forearm for a trapeze, at the top of the piazza steps.

Mr. Whittaker greeted his wife. "You've been paged, sweetheart. The D. A.'s looking for you. Name of Kneeland Babcock. I think he's the McCoy. He's over in the room. Giving it the works."

They entered the Annex. Delia, the waitress, carrying a tray of dishes, stood aside to let them pass. Mary asked, "Are those from Mrs. Heath's room?"

Delia nodded. Mary took the tray from her hands. The waitress stared.

Chris grinned. "Get used to that," he said. "Detectives are crazy." He turned the knob of Nola Spain's room, swung the door open for his wife, said, "See you later, beautiful. Have fun."

A long, pallid man looked up from the rocker as Mary entered. "We didn't order anything," he said.

"I brought it anyway," she answered cheerfully. "Just in case. Tray full of nice fingerprints. Mrs. Heath and Miss

Chalmers and Lord knows who else." She set the tray down on the edge of the dresser.

The room was crowded. Jake Haskell was there, Sergeant Sargent, Sam Dolliver, clustered around the man in the rocker. Sergeant Sargent wore a livid scratch from eye to chin. A man in shirtsleeves was dusting powder over the window sills; a youth crouched on the floor, examining the wood through a glass.

Mary beamed. "Well, well," she said. "Looks like old home week."

The long man assembled his limbs, got up. The crown of his skull nearly touched the swinging light bulb. "I am Kneeland Babcock, attorney for this District."

"I'm Mary Whittaker, who had the bad luck to find a body."

"You *were* Mary *Carner*, I believe." Kneeland Babcock smiled parsimoniously. "I have heard of you. Phyllis Knight was a connection. On my aunt Martha's side. I am glad you're here." He was New England: tight, small features, dignity as rigid as his high, stiff collar. But in his meticulous speech and manner, Mary found reassurance.

"I'm glad you've come," she said and meant it.

He answered, "Will you take my seat? We will commence again from the very beginning. We have, unfortunately, lost some things that are irretrievable. We will do the best we can." He seemed tired and he looked as though he had been locked up in a dark closet for a long while. His pallor made him an alien among the weather-rosy faces of the police. Added to his stooped, narrow shoulders, it spoke eloquently of days and nights bowed over law books, or pleading in musty courtrooms.

After he had listened thoughtfully to Mary's description of the body, the room and the grounds, he said, "It is, then, your opinion that the assailant entered this apartment through that window? But that's doing it the difficult way, isn't it, with all the doors in the house unlocked?"

Mary answered, "Of course. But whatever reason would there be for removing a window screen at night except to enter or leave?"

"To look out. To look for someone. Or look after someone."

"Officer Dolliver and I found a few shreds of gray wool on the window frame," Mary said. "Would you like to know what became of them?" She looked pointedly at Mr. Haskell.

Kneeland Babcock smiled wryly. "I can guess. However, those shreds of wool may have been there for weeks. A bathing suit, possibly, hung out to dry."

"Quite right," she said. "Then there was that extraordinary footprint Officer Dolliver and I saw. The print like a cloven hoof."

"Sam has told me about it. You realize, of course, Mrs. Whittaker, that that may have been an optical illusion, resulting from the fog." He had a nervous habit of cracking his knuckles when he was deep in thought. She found it as disconcerting as his matter-of-factness.

"You're very realistic, aren't you?" she observed.

The stingy smile hovered around his thin lips. "I was born and reared in Salem," he said. "My ancestors sailed from Salem port when Cotton Mather preached in Boston. I was raised on the witchcraft legends. The House of Seven Gables, the Jail, Gallows Hill, paid my way through college. A guide. You'd scarcely expect me to be impressed by supernatural implications at this late date."

She said, "Then you'll certainly put no stock in the little girl's story that a witch attacked her mother."

He shook his head. "No witch ever used a steel spike. Potions. Incantations. Spells. Bat's wing and eye of newt. But never cold steel. Oh, I'm not getting uppity, ma'am. I'm not refusing to consider any evidence. Sam told me about that footprint. We are examining the room thoroughly to see if we can find anything resembling it."

"We can't." The young man on the floor spoke up. "The place is a mess. All scuffed up."

Mary looked at Mr. Haskell again but she restrained herself nobly.

"Sam Dolliver tells me the print was facing the window."

"Right," Mary replied. "As though someone had been looking in or had stepped over the sill backward."

"How about the young woman whom Sam said you found looking in the window?"

"Miss Bean?" Mary frowned. She shook her head. "Sightseer. Nothing more. And sport shoes that left a totally different sort of print. But there is something else. I saw what appeared to be punctures in the wet turf around the house —a double row of little holes. I traced them almost to the sea-wall."

Mr. Babcock looked out of the window. He said mournfully, "Our state police wear good solid leather. Fine for durability, bad for lawns. We'll be fortunate if we find a single one." He sighed. "I fear we shall have to do without prints. I trust the problem will not prove unsurmountable. However, we have other resources. We shall proceed to trace the source of the weapon and we shall investigate the victim's past life and attempt to ascertain who, if anyone, was acquainted with her in Laneport."

"Three people that I know of," Mary ventured. "Paul Donato, the sculptor, and his wife. And a young man from the yacht *Cynisca*. She was out with him last night, I understand. He met her at Donato's. His yacht's anchored down on Johnson's Neck."

Kneeland Babcock said, "Sergeant Sargent, I'd appreciate it if you'd send your men down to the Marine Railways. Locate this boat. *Cynisca*, did you say, Mrs. Whittaker? And what is the young man's name?"

"Prince Charming," she answered.

"Prince Charming!" Kneeland Babcock swallowed hard. But he did not blink or smile. He said, "Sergeant, if you will kindly find Prince Charming and bring him here to meet me. Meanwhile, I shall go over to call on the Donatos. I shall be honored, Mrs. Whittaker, if you will join me. Mr. Haskell finds himself slightly handicapped—congenitally, I fear. The town of Laneport will be grateful for your help."

She said, "I'll be glad to do what I can," but she thought, *What a sucker you are, Mary! It's your honeymoon. It's your holiday and you're already up to your neck in murder.*

Chapter Seven

THE GOLDEN DAGGER

A CRISP WESTERLY BREEZE chased the fog from the shore, drove it out beyond Lane's Island. There it hung, suspended between sky and sea, waiting for a final gust to carry it home to the Newfoundland Banks.

The sun spread a thin gold wash over the winding streets of the town. It glinted on the tops of cars, warmed the freckled faces of a handful of Laneport boys who had heard the news from Judkins' driver and had sped on their bikes to stare at blank, white building walls and evoke imaginary gore.

As Mary stepped from the Rockledge porch into Central Road, she felt the poignant charm which had made this town Mecca for generations of artists. Laneport was old but it swathed its venerable bones in bright shawls of beauty. Time had mellowed its small, square houses. Each had a garden, glowing with petunia, nasturtium, phlox, larkspur, poppy, gladiolus, and hollyhock. At the bend in the road, the sun lay full on an old red building that had one time been a sail loft, made it warm and vibrant as heart's blood. Across the way, the sea was sparkling cobalt and the rocks, rusty in the fog, were burnished copper in the sun.

Peace wrapped the street—a Sabbath peace—impervious to the morbid urchins, to the rigidly corseted, overstuffed dowagers in bouclé, hobbling by twos, with tapping canes, out one way to Johnson's Neck, out the other to the Cape Point, to the troopers whooshing around corners on their motorcycles, to cars swishing on the macadam. A Sabbath peace, centuries old, not to be thrust aside by the transitory turmoils of summer people.

Mary crossed the road at Kneeland Babcock's side, turned a corner and climbed a steep hill to the third house on the left.

A rose hedge, with fat, flame-colored hips like ripe cherries in the dense green foliage, fenced the house. A painted sign on a wrought-iron bracket, above a swinging gate, said *Paul Donato Studio* and a green-bronze dryad on the lawn gave testimony.

Paul Donato's house was a gray-shingled L. The long end of the L, one could see from the road, was a studio. High, ecru-curtained windows, facing north, took up an entire wall. The short end of the L had a mandarin-red door, with a brass lion's head for knocker, and gauze curtains fluttering against the screens of casement windows. A quart of milk and a pint of cream stood before the door and a huge black cat scratched the panel with importunate paws, mewing indignantly.

Kneeland Babcock opened the gate and they went up the path to the red door. The cat whirled, arched its back, glared at them with angry amber eyes. Mary bent down to stroke it, pacifically murmuring, "Nice kitty." Needle-sharp claws struck at her hand. The cat spat, leaped into the air, and was off into the bushes, like a shot.

"Hurt you?" The District Attorney shook an admonitory forefinger. "Don't ever try to pet one of those. Maine coon cat. Handsome as a Persian. Wild as a tiger."

Mary sucked the long scratch on her wrist. "Why don't the Donatos get up and feed it?" she protested. "Any wonder it's wild?"

Kneeland Babcock raised the lion's head, dropped it. He waited, easing his long neck in its confining collar. He raised the lion's head again, and a third time. The knocker echoed hollowly in a silent house. He tapped his foot. **"These artists!"** he complained. "Carouse all night. Sleep all day." His fist beat a tattoo. "But they must be home," he reassured her, his face and voice puzzled. "Of course, they must. Their milk is here. Their windows are open."

They went around the side of the house. The casements were open on that side, too, curtains breeze-flat against the screens. They peered into a large, disordered living-room, at snowballs of crumpled napkins on a Persian rug, crusts of sandwiches and icing rinds on plates and tea cups heaped around a brass samovar, at a staircase, leading to a gallery. As they pressed their noses against the screen, they heard the creak of an opening door, saw a thin, long shadow fall across the carpet, zigzag slowly, irresolutely. And then they heard a soft thud. The shadow was gone and the house was silent again.

Mr. Babcock rattled the copper screens. He tossed off his dignity. He yelled, "Hey! Hey there! Open the door!"

Mary ran around to the back of the house. There was a rear door and she threw her weight against it, shook the knob. It did not yield. Then she saw a small closed window that had no screen. She tried to push it up. It was locked. She ran around the house to fetch Mr. Babcock. "There's a window we can manage. With your height and my figure. You don't mind housebreaking?"

"As a matter of principle, yes. Of expediency, no."

She took off her slipper, gave it to him. With its heel, he smashed the glass near the window latch, reached through the jagged break, unlocked the frame, pushed it up. He boosted her over the sill. She stepped onto a pantry table, strewn with the debris of party preparations. She ran through the house, flung open the front door and then, with the District Attorney striding after, leaped up the steps to the gallery.

On the floor, before a bedroom's open door, lay, flat on her face, a tall woman in a pink silk nightgown.

Kneeland Babcock picked the woman up, carried her into the room, stretched her on rumpled pink sheets. The woman's eyelids trembled, rose slowly over eyes opaque, misty, unseeing. They drooped and shut in sodden sleep.

The face on the bed was supremely ugly—a sallow skin, dusted with gray-chalk pallor, gaunt cheeks, indigo lips. The nose was the muzzle of a thoroughbred collie, narrow, high-bridged. Black hair straggled like Medusa's snakes. Delicate Alençon lace of an exquisite nightgown clung to a scrawny neck, to a flat bosom which rose and fell with shallow, labored breaths.

The District Attorney said, "Alicia Donato. I've met the lady before. Under quite different circumstances. I don't know what you do for this but do what you can. I'll phone for the doctor." He went downstairs.

Mary straightened the sheets, smoothed the pillow slip, watching the tortured breathing of the unconscious woman. What was this? Illness? Drugs? She touched the forehead. The skin was clammy, sweating with the colossal effort of drawing breath. What should one bring to this? Stimulants? Alcohol? Aromatics? Water? What did one do?

She must have awakened, Mary thought; *she must have had strength enough to get out of bed. Unless someone helped her—unless there's someone else here.* She looked around the room. Alicia Donato's bedchamber was a houri's bower of French walnut and rose taffeta, ruffled, scented. A connecting door at the far end of the room stood half-open. Through it, Mary saw the gleaming tiles of a bathroom and another door, beyond the bathroom. She went through the bathroom to the second chamber. This was a man's room. The furniture was massive, highly polished, beautifully grained dark wood and a wide studio couch covered with leopard-dappled velvet.

On the velvet bolster lay a small sheet of white notepaper, held by a golden pin that had a pearl-set dagger hilt. The dagger pin was stabbed through the platinum circlet of a wedding band.

Five poignant words were scrawled on the sheet of paper: *"This is the last humiliation."* There was no signature.

Was this suicide, then? The "last humiliation." But it wasn't the last, Mary realized. Far greater humiliation to seek to end the failures of a life by self-inflicted death and not quite bring it off—to live to face the knowledge that one had failed in dying as in living. She looked thoughtfully at the tragic message. Her eyes and mind paused at the golden dagger.

She went back to the bathroom again and opened the medicine cabinet. On its lowest shelf, she saw a small green bottle with a prescription label that said: *"Twenty drops in water before retiring."* She took out the stopper. The bottle was empty but she sniffed the faint, astringent sweetness of phenobarbital. A glass on the washstand still held the pale rose lees of the sleeping potion.

She caught a glimpse of her own face, pale from lack of sleep, in the mirror over the basin. It faded and in its place she seemed to see the taut, hollow ugliness of the woman who had raised the lethal glass to her lips. *Was she so much hurt,* she asked herself, *because her husband had sent for Nola Spain? Did that make her want to kill herself? Or was there something more? What really makes people take their own lives? Failure, disappointment, or—overwhelming, inescapable guilt?* She clapped her hand over her mouth. A golden dagger for Alicia Donato's husband! A steel dagger for the other woman!

Then she heard the brakes of a car and swiftly striding feet on the path. She came out into the gallery to see, for the second time that Sunday morning, the bald head and solemn length of Dr. Nathaniel Sulloway.

Dr. Sulloway grimaced sourly when he saw her. "Do you specialize in murdered women?" he asked.

"I don't believe this one will die. Tried to. With barbital, I think."

"I'll find that out myself," he said. He entered the bedroom and slammed the door.

Mary went down the steps to the living-room. This was a magnificent room, white-plastered, high-ceilinged, beamed. A long, deep sofa, its blue velvet cushions flattened, stretched before a fireplace. Jewel-toned tapestries, echoing the colors of the Persian rug, hung on the walls. On little tables and pedestals stood torsos and figurines of marble—black, pink, and white. No summer cottage, this, nor artist's garret. A show room, rather. A rich, distinguished room, impressive even in its post-teaparty clutter.

Three steps, opposite the fireplace, led down into the studio. The studio door was open.

The District Attorney stood before the fireplace, frowning at his hands. He held his fists out to Mary. In his sootstained fingers were scraps of stone. She picked out a marble hand, a fragment of draped torso, a diadem-crowned forehead.

Mr. Babcock gestured toward the fire-tongs and a heavy mallet which lay in the cold ashes of the hearth. Mary picked the mallet up. It was speckled with white splinters and crumbs of marble.

"Vandalism," Kneeland Babcock said soberly. "Deliberate destruction."

"Those look like pieces of Paul Donato's famous 'Fairy Princess,'" she answered. "The statue Nola Spain posed for. Donato didn't want his wife to know he'd sent for the model. She came here last night. He wasn't home but Mrs. Donato was. Some time after her guests left, Mrs. Donato tried to kill herself. That's what it appears she tried to do. There's an empty barbital bottle upstairs. And a toy dagger and a wedding ring and a note that says: 'This is the last humiliation.' What does it add up to?"

The District Attorney did not answer immediately. He stood before the hearth, sifting the ember-blackened crumbs of marble through his fingers. Finally, he said quietly, his inflection interrogation rather than statement, "It takes a good deal of vehemence, a good deal of passion, to pound a piece of marble to powder."

"About as much as it takes to drive a steel spike into a human body."

The faint smile fluttered around the District Attorney's lips. "We shall see," he said, "what we shall see."

The door on the balcony opened and Dr. Sulloway called across the rail, "Mr. Babcock, come up here, please."

When the District Attorney had gone upstairs again, Mary paced restlessly about the room. What had happened here last night? Had there been a scene? Had there been a quarrel? Dr. McAlistir had been at that party, and the fat woman in the batik blouse—Miss Godwin. They would know what, if anything, had transpired before Nola Spain had met Prince Charming. But after those two had gone out together—what had happened then? Alicia Donato knew. Would she ever be able to tell? The jealous wife left alone to churn her bitterness into murderous passion. Had she gone to the Rockledge, accomplished her vengeance, and then come back here to end the tragic drama? Where had she found that sharp steel pencil? . . . Why, here! Here, of course! The very sort of tool that had made Nola Spain's form immortal might have delivered her living beauty to death.

Mary hurried down the three steps into the sculptor's studio. At first it seemed to her as if she had wandered into the land of the dead. The drawn tan curtains at the long windows left the room in creamy shadow. Down its length, from the steps to the far windows, stood motionless human forms—some sheeted, some bare. Folding bridge chairs, bunched in the center of the floor, still holding the untidy leavings of the tea, told her that Alicia Donato's guests had been here, too, sipping their orange pekoe among the marble ghosts.

Near the entrance was a small platform. On it, in neat

rows, lay the sculptor's tools, his mallets, chisels, compressed air drill, and a row of fine steel rods, like sharpened pencils. She took one from the row and when Kneeland Babcock came down the stairs again, she showed it to him and said, "There are more where this came from."

Mr. Babcock looked at it thoughtfully. "If Mrs. Donato survives," he said in grave accents, "she'll face a jury."

Within the quarter hour, an ambulance drew up beside the rose hedge. Alicia Donato, her eyes still closed, her silk and lace swaddled in gray blankets, was carried out. State troopers swarmed into her disheveled house.

At the Laneport Hospital, a trooper paced the corridor outside the room where nurses and internes labored with stomach pump and stimulants to save an unhappy lady for the electric chair.

Mary walked back to the Rockledge with the District Attorney. "Is it good enough?" she asked.

He knit his brows and cracked his knuckles before he answered. "We'll try for a confession," he said at last. "But I think we shall have a case without it. There seems to be motive. There is accessibility to the weapon. There is evidence of guilty conscience. After we have spoken with the husband, of course (Where do you think he can be, Mrs. Whittaker? Does anyone know?), and have verified the grounds for the lady's jealousy, I think we shall have clear sailing. And to be sure, we have an eye-witness. The little girl. Having seen what we have seen, one can hardly blame her for thinking she saw a witch." The wan smile fluttered around his mouth. "This is a difficult world for unattractive women. . . . Tomorrow morning, I should like to have the little girl brought to the hospital, for identification. The autopsy will be done by Monday evening. We shall be ready for the inquest Tuesday morning. I do not believe we shall require your presence after that, unless you choose to honor Laneport with a longer stay."

Mary shook her head. "It's not on the calendar. Oh, I don't deny that this place has charm. But it's scarcely what we're looking for right now. Too much excitement."

"I understand." His chill courtesy warmed. "You've just been married. This is a rather disconcerting beginning. May I sincerely trust that it is no omen."

She smiled. "I'm not worried about that. I'm not afraid of murder. It's responsibility that gets me down. I wish I'd never heard of Nola Spain. For now I know I'll never stop thinking of her until I know why she died and at whose hand."

"You'll know that, too. And very soon." He seemed to gain assurance as he spoke. "Our problem, I believe, is solved. Your concern with it is nearly ended. And mine begins. There is, unfortunately, many a slip between arrest and sentence."

Sergeant Sargent was waiting for them on the front porch of the Rockledge. He touched his hat brim. "Mr. Babcock," he faltered, his eyes shifting unhappily, "I regret to report—I went down myself—The yacht *Cynisca's* gone. She left this morning, sir. In the fog."

"Prince Charming's gone!" Mary's chin dropped.

"Regrettable," the District Attorney said. "But not *too* bad. We do have a case without—why, Mrs. Whittaker, whatever is happening to you?"

Mary's face had gone blank. "I saw it leave," she cried. "This morning. That silly little Mr. Parsons told me not to believe my own eyes. Said no ship could possibly go out in that fog. . . . We've got to bring it back."

"Have you any idea how large the Atlantic Ocean is?" Mr. Babcock began. He snapped a knuckle and inspiration came. "Sergeant Sargent, will you be good enough to communicate with Lane's Island and ask them to send out a seaplane to locate the yacht *Cynisca?* And notify me at the Laneport Hospital when the vessel is sighted."

A gong reverberated inside the lobby, calling the Rockledge guests to chicken and biscuits.

Mary said, "Will you lunch with us?"

The District Attorney bowed. "I should be delighted. But another time. I have an engagement. At the Laneport Hospital. I must begin at once—to prepare for trial."

Miss Templeton jostled Mary as she hurried back to the Annex to find Chris. Miss Templeton smiled saccharinely. "Oh, how do you do, Mrs. Whittaker, and have you solved your little murder?" Mrs. Heath, her chin set defiantly, scuttled past. Mrs. Bean, gray-faced, caught her sleeve: "Oh, Mrs. Whittaker, I've been advised to ask you—my daughter—"

Mary paused a moment for Mrs. Bean. "You'd better ask the police where she is," she said sardonically. "Down at the morgue, probably, viewing the remains."

Chris was alone in the room, rocking disconsolately. "Time you came," he wailed. "Deserting me for another man. These fickle women."

"I came as quickly as I could, darling. There's more trouble. More and more. Mrs. Donato took barbital last night."

"I wasn't talking about you and your corpses. It's Baby Doll. She walked out on me. Gave me up for another man. Your pal. The little man with the funny ears. Been sitting out on the rock with him all morning, talking about witches. And darned if she didn't march off to lunch with him. . . . Say, why don't they fix that plumbing?"

The tapping had commenced again. Tap, tap—tap, tap, tap—tap, taap—tap, taap, taap—tap, tap, tap, tap—tap—tap, tap, tap. It made a rhythm. It stopped. And then it began again, the same tempo, the same short and long taps.

Chris took out a pencil. On the white dresser cover, he made two dots in a row, then three, and after he had written down the three, he shouted, "That's an S."

"Do you know Morse?"

"I know SOS. . . . Be quiet! Let me listen." He wrote

down all the dots and the dashes. "No," he announced finally, "it isn't SOS." The tapping had stopped. The house was still now, as though it were listening too—listening and waiting. And then the tapping commenced again. Chris followed the rhythm of the taps on his penciled pattern of dots and dashes.

He said, "It's a message. There's no doubt about it. I don't know what it means. But somebody's trying to get something across."

They moved together toward the door of their room and the tapping seemed louder, nearer. Chris opened the bathroom door. The rat-tat-tat filled the little room. "I was right the first time," he said, disgruntled. "It is in the pipes."

"Chris," Mary's voice rose with excitement. "It's the third time I've heard that sound. First when I woke up, right after Nola Spain was killed. And then again when Mrs. Heath was downstairs, putting on her fainting act. And now." She spaced her words to make them impressive. "When—Mrs. Heath—is—over—in—the—other—building—for—lunch. Twice—when—Mrs. Heath—was—out—of—her—room." She gripped his wrist. "Come on. Somebody up there's trying to say something."

Chris trod on her heels as they flew up the steps. They rapped on the door of Mrs. Heath's room. It opened slowly. The short, wide bulk of a woman in black filled the doorway. Three pale chins disengaged themselves from a mammoth bosom, wobbled in what seemed to be a greeting.

"Did you understand my message?" The voice was small, sweet, cultured—a surprising voice to issue from that gash in the doughy face. It was as if another, different person was hidden within the grotesque body.

Chris said, "What were you trying to say?"

The pleasant voice replied unhesitatingly, "I saw her. I was trying to tell someone that I saw her. . . . Won't you—" It faltered. "Won't you step in?"

Miss Chalmers waddled into the bedroom ahead of

them. She was a dwarf in height, a giant in girth—more than 300 pounds on less than five feet of frame—small features and eyes almost lost in shiny layers of fat. Miss Chalmers' hair was gray, brushed smooth, rolled into a neat bun. A rusty, black Mother Hubbard hung down to her ankles. She squatted on the edge of the bed, played nervously with a steel knitting needle.

Hers was a trim, white room, like all the rest in the Annex, but unlike the others, it seemed to be a room in which people lived. There were personal things, home-like things—a hand-embroidered antimacassar across the back of the rocker, faded sepia photographs in raffia frames on the dresser: a lady in a bustle, a gentleman with mutton-chop whiskers and seals dangling from a watch chain. A rotogravure cutting of a child and puppy was stuck into the mirror frame. The glass was plastered with drying handkerchiefs and underneath it stood a little shelf of well-worn books. The night-table held a sweet-grass sewing basket, a vase of paper flowers, and, on the bolster of each bed, an embroidered lace-trimmed heart reposed, one monogrammed R, the other I. There was a certain pathos in the attempt to make the bare room livable. It reminded Mary of cells she had seen in the Women's Prison—steel and stone cubicles brightened with bits of handwork, family pictures. This was Isabel Chalmers' prison, too—a prison whose windows looked out on the free sky and the restless sea—a room in which a woman was jailed because nature had been unkind.

Miss Chalmers looked over her shoulder toward the door. "I haven't much time. Ramona will be back any moment. My sister, Ramona." Her fingers twiddled with the steel needle. She held it up. "I used this," she said. "To tap the message. I hoped I had the code right. I hoped someone would understand. . . . I've been trying to tell someone, ever since. But Ramona wouldn't let me. Ramona was afraid. Ramona was afraid I'd be—bothered."

Mary said, "It's gracious of you. After all that trouble with the trooper this morning."

"That!" Miss Chalmers' voice grew strained. "That was Ramona. I really can't understand why she had such tantrums. I wanted to talk to him. I wanted to tell him. But she locked me in the bathroom. She wouldn't let me out to talk to him."

"What did you have to tell him?" Mary asked.

Miss Chalmers bent forward. "I saw her," she whispered. "I saw a woman come up from the sea. Ramona didn't see her. Ramona was fast asleep. But I wasn't asleep. I sat right there by the window and I saw her. Floating up from the sea, in the mist. A tall woman, with a light before her and a cloak over her face."

"You're sure it was a woman?" Mary asked. "No doubt of that?"

"Why—I—" Miss Chalmers seemed confused. "Why, I believed it was a woman. Why, yes, I believed at once it was a woman. One associates a woman with that sort of thing."

"With what sort of thing?" Mr. Whittaker's tone was sharp. "With murder?"

Miss Chalmers' chin dropped to her bosom and she seemed lost in thought. At length, she raised her head. "It might have been a man, of course. The fog is so confusing. It distorts things so. But when I saw it coming up from the sea, out of the mist, I said to myself. 'Why, there's a woman, out in the fog. And the footsteps were a woman's. . . .'"

With the print of the devil! Mary thought.

Miss Chalmers went on. "When she came up the stairs to the porch, her footsteps seemed hard and firm and then she bent down and I couldn't see her any more. But I heard her walking softly, as though—as though she had taken off her shoes."

Mary gasped.

"Oh, my ears are very sharp," Miss Chalmers said with a

lilt of satisfaction. "And my eyes. I know everything that goes on here. That's how I live. That's how I manage to endure it here alone. The walls of this house are alive. They speak to me. They tell me everything."

"Tell me something," Mr. Whittaker said suddenly. "Where did you learn Morse?"

"Where did I—?" It was impossible to mistake the expression on Isabel Chalmers' face. This was naked terror. Her hands fluttered; the knitting needle rolled to the floor. "Oh I—we—" Miss Chalmers choked.

The door opened. Mrs. Heath stood on the threshold. She stared at Mary and Chris, and her pale face turned to tallow; her eyes bulged. Delia, the waitress, behind her with the tray, gaped at the strangers in this inviolable room.

"Darling!" Mrs. Heath recovered. She flew to her sister's side, circled her shoulders with protective arms. "How dare you!" She glowered at Mary and Chris. "How dare you intrude on my sister!"

Miss Chalmers smiled. "I'm afraid I shall have to ask you to leave," she said, wistfully. "I'm not allowed to have company. Thank you very much for dropping in."

Chapter Eight

THE STUDIO

A COUNTRY INN IS a percolator. News seeps, simmers and bubbles. No one had posted a bulletin but the Rockledge guests all seemed to know when the Coast Guard plane was to leave and why. They lined the porch rails to supervise its going.

Lane's Island was plain before them—low, white buildings on a gull-flecked rock in the restless blue of the outer harbor.

A sleek gray seaplane rolled down a runway. The air filled with the frightened wings of birds, the creaking of hundreds of rusty hinges. The plane skimmed the waves, rose slowly, streaked across the sky, vanished in the opalescent haze.

"There she goes!" Miss Templeton shrilled, quite superfluously. "To find the *Cynisca!*"

Fern Godwin tapped Mary's arm. "Miss Dow said you'd want to talk to me." She linked her arm through Mary's. "Let's go up to my room. Away from the maddening crowd. . . . Oh, you can come too, Mr. Whittaker. Delighted to have you."

Chris Whittaker said, "No, siree. I know my place. I'll go swimming."

Fern Godwin's was a cluttered corner chamber, one flight up in Main, redolent of turpentine, crowded with stacked canvases, paint boxes, artist's odds and ends. It had a tiny balcony facing the ocean.

Miss Godwin led the way to the balcony. "My little hideaway. Where I refresh my spirit. . . . Do take this chair, dear. It's the most comfortable—reliable—one. Do you smoke?" She passed a crumpled pack of cigarettes, lit one for Mary and one for herself, inhaled deeply. "I never smoke in the dining-room. Some of the older ladies mind." She stretched her ample torso on the faded Indian blanket over the lumpy divan. "You won't mind if I just relax? A few minutes on my back and I'm a new woman." She puffed her cigarette and chirped, through a nimbus of smoke, "Well, my dear, Miss Dow told me you were asking about poor Alicia. She thought I should be the one to tell you."

"Tell me what?" Mary asked cautiously.

Miss Godwin chuckled. "You know perfectly well what. About Alicia and Paul. Everybody in Laneport knows all about them, of course, but Miss Dow felt that one responsible person who knows all the details ought to give you the correct information."

Mary flicked a speck of loose tobacco from her lower lip. "Miss Dow did mention that you were at the Donato studio last night," she said, feeling her way, distrustful of the other woman's exuberance, forewarned by her fruitless session with Mr. Parsons. "Were you there, by chance when Nola Spain—"

Miss Godwin did not let her finish. "I can't get used to hearing her called Spain. She's always been Nola Andrews to me."

"Nola Andrews!" Mary repeated the name to fix it in her memory. "You knew the woman before?"

"Knew her. Of course. Years and years."

"Swell!" Mary shifted forward in her seat. "You're the girl we're looking for. Is it true—do you know?—that Mrs. Donato disliked Nola Spain? Was jealous of her?"

"Jealous! That's hardly the word, my dear. Have you ever seen Alicia?"

"I've seen both women." Mary smiled grimly. "Can't say that either was at her best."

"Of course not. Poor things! Jealousy does such dreadful things to people. Hate. There's far too much of it in this world, don't you think so, dear? Why can't people just live and let live?" Her smug mouth drooped in what might pass for sympathy. She wriggled upright, settled back on the sofa. "I can talk better sitting up. Well—" She puffed deeply. "You know Paul married her for her money, don't you? . . . You don't! Why everybody knows that. One look at her and it's obvious. . . . Alicia's an Avery. Back Bay, my dear. Money to burn since the Civil War. . . . They met in Paris. About twelve or fifteen years ago, while Paul was still studying. She fell for him like a ton of brick. He saw the main chance, took it. That's all there was to that." Miss Godwin gestured expansively. "Oh, her family had kittens over it. But there wasn't much they could do except hold conferences and fume. Alicia was—well, over twenty-one—and her money was in her own name. And once Paul had decided he was willing to marry her, all the king's horses and lawyers couldn't have pulled Alicia out of it. She got her money's worth for a while. Paul's *magnifique!* Handsome. Virile. Twirling the mustache, bowing from the waist, kissing the hand." She sighed. "Wait till you meet him. . . . Are you rich?"

"Just a poor working girl."

"Heaven protect you," Miss Godwin chortled. "But, alas, you won't see Paul at his best. He really puts himself out for the well-to-do. The others?" She grinned maliciously. "They put themselves out for him. Of course, it's good business. Wealthy ladies have houses. Houses have gardens. Every garden has a Donato fountain. It's practically a law. . . . Are you comfortable? Sun's not in your eyes? I can draw the blind."

"Thank you. I like the view."

"So do I. So peaceful, so serene. It gives me my sublimest thoughts. . . . Well, let's get back to Alicia and Paul. She financed him in the beginning. Marble and bronze casting cost real money, you know. And she introduced him everywhere. But after the first few months, Paul seemed to get along very nicely by himself. He *is* talented, make no mistake about that." She seemed sincerely anxious to correct any adverse impression she might have given. "He knows his mediums, he knows his anatomy."

"His anatomy?" Mary echoed.

"Of course. A good sculptor has to know almost as much anatomy as a doctor. Even a painter who paints the human form knows—"

Mary interrupted again. "Would a sculptor's wife by any chance know anatomy too?"

"Alicia? You mean would Alicia know where to locate a vital spot?" She shrugged. "That would depend on how much she was interested in her husband's work. Technically, I mean. Alicia was interested in Paul's work but I don't think that way. Considered herself a sort of business partner—making contacts, suggesting subjects for his work. . . . Paul's things are pretty without being sugary. Conventional, of course, but pleasant. Like the 'Fairy Princess.' Nola was the model for that."

"He did that a good while ago?"

"About six years. That was the beginning of the real trouble between him and Alicia. She went to Reno while he was working on it. Went all the way out West. And then came back. I don't think she could bear to give him up, no matter what he did. Half a loaf, you know. Better than none."

Mary snuffed out her cigarette. "Exactly what did he do?"

"Do? He fell in love with the model. Oh, my dear, you didn't know Nola then. Her name wasn't Spain (I can't imagine where she picked up that ridiculous appendage). She was the most radiant, most exquisite creature in the world. I don't know where she came from, who her people were. All I know is that Paul inherited her from another artist, Denny Rodman. Paul had a studio in New York that year. Had got fed up with Boston. Came down to the Village with the hoi polloi. I used to see a good deal of him (I live in New York, too, you know, or don't you?) at exhibitions, mutual friends' studios, restaurants. Usually, Nola was with him. Won't you have another cigarette, Mrs. Whittaker?"

Mary said, "No, thanks."

Miss Godwin lighted one for herself. "You don't mind if I do? I'm a chimney when I'm up here. Good little girl downstairs, but in the privacy of my balcony—" She blew a doughnut ring, stabbed the hole with the lighted tip of her cigarette, giggled like an adolescent. "The mice will play—well, let's get on with Paul and Nola. A model was just female flesh to Paul before he met Nola. He went to bed with them as a matter of routine. But they meant nothing to him. Ships in the night! Until he met Nola. She was the great love of his life—the dream girl. He followed her around like a pet poodle. That was when Alicia went to Reno. Can't blame her, can you?" She laughed throatily. "She had condoned his passing infidelities but this public adoration of another woman was just too-too. He didn't seem to care who knew that he was crazy about Nola. Well, a wife will stand just so much—even an artist's wife. But—" Miss Godwin frowned. "The joke was on Paul. Nola wasn't interested. Whenever I saw them together, she was acting pretty much like Her Royal Highness, permitting the devoted slave to touch the hem of her garment. But when Alicia went to Reno, Nola dropped out of the picture. No one ever saw them together any more."

"And after Nola left Paul, the Donatos came together?"

Miss Godwin nodded. "After a fashion. Anyway, Alicia came back home and first thing we heard, she had bought this Laneport place, spent a fortune remodeling it, fixing it up to make a big splurge. Salon for the famous sculptor.

We gathered that everything was hunky-dory and that
Paul had promised to be good. He'd been humbled, you
see. Hadn't been able to get the woman he wanted. It was
a new experience for him, I can tell you. Must have scared
him. Made him feel he was losing his sex appeal. . . . Of
course, the 'Fairy Princess' was a tremendous success. He
exhibited it at the Academy Show. Some manufacturer
bought the rights to it and the public ate it up. I think myself that's a mistake. Cheapens a work of art. Cheapens an
artist. But just the same I wouldn't mind having some of
the money Paul's made out of it. Wouldn't be at all surprised if it's made him quite independent of Alicia's fortune. Poor thing! She hasn't even that to hold him with
any more. She always hated the 'Fairy Princess.' Couldn't
bear to have you mention it. More than once Alicia's said
to me, 'I'd like to smash that damned thing!' "

"Someone did," Mary said. "Last night."

"Really! That's news! Alicia smashed it. Of course she
did. No one else. She was boiling!" Miss Godwin lit a third
cigarette from the butt of the second. She puffed
thoughtfully for a moment. Then she said, "But why did
she go out and kill Nola? She'd had her sublimation. You
know, destroying the image of the hated one, instead of
the person himself. It's supposed to be effective."

"We don't know that she did kill Nola Spain."

"Of course, dear," Miss Godwin smiled tolerantly. "You
must be careful. A person's innocent till proven guilty. But
there isn't much doubt about Alicia. That sculptor's point
of Paul's."

Mary said, "You know about that, too?"

"Oh, my dear," Miss Godwin put her hand on Mary's
arm. "Everybody knows everything. Sam Dolliver reports
to Jake Haskell. Jake passes Phoebe Dow in the lobby and
Phoebe in her innocent, artless way asks, 'Have they found
out anything yet, Jacob?' and Jake stands there on one foot,
pretending he's in a hurry and it's all very secret and tells

her the latest and she tells it to the next person who stops and asks her. We know that you and Sam Dolliver saw a peculiar footprint on the porch—like a cow's, wasn't it, dear? (Mist does play such tricks.) We know that you caught Lorna Bean looking in that window. (She must have been *so* embarrassed. She hasn't dared to show her face around here all day. Must be moping somewhere on the beach. Her mother's almost frantic.) And we know that poor Mrs. Heath scratched Pat Sargent's face when he tried to search her room. And Miss Chalmers was locked in the bathroom. (That was a shame. I've known the poor things for years and years. They're so terribly sensitive.) And so of course we know about the steel point that Nola was killed with. And we know about that funny, adorable, little girl calling Alicia a witch. It was a little cruel but you can't blame her too much."

"You do know everything!" Mary raised her eyebrows.

"Oh, my dear, don't do that to your forehead! You're really quite attractive till you frown. Yes." Miss Godwin leaned forward, professionally critical. "Yes, you've got a fine face. Good bones. Nice coloring. Your eyes are awfully good. . . . Have you thought of sitting for a portrait while you're in Laneport?"

Mary shook her head. "Not stopping more than a day or so. No time for art."

"Don't say that. There's always time for art. There must be. . . . What sort of a world would this be if everybody said 'no time for art'? Besides, you aren't going to leave now, while Mr. Babcock's depending on you. Dear Mr. Babcock, he's so conscientious. Hunting clues and solving mysteries isn't really 'his business. But he knows Jake's limitations. . . . Just two sittings. Yes, I could do you in just two sittings. It would be such a lovely gift for your husband."

Mary protested irritably, "Please, we'll talk about it some other time, if you don't mind. I'd like to go back to what you said a while ago—that Alicia Donato was boiling last night. You saw her with Nola, didn't you?"

Miss Godwin, miffed by the abrupt rejection of her overtures, merely bobbed her head with dignified reserve.

"You haven't told the police anything about it, have you?"

Miss Godwin shrugged. "Nobody asked me, sir, she said."

"I'm asking now. Every detail you can remember of what happened last night at Donatos, please."

"Well. That's a large order." Miss Godwin pulled up her plump legs, tucked her skirt around them, slewed herself into a more comfortable position on the divan. "Well, at first it was the usual sort of Laneport evening. You know, business and pleasure. Summer visitors who have money, simply thrilled to be in an artist's studio. *La Vie de Bohème.* Mrs. Merrill and Mrs. Prentiss were there. I brought them. They were so anxious to meet Paul. All the summer visitors know about him. (That's the effect of the 'Fairy Princess.') And Dr. and Mrs. McAlistir and a Mr. and Mrs. Morgan from the Beachview and a Professor MacDougall from the Lane Head Inn and some other people whom I didn't know. They oh'd and ah'd over all of Paul's things and they seemed so dreadfully disappointed that Paul wasn't there. And you can believe me that Alicia was disappointed too. She made some lame excuse about his being called away for a consultation with some architects about a fountain for a client. (There's a new woman, I believe. Newton or Brookline. Somewhere near Boston. No details yet. We never get details till it's near the end. Paul's very discreet until he loses interest. And then he blabs and brags.) Well, around nine o'clock Nola Andrews came in. I thought I'd seen her in the dining-room at dinner but I wasn't sure. I hardly recognized her. She looked so much older, so sickly. She opened the door and she asked rather timidly, 'Is this Paul Donato's studio?' Alicia was pouring. . . . Won't you have another cigarette, Mrs. Whittaker?"

Mary said, "Yes, thanks," this time.

Miss Godwin held the match for her. "That's better. I always feel like such a pig, smoking when my guest isn't. Well, Alicia was pouring but when she heard that voice, she looked up and went white as a sheet and her hand shook so that she nearly dropped the cup. But she went to the door. I distinctly heard her say, 'What do you want here?' As though Nola was a beggar or a peddler. But Nola answered quite calmly, 'Paul sent for me.' 'He isn't here,' Alicia said. They stood in the open doorway, looking daggers at each other. Then Nola said, 'Aren't you going to invite me in? It's quite chilly out and you have a very nice fire.' She was inside the door by that time and Alicia had to either push her out bodily or let her come in."

"Alicia was a lady and let her in, I gather?"

Miss Godwin nodded. "Alicia stood aside. Pulled her skirts tight so they wouldn't touch Nola. As though she was afraid of catching something. But Nola strolled in, with that easy graceful cat walk of hers. It's a pity you never saw her walk. Graceful. Proud. Like Alicia's coon cat."

"A young tree swaying?" Mary ventured.

Miss Godwin's face brightened.

"My dear, how poetic! How did you ever come to think of that?"

"I didn't. Mr. Parsons did."

"Did he really! I've always suspected there was something special about him. He never says much. Rather unsocial. But he's sweet. He's awfully sweet. And very much up on things, if you can get him to talk to you. . . . Well, anyway, Nola came in, like a tree or a cat, whichever you want, and she saw me and she said, 'It's like old times to see you, Fern. How are you? You look prosperous.' She shook hands with me. Her fingers were icy. Then she went over to the fireplace and stood there for a few minutes rubbing her hands. I was really quite shocked at how thin she was. The room was quiet. Everybody was watching her. You know how it is when a stranger comes into a room where people have been talking and the conversation dies away while everybody sizes up the stranger. Nola must have realized she had barged in. She turned around and smiled at them all and said, 'Don't let me interrupt,' and, 'Fern, aren't you going to offer me a cigarette?' It was a little embarrassing to me because I never smoke in public in Laneport and Mrs. Merrill and Mrs. Prentiss don't know I do. But I got my bag and gave her one and I heard Doctor McAlister say, 'Too much tobacco. Needs Vitamin B more than she needs nicotine.' These doctors!

"Well, Nola lit the cigarette and stood there in front of the fire. Suddenly she looked up and saw the 'Fairy Princess' on the mantel. She picked it up. 'Paul's done rather well with it,' she said. Her voice was just the least bitter. Then she set it carefully back on the mantel shelf and stood off and stared at it and said, 'It's hard to imagine I once looked like that. It seems so long ago.'

"Well, my dear." Miss Godwin leaned over the arm of Mrs. Whittaker's chair. "You should have heard them. 'Are you that?' You know how people are. Always excited about models. Think there's something very glamorous about them. Yes, everybody got quite excited about Nola but they seemed to bore her. She saw the steps to the studio. And she said, 'Alicia, do you mind? I'd like to see Paul's latest work.' She went down into the studio. After a minute or so, Alicia followed her and they had some words. I don't know what was said because I really couldn't hear a thing up in the living-room and I hadn't a decent excuse for going down into the studio myself. Well, after a while Mrs. Merrill helped me out. She said, 'Why don't we go into the studio, too, and see Mr. Donato's latest work?' Those two stopped talking the second they saw us coming. But I noticed that Alicia was quite red in the face and the cords in her throat were like wires. But Nola was cool as iced tea. She had one of Paul's little points in her hand and she was playing with it, stabbing a piece of wood with it, as if it was a dart."

Nola Spain, playing nonchalantly with the instrument that was to bring her death. Unafraid of it, unsuspecting. It was macabre. Mary shuddered slightly.

The artist's bright eyes caught her little tremor. "I don't blame you. Sounds quite ghastly, doesn't it? Now that we know what we know. Well, there might have been a murder right then and there—Alicia was so mad—if that young man hadn't arrived. He knocked at the door, and Alicia went to open it. He was dear! About twenty-two or twenty-three, I'd guess. Dewy-looking. Golden curly hair, short, freckled, sunburned nose. I'd like very much to paint him. . . . Mrs. Whittaker, you really mustn't mind my comments. A painter, you know, always sees people from a certain point of view."

Mary said, "Of course I don't mind. Your observations are most interesting. And you don't know how helpful."

"Helpful? I can't see how. But you know best. All I know is that I'm having a wonderful time talking. And you're such a marvelous listener."

"The young man came in," Mary prompted.

"The young man? Oh, yes. You're not easily sidetracked, are you? . . . Well, he looked around, rather vaguely, and asked, 'Is Nola Spain here?' That was the first I'd ever heard her called Spain. Nola must have heard his voice because she called out from the studio. 'In here, Todd. I'm in here.'"

"Todd?" Mary repeated.

"Yes, I think that was the name. Do you know who he is?"

Mary shook her head. "Her child has mentioned him."

"Friend of the family, evidently." Miss Godwin smirked.

"Well, he dashed for the studio. She held out her hands to him and for a second there was the same beatific expression on her face that you can see on the 'Fairy Princess.' They stayed in the studio for about a minute and then they came up arm in arm and she said to Alicia, 'I'm sure you won't mind if I leave.' Alicia showed her teeth. She said, very nastily, 'Playing in the kindergarten? Robbing the cradle?' Nola got red in the face but I'll say to her credit she gave back as good as she got. 'Not entirely,' she answered. 'I'm still interested in my contemporaries,' and she gestured toward the studio with that little point of Paul's."

"What did she do with that point? Did she, did you notice, by any chance carry it out with her?" Mrs. Whittaker was clearly excited now.

Miss Godwin rested her chin on her palm. "Why, yes," she said finally. "I believe she did. . . . Oh!" Her eyes narrowed. "Oh," she said again. "Then it could have been someone besides Alicia!"

"Exactly."

"And that's why the Coast Guard's hunting for the *Cynisca?*"

Mary nodded.

Miss Godwin squirmed back on the divan. "It never occurred to me—I never dreamed that that would be—I must have another cigarette on that."

Mary said, "You haven't finished the evening. You haven't told me what happened after Nola Spain left. What Alicia Donato said or did. We haven't finished with her, by any means."

"There isn't much more to tell." Miss Godwin's eyes had a faraway look, as though they were pursuing the vagrant yacht *Cynisca.* "Nothing important happened after that. We left in a little while. Mrs. Merrill and Mrs. Prentiss and I. We just stepped down into the studio for a few minutes more. Mrs. Prentiss wanted another look at the Bacchante that Paul's planning to send to the Laneport Art Society

Show. (You must come, my dear. It's opening this week. I'll get you a card for Varnishing Day. It's such fun. That's when the celebrities come. And all the artists.) Well, we went into the studio again. And while we were there, Esther Lyndall came in. Alicia was quite surprised to see her, too. Because you see, Laneport's informal and people do drop in at studios at all hours, but Esther Lyndall isn't one of the droppers-in. She's town folks. Her people have lived on the Cape for hundreds of years. And we're outsiders, nobodies, Bohemians. Lord knows we bring more money into Laneport than the fishing boats do. But even if we do come back every summer, to people like Esther Lyndall we're still only interlopers. She turns up at the big shindigs, like Varnishing Day, and shows off her best manners, but outside of that she's veddy-veddy formal. . . . Well, anyhow, Alicia said, 'Oh, how do you do, Mrs. Lyndall. Won't you have some tea?' Mrs. Lyndall said, 'No.' Not even a thank-you. But she came in anyway and sat down for a minute. And then she got up as if she had an itch and went into the studio. And then she came out again. Alicia asked, 'Are you looking for someone, Mrs. Lyndall?' And she said, 'Yes, for Ryon. Has he been here?' Alicia said, 'I haven't seen Ryon in a month of Sundays. What's happened to Ryon?' 'Nothing,' Mrs. Lyndall answered her, in that curt way she has, as though you had no business even to address Her Majesty. And then she stomped out. That didn't make Alicia any happier, I can tell you. She's an Avery, remember, and Esther Lyndall certainly had no right to act as if she was slumming in Alicia Donato's house. Well, we got our things right after that and went home. I don't know how long the others stayed."

"What time did you leave?" Mary asked.

"About ten, I'd say. A bit after that perhaps."

"Did you see Nola Spain and her young man on your way back to the Rockledge. . . . Did you see anyone on the streets at all?"

"Not a soul. Too early for the movies to be out. Too damp for strollers. . . . Although I can't bring myself to like the creature, I did feel sorry for Esther Lyndall, running all over town hunting that son of hers. Humiliating. Of course I didn't know then what I know now or I might have felt sorrier . . . Ryon getting drunk. Disgracing himself, waking up the whole town—"

"I know," Mary said drearily. "The white fox. The white woman."

"I don't know what you're talking about," Miss Godwin answered crisply. Then she sighed. "Poor Ryon!"

"Why, *poor* Ryon?"

"Oh, my dear." Miss Godwin waved her hand. "If you knew Ryon—the most pathetic case. You see, he can't paint, but *he* thinks he can and *she* thinks he can. Oh, he gets things on canvas fairly well—in an academic sort of way—but his work is so drab, so spiritless. Does the same things over and over. No growth. Learned a few tricks in art school and goes on repeating them. It's a mistake—" her voice grew stern—"to tell youngsters who have only a mediocre facility that they're artists. It ruins their lives. Of course, if Ryon Lyndall had to earn a living—if he got out and had some contact with life. . . . But when a man's tied to his mother's apron strings. My dear, he's at least thirty— oh, more than that—but the way Esther Lyndall babies him, you'd think he couldn't find his way to the wee-wee room alone."

Mary yawned behind her hand.

"I'm boring you. I'm so sorry, my dear," Miss Godwin cried.

Mary got up. "You've been grand and I'm just rude and sleepy."

"Must you go? We haven't had a chance to really get acquainted. I'd like so much to show you some of my canvases. Do drop up again, dear, and bring your handsome husband. I'm sure he'd be interested in some of the portraits I've done. Of quite important men. And tell him," she lowered her voice to a coy whisper, "that I've a lovely bottle of rye. . . . Good-bye, dear, so nice of poor Nola's murder to bring us together."

Chapter Nine

PRINCE CHARMING

MR. PARSONS WAS waiting in the lobby, sitting on the edge of the sofa. When Mary came down the stairs from Miss Godwin's room, he got up, stumbled toward her, his nose quivering like a puppy's. "I must speak with you at once —of the utmost importance."

Miss Moffett rescued Mary. She crooked her finger. "Message for you. Mr. Babcock called." Miss Moffett consulted a slip of paper. "At three-fifteen. You're to call him right back at the Laneport Hospital."

"Mrs. Donato has recovered consciousness," Mr. Babcock drawled over the phone. "She's admitted taking the sedative. To quiet her nerves, she claims. She's admitted she had no great affection for Nola Spain. (She calls her Andrews. Spain is either a marriage name or an alias.) But she insists emphatically that she had no knowledge whatever of the woman's demise. . . . I can't say she appears particularly grieved. . . . Naturally, she is not prepared to plead guilty." A sigh floated over the wire. "Ah no, none of these people have the slightest intention of making life simpler for a district attorney."

"Have you considered that she may be telling the truth?"

"I have," he conceded. "But not as seriously as I have thought that she is not. We consider each suspect to be lying until he can prove otherwise. We expect the lie. . . . May I ask a service of you? You spoke this morning of certain threads of wool on the sill of Mrs. Spain's room, unfortunately now unavailable, which there is some likelihood were left by our mysterious nocturnal assassin." His stilted phraseology amused her. It seemed to belong to some artificial Victorian shocker. "I should appreciate it if you would find time to go to the Donato residence, and make a comprehensive search of the wardrobes there, to ascertain whether there is any garment which, conceivably—"

"Of course. I'll go at once."

"Thank you. I'll telephone Officer Haskell to admit you to the house. And you will kindly let me know?"

Mr. Parsons followed her out of the door. He crossed the road beside her and climbed the hill, panting to keep up with her swift stride. "I trust I am not intruding," he rasped. "I find it quite essential to discuss—"

"I'm hardly in the mood," she interrupted, her tone distinctly snappish, "to talk about spooks and witches."

"Well, ma'am." He cleared his throat apologetically. "I have talked the matter over at length with the little girl and have carefully considered—"

She said, "Some other time, please."

They had come to the Donato house. The magnet of murder had drawn tourists and townspeople. Parked cars lined the narrow road. A state trooper sweated in the middle of the path, struggling to keep traffic moving. An archaic limousine, chauffeur-driven, pulled up its brakes. A white-haired dowager stuck her head out of the rear window, cried, "This is the house. This is the place—isn't it, officer?—where the murderess lives? . . How exciting!" Her bright old eyes darted over the façade and the lawn. She sighed blissfully. "You may drive on now, Evans. We'll visit the Rockledge next."

A small boy dashed under the trooper's arm, tore a rose hip from the hedge. The foliage, Mary saw, was ragged as though birds had been at it. "I got it," the urchin crowed to his companions. "I got me a souvenir."

Mary cut through the crowd. Jacob Haskell saw her from the doorway, came down to the gate, opened it ob-

sequiously, scowling at Mr. Parsons. "Only the lady," he
said.

Mr. Parsons sat down on the running board of a parked
car. Looking at this small, withdrawn, mouse-like person,
it was hard to guess that there sat a man whose heart was
leaden and whose pride was bleeding. For Mr. Parsons had
made this murder his personal responsibility. In his profound concern, he had turned heart and mind inside out
before a stranger and he had met, as he had known he
inevitably must, lack of understanding and rebuff.

Alicia Donato's black coon cat crawled from the hedge,
watched Mr. Parsons with hungry, frightened eyes, padded
toward him, rubbed its side against his leg, mewed for
sympathy. Mr. Parsons stroked its head. Comforting the
cat, he himself felt comforted, less lonely.

The sumptuous little house was silent and untidy—
exactly as it had been when Mary had seen it first. A state
trooper stood at the studio threshold and a stocky man in
shirtsleeves knelt by the fireplace. On the sofa lay a pasteboard suit box and in it were the fire-tongs, the mallet, the
blackened shards of marble, Alicia Donato's wedding ring,
her note, the dagger pin, the green medicine bottle and the
glass.

"He's from Mr. Babcock's office." Officer Haskell indicated the stocky man. "Getting together all the evidence.
We're doing a thorough job, ma'am." He spoke humbly,
placatingly. "Not missing anything. . . . D.A. said he
wanted you to look for something special."

She went upstairs to Alicia Donato's room and opened
the closet. Mrs. Donato's wardrobe was ample and expensive. There were labels of Saks-Fifth Avenue, Bergdorf
Goodman and Bonwit Teller of New York; Molyneux,
Paquin and Schiaparelli of Paris; Norman Hartnell of Lon-
don. There were sports frocks and spectator sports dresses,
chiffons for evening, voluminous negligees, adorned with
rich laces, suits and wraps. But no such garment as she

was seeking. She looked in Paul Donato's bedroom. She went downstairs again, searched carefully through the house. Behind the open front door she found another closet. A dozen empty velvet-covered hangers swung from a rod, but on the floor, as though it had been tossed by some reckless hand, lay a gray tweed coat. She picked it up. It had a hood. Something hard smote her thigh. She looked in a pocket. She found a metal flashlight. She folded the coat and placed it in the suit box beside the hammer and wedding ring and broken marble. She used the Donato telephone to call Mr. Babcock. "There's a gray tweed coat and a flashlight. Witch's cloak and witch's fire. All that's lacking is the broomstick."

"Excellent," he answered. "It's shaping very well, don't you think? I'm leaving the hospital, coming up your way. There has just been word from the Coast Guard. Radio. Their plane sighted the *Cynisca*. Off Marblehead. She was heading north, returning to Laneport harbor. They're escorting her in. If you would care to meet me at the Marine Railways on Johnson's Neck, in half an hour or so—"

Mr. Parsons popped up from the running board, fell into step beside her. "I trust you have completed your mission?" he asked diffidently.

"I think we have." She could afford to be indulgent, since the case was so near its solution. "I think we've found our witch."

"Mrs. Donato?"

She nodded brusquely.

"That's what I wished to talk with you about. That's exactly what I wanted to say. My plan was to have the child—"

"Identify her witch." She finished for him. "We've thought of that ourselves."

Bathers, returning from the beach, were straggling up Central Road. She looked at them jealously and thought, *Everybody's having fun while I'm working. Why do I let myself in for these things?* She darted into the lobby, said to Miss Moffett, "When my husband comes back, tell him, please, that I've gone down Johnson's Neck."

"To meet the *Cynisca?*" Miss Moffett inquired promptly. "I knew they'd find it. Good old Uncle Sam. Always gets his man."

When she came out again, there was Mr. Parsons once more. *Oh, dear,* she thought with genuine irritation, *is he my shadow? Is he going to haunt me?*

"You don't mind, I trust," Mr. Parsons commenced, "if I walk along with you. I must talk to someone. The little girl seems to have disappeared. And Doctor McAlistir. I talk things over with him sometimes. He is quite understanding. But his wife seems to have taken him away, too."

So that was it. He wasn't butting in. He was just distressed over what had happened and anxious for the comfort of companionship. Mary softened. "You must excuse me," she said. "I've a great deal on my mind, so that if I don't seem to be listening—"

"My mind is full too," he answered patiently. "I have been thinking over the last information you gave me." He hop-skipped to keep step with her. "I cannot quite—" he broke off suddenly. "There's Mrs. Lyndall's garden. The one I mentioned this morning. You really ought to stop and see it if you have the time."

Behind a gold-on-blue swinging sign, announcing *Ryon Lyndall, Studio,* a blue and white house nestled in a flower bed. Scarlet and gold poppies nodded their tulip heads, zinnia and snapdragon, larkspur and marigold wandered in incredible colorful profusion around both sides of the house. Petunias bordered the path all the way out to the road. Morning-glories, from ice-blue to deepest purple, climbed the walls. A canary-yellow butterfly whirled drunkenly over a bed of white and scarlet roses.

In the back of the garden, where the flower beds ended near the water's edge, a drooping, bearded lily sprawled in a steamer chair, with an ice-cap on its head, its hands hanging listlessly.

"That's Ryon," Mr. Parsons chuckled, "doing penance."

Mary slowed her pace, glanced at the lolling figure. As she stared across the flower beds, a cloth hillock detached itself from a clump of rose bushes, unrolled, straightened. The high bosom and wide shoulders of a female towered above the posies.

"Mrs. Lyndall!" Mr. Parsons exclaimed. "I didn't see you."

Mrs. Lyndall answered, "Humph."

Mr. Parsons smiled tentatively. He looked again toward the rear of the house. His smile broadened. "How is Ryon?" he asked.

Mrs. Lyndall's spine became a ramrod. "Quite well!" Her face was stony.

Mr. Parsons took a single diffident step toward the garden. "You mustn't be too upset, Mrs. Lyndall," he ventured. "Even if people do know. They're really quite understanding about these little derelictions. Artistic temperament. Now I—when I heard him singing last night—a song about a fox—I don't know whether you heard it—I had a premonition. I saw the white woman. The fisherman's white woman."

Here we go again! Mary thought dismally. She moved on.

"It's the death omen," Mr. Parsons explained. "And of course there was a death."

Mrs. Lyndall said, "Please. Not so loud. Disturbs Ryon. His poor head."

Mary strolled away, down Johnson's Neck. Mr. Parsons' voice drifted after her, wheezing, "Quite amazing. The child said it was a witch," and Mrs. Lyndall's interrupting him, "Won't you come in and let me give you some tea?"

She walked slowly down the road. Mr. Babcock had said half an hour. There was time to look in the shop windows.

Johnson's Neck was a fair. Its little studios were pastel-tinted blue, yellow, pink, and each had its flower bed or box. Between the houses were the gift shops—windows crowded with copper and brass, ruby and cobalt glass, wood carvings, old silver, peasant linens, straw angels, with tin halos, and painted wooden horses from Sweden; pewter from Denmark; porcelain figurines, toiles de Jouy from France; tulip-patterned Dutch pottery; ceramics, enameled copper from India and Iran; serapis, tin altars, raffia donkeys from Mexico; framed lithographs of Currier and Ives, out of old New York. The whole world had poured its treasures into this narrow peninsula on the New England seacoast.

The Neck grew narrower and studios and shops, she saw, were propped on piles, and sunk into the silt. A long yellow barracks, rear end high above the oily, scummy water of the inner harbor, bore the sign *Laneport Art Society* on its portal and a little balcony at its side where art viewers, coming up for air, promenaded genteelly in the afternoon sunshine.

"Hey, Mary—where's the fire?" She whirled around. Chris and Baby Doll were racing, hand in hand, down the road. Chris, she saw with deep envy, had a sunburn. He linked his arm in hers. "Can't shake me any more. Can't shake *us*. We're staying together, Mrs. Whittaker. And to hell with crime. . . . Baby Doll, don't look at me like that. You can't bully me. You're not my grandma. If you don't like my cussing, you can't be my girl."

At the tip of Johnson's Neck they came to a graveled open space, which ended at elevated wooden tracks, sliding down to the water's edge, a maze of docks, a crowded bay where yachts and fishing schooners rode at anchor. The *Rosabelle*, three tall masts and a black and green hull, towered over them from the height of the tracks.

Chris said, "They pull 'em up for greasing and oiling. Or scraping barnacles. Or is it binnacles? . . . Psst. There's your pal, Sergeant Sargent."

The sergeant's shoulders twitched as his name was taken, but he did not turn around. Instead, he stared moodily out to sea, straining for sight of a seaplane and a yacht.

The tires of a car ground the gravel. Brakes rasped. A car door slammed. Kneeland Babcock's tired voice said, "Good afternoon, Mrs. Whittaker. . . . Ah, your little family!"

Before she could make introductions, she heard the drone of a motor overhead. The gray plane swooped out of the sky, down to the water's surface, skimmed the sea in a whirl of rainbow spray, cut its motors, drifted toward the dock. Then around the bend, from the open sea into the land-locked harbor, came a superb white ship, gliding as smoothly, proudly as a swan, polished wood and polished brass and white paint gleaming. It turned gracefully in mid-harbor, slid alongside a dock. A blue-clad sailor threw a rope. Sergeant Sargent caught it, made it fast. Two sailors laid down a gangplank. A young man in sweater and slacks, golden hair glinting in the sun, sunburned throat and chin held stiffly, came out on the deck, leaned against the rail. Sergeant Sargent and Mr. Babcock moved swiftly toward the gangplank.

Baby Doll's small figure hurtled between their legs, leaped at the blond young man, screaming, "Toddy! Tod-deee."

The young man took one startled step back and then two quick, eager strides forward. He scooped up the child, hugged her. "Baby Doll! Did Mommy send you to meet me?"

"Oh, Toddy!" Baby Doll hid her face in his sweater. "Mommy's dead. A big bad witch killed her dead."

The young man set the child down on the deck. "You mustn't say such things." He shook a reproving finger. "Mommy won't like it if you tell stories like that."

Mr. Babcock looked quickly at Mary. Then he strode up

the gangplank. He said, "Babcock's my name. I am the District Attorney of this county."

The young man scowled but he answered courteously, "I'm Todd Amroe. What can I do for you, sir?"

The District Attorney looked at him steadily. "I requested the Coast Guard to bring you back," he began.

"You sent the Coast Guard for me?" The young man seemed thoroughly bewildered. "My radio man did say something of the sort. Said he got some silly message from the Coast Guard plane to return to Laneport. But we were on our way back. . . . Did you know we had the girl?"

It was Mr. Babcock's turn to look baffled. "Which girl?"

"Here. Come with me, sir." Todd Amroe led the District Attorney into the ship's lounge. After a minute they came out again, an unwilling young woman, with downcast, tear-stained face, shuffling behind them.

"Good lord!" Mary exclaimed. "It's Lorna Bean!"

Miss Bean raised her head. When she saw Mary her cheeks flamed; her eyes glowed sullenly. Mary went up the gangplank.

The District Attorney turned to Mary. "Are you acquainted with this young woman?" he asked.

"Slightly. We've met before. At Nola Spain's window."

"What's all this talk about Nola?" Todd Amroe demanded.

Mr. Babcock answered him. "Mrs. Spain is dead. I presume you are aware of it."

Todd Amroe stared at Baby Doll and then at the District Attorney. "It's not true. It's not possible." He looked from one to the other, seeking assurance that it was not true, but their solemn nods affirmed the fact.

His lower lip trembled. Abruptly he turned away from them, dug into his pocket, pulled out a cigarette case, lit a cigarette with shaking fingers, walked away, leaned over the stern rail, staring down at the water, dribbling ash into it. They saw him raise his arm, wipe his eyes with his wrist. Then Baby Doll went to him, looked anxiously up at his face, and put her hand into his. "Don't cry, Toddy," she said. "See, I'm not crying. Only babies cry."

It was a moment in which it would have been natural to forget that they were minions of law and justice. But to Kneeland Babcock, at any rate, the passing of Nola Spain was death without tears. He turned to Miss Bean and said gruffly, "Now young lady, suppose you tell us what you're doing here?"

Miss Bean hung her head. She did not answer.

Mary said, "Miss Bean has a habit of turning up in strange places. When I last saw her—at three-thirty this morning—she was leaning over the window sill of Mrs. Spain's room."

"I didn't do anything. You know I didn't," Miss Bean whined.

The District Attorney said coldly, "Young lady, I advise you to tell us the truth. For your own good. You were acquainted with Mrs. Spain?"

"I? Oh, no." Miss Bean shook her head vigorously. "I never saw her but once. In the dining-room last night. And after she was dead."

"But you knew that Mr. Amroe was a friend of hers?"

"He was a friend of hers? Was he really? I didn't know that."

"You didn't, eh? Then why else, may I ask, did you go to him after it was over?"

"I didn't go to him. I went to the boat."

"To escape?" Mary asked brusquely.

Miss Bean nodded.

The District Attorney and the detectives and the state trooper stared at one another, open-mouthed. This couldn't be what it seemed. It was too silly. This teary girl had stabbed a woman through the heart! Alicia Donato, burning with murderous jealousy, while this slim, slouching young woman was serving her as executioner of a hated rival!

"What were you escaping from, Miss Bean? The police?" Mary persisted.

"The police?" Lorna Bean's eyes were pin-points of terror. "The police? Oh, no—my mother!" Her face flamed again. She snuffed back tears.

"Your mother? What has she to do with the death of Nola Spain?" The District Attorney's neat and compact case, so nearly complete a few hours ago, was falling apart with each incomprehensible word that dropped from the lips of this girl. He was upset and his agitation was plain for all of them to see.

"My mother has nothing to do with Nola Spain," Miss Bean answered. "Only with me." Her words came reluctantly, weighted down with embarrassment. "I didn't want her to know. I didn't want her to know I looked in that window. I was so ashamed. When you caught me, I had to get away. Far away from that place. . . . I thought they'd take me. I thought when they found me on the boat, they'd treat me as if—oh, I don't know what I thought. I just wanted to get away. Don't tell my mother. Oh, don't tell my mother." Her shoulders shook. Tears raced down her nose. "What'll I do now?" She gurgled. "How'll I go back and face them?"

They sat under an awning on the deck of the *Cynisca*, on seat cushions six inches high, and watched the sun slowly dipping behind the spires and spars of Laneport, transforming the inner harbor into a lake of gold, while Baby Doll swung gleefully on the shining brass rails of the hatchways and Miss Bean sat alone, weeping into a claret lemonade.

Mr. Babcock asked again, "You came back only because you had that girl aboard?"

"That's right." Todd Amroe's face was flushed. The butts of the cigarettes he had lighted, left burning, unsmoked, made a smouldering volcano in the glass ash-tray on the table. "We discovered her after we passed Marblehead. She had locked herself into a washroom. Stowaway. I ordered the captain to turn back at once. I didn't want her. I wasn't going to assume responsibility for her. She raised Cain. Said she wouldn't go back. Said she'd throw herself overboard if we tried to bring her back. I think she's slightly off." Mr. Amroe looked uneasily at Miss Bean.

"A good many things are—er—slightly off," Mr. Babcock observed. "For instance, your own departure in a heavy fog. What was your hurry, may I ask?"

The young man bit his lip. "I had no reason to stay."

"You insist that you had not heard of Mrs. Spain's death before you left? That you escorted her back to the Rockledge and left her there before midnight?"

"Yes, sir, I certainly do."

"Er—eh—" Mr. Babcock seemed uncomfortable. "What condition was Mrs. Spain in at that time, may I ask?"

Todd Amroe pushed back his chair. "What do you mean, sir?" His face was full of fight.

"Please remain seated," the District Attorney answered calmly. "Was she, by any chance, intoxicated?"

The young man's ears turned scarlet. "We had champagne," he conceded. "Oh, we weren't drunk. Not really drunk. . . . How many glasses are there in a quart? That's all we had. A quart between us. And Gregory—he's the steward—he'd made some sandwiches. Chicken and caviar."

Chris Whittaker said, "The condemned woman had a fine supper. She went out in style."

Todd Amroe glowered at him.

"That's probably why she didn't wake up when her murderer came," Mary suggested. "Alcohol's an anesthetic, too."

"What was this? A celebration?" the District Attorney asked.

Todd Amroe lowered his head. "We were drinking," he mumbled into his chest. "Our farewell."

"Your farewell?" Mary echoed sharply.

He nodded. "It was over. We drank to our friendship— to our memories."

"She had someone else?" Mary asked. "A new love?"

"Oh, no." He shook his head emphatically. "I'm quite sure there wasn't anyone. . . . Must I tell you all these things?"

"I'm afraid you must," the District Attorney said. "You were the last person known to have seen her alive. And more than one man has killed a woman because she said good-bye before he was ready to let her go."

The young man squirmed. He writhed within his sweater as though he were caught in the toils of something slimy.

Mary said, slowly, impressively, "That is particularly important, since Nola Spain carried out with her, in her own hand, when she left Alicia Donato's house, a weapon like that with which she was killed."

The District Attorney looked at her reproachfully. "Why was I not told of this?"

"No chance to tell it," she apologized. "I just learned it myself a little while ago."

Todd Amroe stared at them both. "What weapon are you talking about?" he asked.

"Didn't you notice that Nola Spain had in her hand a small, sharp steel rod? I've just been told that she carried it with her when she went out of Donato's."

"Oh, that!" His face brightened. "Of course. Nola noticed it right after she came out of that house. She said, 'How silly of me! I've carried away one of Paul's points.' "

"And?" Mary prompted.

"And," Todd Amroe went on, "she threw it away."

"She threw it away? Where?"

The young man mopped his forehead. "Where?" he repeated petulantly. "How do I know where? Anywhere. She just threw it away."

"Near Donato's? On Central road? On Johnson's Neck?" Mary persisted.

"I haven't the least idea."

"Was there anyone about when she threw it away? Any other people on the road?"

"If there were, I didn't see them. I wasn't interested in anyone but Nola." His voice broke on the syllables of her name.

"But you're certain she threw it away? She didn't by any chance bring it aboard this ship? Or possibly give it to you?"

He answered tartly, "I'm not in the habit of lying. Particularly about small matters."

"This is no small matter," the District Attorney said somberly. "Mrs. Whittaker did not have time to inform me that Mrs. Spain carried this instrument with her. It alters the situation considerably." He hitched his chair closer to the table. "You had best be completely frank with us, young man."

Todd Amroe asked quickly, "Am I under arrest?"

"No."

"Am I under suspicion?"

"Definitely."

"Suppose I say that I won't talk until I have advice of counsel?"

The parsimonious smile played around Mr. Babcock's lips. "In that event," he said, "we shall have no choice but to put you under arrest immediately."

Todd Amroe lit another cigarette, puffed it quietly, as if trying to pull himself together. Finally, he said, "If you arrested me, it would be in the newspapers. My father would know. I can't have that. I can't have that at all." He put his cigarette down on the rim of the table, folded his arms, leaned against them. "I'll tell you everything," he said. "Everything about me and Nola. It isn't very much. Just that I loved her, worshipped her. But that's enough, isn't it?" His lip quivered. His anguish was plain in his face.

"Nola Spain was older than you, wasn't she?" Mary asked.

Todd Amroe's ears reddened. "Does that matter? There were lots of ways we were different. . . . But lots of ways we were alike. In the things we loved and the things we hated. That's what counts. We understood each other perfectly. She was the only person who really knew me. . . . I realized that the very first time I met her. . . . It was at a party. One of those parties people were forever giving for Spain—a couple of years ago. That's where she got her name. Didn't you know that? Spain's not her real name. You see, she was married. I suppose you'd call it married. To a young fellow who went over to fight in Spain. Abraham Lincoln Brigade. At least she'd been living with him before he enlisted. His name was Pincus. Martin Pincus. I think he was the father of the little girl. He died. In the valley of the Ebro. And then Nola took the name of Spain. She told me why she did that. 'People forget idealism too quickly. I want to keep reminding and reminding them as long as I live.'"

The portrait of Nola Spain was taking shape and color. The marble beauty of the fog-filled room was coming alive—a vivid, dramatic personality—a quixotic woman who had scorned conventions but had made a code of her own by which she had lived and died.

Todd Amroe's unhappy young voice went on: "I suppose I had no business at that party. You know who my father is, don't you? Carson Amroe. Look him up in *Who's Who*—or in Lundberg's *Sixty Families*. Columbus Steel, Empire City Bank, Industrial Trust, Porcellian, Union League, Sands Point, Palm Beach, Fifth Avenue and Seventy-sixth. . . ." He flicked his father's qualifications off, with an airy motion of his hand, as if they were of little account. "My father and I—we don't see eye to eye politically."

"Merely agree on the desirability of yachts," Chris Whittaker suggested.

Todd Amroe blushed again. "You don't think I give a hang about all this," he protested bitterly, "and what it stands for. I borrowed the boat from dad. He doesn't know why I wanted it. Nola wrote me she was coming up here. I brought the boat for her sake. Hoped she might get some good out of it. A little air and sun and relaxation. But dad's not to know. I want your promise on that, Mr. Babcock." His eyes were very anxious now. "Dad's to be kept out of this. Dad doesn't know about Nola. And I don't think he'd understand. We haven't been getting along so well, dad and I. Not since I went to college. . . . Would you believe it, I didn't know till I got to college that there actually were families that didn't have butlers! All the families I knew did and I thought that was the way the whole world was. . . . I didn't know what dreadful inequalities, dreadful injustices there were." His voice held an odd note of awe, as if he were still dazed by his discovery of the facts of life. "Oh, I learned, I learned. I learned that a wonderful person like Nola had to live in a one-room hovel, had to depend on that baby to support them both. Poor and sick. But she wouldn't take a dime from me. Most I could ever do for her was take her out for dinner once in a while. Last night I asked her to marry me. And she"—his voice dropped to a whisper—"said no."

A woman with a dollar in her purse had rejected a millionaire's son who came courting on his yacht! "She must have been a most amazing person," Mary said.

"You don't know. None of you can imagine how wonderful she was." Todd Amroe's lower lip trembled again. "I'll tell you what she said last night. She said, 'Todd, I can't marry you. You deserve better. You deserve a virgin. A virgin in heart and body. I'm worn out. I'm used up. I can't wish a burned-out wreck on a boy like you,' she said. 'Todd, I've been pushed around so much. I'm so tired. Twice I thought I had got a little hold on happiness. And both times it was snatched away from me. The first time I was very young and it seemed as wonderful as the moon and stars.' She talked so beautifully. 'And then there was cold emptiness. . . . But Martin came. And that was like the sun. Burning bright.' She was a poet. A poet at heart. 'And then that was over,' she said. 'But this emptiness won't last long. I'm not going to live long.'" His voice broke. "'I'm not going to live long,'" he repeated. "It was as if she knew. But she didn't know. She couldn't know. Just talked that way because she was very tired, distressed, a little bit scared."

"Scared?" Mary asked quickly. "Of what? Of whom?"

Todd Amroe shook his head. "I don't know. I really don't know. I'll try to remember just what she said. It was something like this: 'I'm sorry I came here, Todd. I thought I was going to be happy here. But it doesn't look as if I am. She doesn't like me. She really needn't worry. I'm not going to take her precious away.'"

"Alicia Donato?" the District Attorney suggested.

"The woman at whose house I met her?" The young man shrugged. "They did have words. A sort of catty, female nastiness. . . ." He flushed. "I'd rather not repeat it."

Mary said, "Don't. I know what it was."

He flashed a shy smile at her. "Thank you," he said quietly. "Probably she was the one Nola meant. She said, 'You'd think they'd be patient with me, tolerant. I have so little time.' We talked about Baby Doll too. She said that was the thing that worried her most. Leaving the little girl. She said she was trying to make arrangements for her."

"What sort of arrangements?" Mary asked. "Had she family? Or money?"

"Of course not." The young man's voice was impatient now. "I've told you she was poor as a church mouse. Perhaps there's some relative. . . ." He hesitated again, his forehead screwed up as if he was making a great decision. "If there isn't anyone else—Baby Doll knows me. I think she likes me. I'd be glad to take care of her."

"Not so fast, my fine-feathered friend," Chris Whittaker said. "I got there first."

Chapter Ten

THE CREATOR OF BEAUTY

MISS MOFFETT WAS SURE they'd want to change quarters, especially since they were taking care of the little girl. One really couldn't ask the child to sleep in *that* room. And since the Whittakers seemed to have assumed the moral responsibility for Baby Doll, were they prepared to assume the financial too? Miss Moffett devoutly hoped so because this trouble was going to cost her and Miss Dow Lord-knows-how-much, coming in the middle of the season like this. Some guests ran like rabbits when anything unusual occurred.

It would be half rate for the child. "Miss Dow and I have talked it over and we've decided, unless there turns out to be an estate, not to put in a claim for the one night. After all, she did have only one meal. Saturday night dinner. We don't know whom to ask to pay for it, except Paul. He did make the reservation. Guaranteed the bill. But poor Paul has so much trouble now, so much expense, with Alicia in the hospital, and if he has to hire lawyers—"

Miss Moffett offered a suite, two flights up, in Main, above Miss Godwin—a double and single with connecting bath and balcony. The Boston family which had occupied it all week had just gone home. Miss Moffett prayed, with hands clasped and eyes rolling, that *they* wouldn't talk.

Marcus Aurelius Smythe did his share to appease and hold Miss Moffet's guests. He provided steamed clams and broiled lobster for Sunday night supper, golden bantam on the cob, fluffy pop-overs, home-made Saratoga chips and flaky, oozing, altogether heavenly blueberry pie. The spice of excitement seasoned the Lucullan fare.

The day was done and on the wings of night rode the scented sweetness of country evening and the pleasant weariness that follows a diverting day. Long, long ago—hours so crowded seemed like days—death had stolen into the inn and fear had floated in the mist. But fresh breeze and bright sun, troopers on their champing metal steeds, the whirring Coast Guard plane, had chased the horror and left the thrills.

Mrs. Heath had kept to her room and Delia had carried supper for two over to the Annex. It was a relief, the guests agreed, not even to have to look at Mrs. Heath's unhappy face.

Mrs. Bean came over to the Whittakers in the dining-room. "I don't know how to thank you," she fluttered, "for bringing back my bad little girl. I really can't imagine what got into her."

Miss Bean drooped over her plate, pecked at a claw, her cheeks as red as the lobster shell.

Miss Godwin, dressed for the evening in undulant purple velvet, bald at the armpits, jangled her earrings archly and cooed across the room, "Welcome to Main. You must drop in and let me show your husband some of my canvases."

Miss Templeton, at her right hand, exposed her teeth. "We'll miss you. It was so nice to have you in the Annex. So reassuring to have our own, very own, detectives to protect us."

"Protect us!" Dr. McAlistir scoffed. "Protect us, indeed! Murder right under their noses!"

"Please. Please. Not now." Miss Hays shuddered delicately. "Let's not talk about that before bedtime. I'd like to get my sleep tonight."

Only Mr. Parsons had nothing to say. At his solitary table, he toyed with a fragile pop-over, studying his fellow lodgers with remote, speculative eyes.

After supper, they all went out to the piazza for the mass patrol which settled the meal and decided on tomorrow's weather. Miss Bean sidled up to Mary, murmured into her ear, "Can I talk to you?"

Mary dropped Baby Doll's hand, moved a little way off from the main stream of traffic.

"You must think I'm a perfect fool," Lorna Bean began, her voice and her chin low.

Mary's silence gave assent.

The girl raised her head. "Well, I am," she blazed. "I was a fool to think he'd even look at me."

"You'd never seen Todd Amroe before?"

"Of course not. I'd seen the *Cynisca*. I saw it when mother and I went for our walk. . . . She'll take me again. In a minute, she'll say, 'Lorna. Where are you, Lorna-dear? Time for our little walk.' She'll make me walk down the Neck with her. She'll buy me ice cream. She thinks that ought to make me happy. A dish of ice cream at the Copper Kettle. And then at ten o'clock she'll say, 'You're tired, Lorna-dear, time to go to bed.'" Bitterness oozed from every word. "I never meet anybody. I never do anything. Nothing ever happens to me. I can't stand it any more. . . . I'll kill myself."

Mary said sharply, "Stop that nonsense."

The girl's nervous fingers drummed the porch rail. "Well, what've I got to live for? You've got your husband. She had *him*." Her voice sharpened. "Wasn't she an awful fool? If she had accepted him—"

"If Booth had missed—" Mary shrugged. "If this or that was changed. If Paul Donato hadn't been away. If Nola Spain hadn't drunk too much champagne. If's make conversation but they don't alter facts."

"She drank champagne," the girl murmured. "She had men at her feet. She died. But she lived before she died. I'd be glad to die too, if I could live for just a little while." She studied the dark, noisy sea for a moment. "Oh, what's the use!" She turned again to Mary. "There's something I want to ask you. . . ." She hesitated. "Do you think Todd Amroe's a Communist?" she stammered.

Mary laughed. "He probably imagines he's something of the sort. Fellow traveler."

"Mrs. Whittaker,"—Lorna Bean clutched at a straw—"do you think he believes in free love?"

Mr. Parsons strolled by with Dr. McAlistir, his head tilted toward the doctor's ear. He saw the women at the rail, stopped talking, smiled in friendly fashion at Miss Bean, nodded coldly at Mrs. Whittaker.

When he had passed, Miss Bean said, "He's queer, but he's nice. He's the only one that's even noticed me. Only the old ones ever notice me. Oh, it's so lonely. . . . It's so lonely over there."

Mr. Parsons was lonely, too. After he had said "Good night" to Dr. McAlistir, he sat dolefully down in his rocker. The night without sleep, the day without rest, dragged at his limbs. The silence of the Annex oppressed him—the thought of the two vacant rooms across the hall. The incoming tide lapped mildly against the rocks. Feet shuffled overhead in Mrs. Heath's room. In Mrs. Heath's room. Mrs. Heath and Isabel Chalmers. He rolled the names over in his mind.

He took out his diary and in it he wrote:

It is a serious mistake to admit a stranger to one's thoughts. But it seemed essential at the time. I was bewildered, I confess. Never could I have conceived a tale like that which happened here today. I have an explanation for some of the strange phenomena. It is my belief that certain persons invariably present themselves to certain other sensitive persons, not in the light of their physical appearances, but in the light of their true natures. I may look at what passes for a man and may see only a hog —a gross, overstuffed porker. Or I may look at another and see a predatory buzzard. Thus, an intuitive person like

Mrs. Spain's little girl may look upon the face and form of a female and recognize at once the basic character of the witch. This is not illusion but true understanding. To that person, that female will, at all times, under all circumstances, appear as a witch. Therefore, if the child is permitted freely to hunt for a witch, she will unerringly discover her mother's murderer. And it is my conviction that she will recognize, not Mrs. Donato, as the authorities seem to believe, but Mrs. Heath.

I have attempted to discuss this line of reasoning with several persons. I here record their responses:

Mrs. Whittaker: Dismissed with impatience. Yes, yes, we've thought of that, too.

Baby Doll: Great enthusiasm and clear understanding. Willing to co-operate.

Mrs. Lyndall: Very interesting. No other comment.

Dr. McAlistir: Excuse me, Gorham, some other time. My wife's calling me.

I am disappointed in Alpheus. I had taken him for a man of insight.

He put down his fountain pen, screwed its cap on, laid his diary away in his dresser.

As Mary tucked the blankets around Baby Doll, the child said suddenly, "Mary. I don't want to."

"Don't want to what, dear? Sleep?"

"No." The little girl shook her head vehemently. "I don't want to dentify witches." Her eyes were wide and dark with fear. "I'm scared of witches."

"Darling, you don't have to. Who says you must?"

"He does. That old, old man does."

"Mr. Parsons?" She was piqued. *Why's he annoying this poor baby?* she thought. She comforted the child. "He can't make you do anything, dear. Chris and I will watch out for you. We'll find that big, bad witch and lock her away where she can't ever hurt anybody again. We won't let anything frighten you ever. Good night, darling." She kissed the little girl's forehead.

The child sighed. "Todd's nice too," she said. "He was always so good to Mommy."

Mary closed the door and went into the larger bedroom of the suite. Her husband got up from the rocker. "Alone at last," he said. "Can we be Mr. and Mrs. now, or do we go on being detectives?"

She caressed his cheek. She said, "One more thing before we go back to private life. I want to send a telegram. To New York. To Johnny Reese."

"That hound!" Chris rubbed his jaw reminiscently. "Stolen car! Your pal!"

"Johnny's the boy to send on an errand and this isn't the time to promote a grudge." She found a sheet of Rockledge stationery in the dresser, wrote a few words on it.

When Chris had gone, grumbling under his breath, to hunt for the telegraph office, she let down her hair, brushed it. She put on her nightgown, slipped her negligee over it, took a few sheets of writing paper from the dresser. She was sitting up in bed, her forehead furrowed over penciled notes, when Chris returned.

"Homework?" he asked.

"Addition and subtraction," she answered. "When you begin to fit things together, it's surprising how much is left over."

He took the paper from her, glanced at it, crowed like a rooster. "Information please. Time to stump the experts." He read aloud: "One: *To what extent can we believe Baby Doll? Did she actually see anyone in the room or did she merely imagine she did?* . . . Of course, she did. If she said she saw a witch, she saw a witch."

"You too," Mary groaned. "Is everybody crazy?"

"Two: *What sort of creature could have made that print with the cloven hoof?* . . . A cow looked in the window. Or maybe old Nick, himself. These are a cinch, Mary.

"Three: *How did Alicia Donato know what room Nola occupied, what window to enter?* . . . That's a good one. If the murderer wasn't sure, he, she or it might have dropped in on us. Ugh! Ten dollars and a set of the *Encyclopædia Britannica* goes out to Mrs. Whittaker. . . . How *did* she know, Mrs. W.?"

"That's what I hope to find out. Haven't found anyone yet who told her. Both Miss Dow and Miss Moffett deny she asked them."

"Four: *Did Nola Spain actually come into the Annex alone?* . . . You mean she might have brought the pretty boy in with her?"

"He says no. But everyone's a liar till he proves otherwise."

"Five: *Could Todd Amroe have brought himself to kill Nola Spain out of jealousy—desire to keep any other man from having her?* . . . Nix, Mary, that's no good. He's not the type.

"Six: *Was the sculptor's point which Nola Spain carried with her out of the Donato House actually thrown away?* . . . Well, if it was, anyone out on the streets of Laneport after ten o'clock might have picked it up. Check?"

"Double check. But if she didn't throw it away, Todd Amroe might have used it. It's his word against the probabilities."

"I catch on. But if she did throw it away, there's no telling in whose hands it might have landed. You've got the whole blamed town to choose from. . . . Seven: *Who or what in Laneport was Nola afraid of?* . . . Amroe's yarn again. You've got the answer. The Donato dame.

"Eight: *What was the first happiness that was snatched away from Nola Spain?* . . . Golly, you certainly memorized Toddy-boy's tale. From what I gathered Paul Donato was number one. And the dead Red number two.

"Nine: *What arrangements was Nola Spain trying to make for her child?* . . . Time will tell, Mrs. W., time will tell." He put down the sheet of paper. He contemplated it. Then he picked up his wife's pencil: "Add another question," he said. *"Where did Isabel Chalmers learn to tap on water-pipes in the Morse code?"*

Early next morning they had the answer to Christopher's question.

Miss Dow knocked on their door. "Mrs. Whittaker," she called through the panels. "Mr. Babcock's here. He's in a hurry. He says will you please come down."

Mr. Babcock was at the telephone with Sam Dolliver at his elbow. The policeman waved a cordial greeting but Mr. Babcock went ahead with his own affairs, listening with one hand and writing in a little notebook with the other. His eyes were red-rimmed, blood-shot, his clothes crumpled as though he had not had them off all night. At last he said, "Thank you very much," to the telephone, hung up the receiver, said "Good morning" to Mary, and, "I must thank you, Mrs. Whittaker. You have done us a real service. When you brought us that tray of dishes, you delivered to us—" he paused, rolling his tongue over his lips, savoring his tidbit of surprise—"the fingerprints of a murderess!"

Mary gripped the newel post. "Mrs. Heath? Miss Chalmers?"

"We have found the fingerprints of one Eulalie Hendrix, who in September, 1909, was arrested in this state for stabbing a woman to death with a kitchen knife. Eulalie Hendrix was fifteen years of age at that time. As a juvenile, she was not eligible for the death penalty. She was committed to the State Reformatory for Girls until she reached twenty-one. She was released in 1915. My office has been in communication with the Reformatory. I have just received a report." He opened his little notebook, read from it: *"Description of Eulalie Hendrix on admission: Age fifteen, height four feet, nine inches, weight two hundred and forty-eight pounds. . . ."*

"Isabel Chalmers!" Mary gasped.

He nodded. "The resemblance is striking. Short. Obese. And a singular similarity in the type of crime. Miss Hendrix, or Chalmers as we know her, stabbed a beautiful young woman in a fit of anger. Her defense was that the woman had taunted her because of her appearance."

A number of things came into Mary's mind and she spoke of them all in a bunch: "So that's where she learned to send messages. In prison. That's why her sister guarded her so carefully. So that no one would see her, rouse her temper by making fun of her. . . . She was out of her room that night. I saw her myself at the top of the steps. . . . She tried to shift the blame. Tried to tell us it was someone else. . . . Chris and I were up in her room. She told us she saw a woman in a cloak, coming up out of the sea. She seemed anxious to talk, but her sister drove us out of the room."

"Her sister," Mr. Babcock added, "is apparently a Mrs. Elmer Watson. The records state that Eulalie Hendrix was paroled in the custody of this sister. They have taken different names. Yet one of them could not change her fundamental nature." He consulted his notebook again. "There seems no record of mental disturbance. The Reformatory report is: 'Well-educated, refined, co-operative, no bad habits.'"

"No vice but murder," Mary observed cynically. "Suppose she does do a little killing—as long as she doesn't smoke."

Miss Dow's face, behind the counter, was piteous. "Dear me," she moaned, "I trusted them. I had a murderess here. Under my roof. Dear me, Mr. Babcock, will it come out in the papers? Will everybody know?"

The District Attorney said, "We shall remove them from your premises as quietly as possible." He signaled to Sam Dolliver. He strode through the lobby to the back door and across the porch to the Annex.

Mary tagged beside him. They entered the Annex. The

District Attorney rapped imperatively on the door of the room at the head of the stairs. He got no answer. He rapped again. Then he touched the knob. The door swung open.

Smooth spreads covered unslept beds; closet door stood ajar; hangers hung empty; dresser drawers held no more than a lone wire hairpin, a crumpled bit of tissue paper. On the dresser top lay a sealed, bulky white envelope of Rockledge stationery, addressed in a round, juvenile hand to *Miss Dow, Miss Moffett.*

Mr. Babcock pocketed the envelope. "The birds have flown," he said grimly. "But they won't fly far. Not with the weight they carry."

They brought the envelope to Miss Dow. She tore it open and she found a note, a heap of bills and coins. She read the letter, silently at first, with moving, trembling lips, and then she read it aloud: *"We have found it impossible to remain any longer. Thank you for your many courtesies."* Her voice broke. She gathered its splinters, went on: *"We trust the enclosed amount is correct to date. We have put in a dollar more than our calculations, in the event that our mathematics are not quite accurate. If it is superfluous, kindly divide it between Delia, the waitress, and Marian, the maid. In the event that it is not, we have added fifty cents for each of them."* Both women had signed their names. After the signatures there was a postscript: *"Our behavior may seem odd to some but we feel we cannot remain in any place where our privacy is not assured."* . . . "Privacy not assured!" Miss Dow's bosom rolled. "Privacy! When I myself told Jacob Haskell yesterday—"

The front door opened. A lusty masculine voice said, "Yes, yes, go on, Phoebe darling, what did you tell Jacob Haskell?"

They swung around. An olive-skinned man, black-mustached, black-eyed, black-browed, attired in green corduroy jacket and brown tweed trousers, grinned at them with good-natured insolence. Miss Dow gasped, "Paul! It's you!"

Paul Donato came forward, laughing. "In person and famished. Tell Marcus Aurelius to rustle up some ham and eggs. Alicia's walked out on me. Send one of your maids over, will you, Phoebe, like a good girl. Alicia left the place a holy mess. Must have had a riot there. Window broken." He bent his head to Miss Dow's ear: "Did Nola get here?" But before Miss Dow could answer, his keen, restless eyes had taken in the District Attorney and the policeman. His heavy brows leaped up and made a fringe across his forehead. "Mr. Babcock, I believe! An early bird! Business or pleasure?" He glanced at Mrs. Whittaker, swiftly, acutely.

Mr. Babcock answered, "We can dispense with pleasantries, Mr. Donato. We have been waiting for you. Nola Spain is dead and your wife is at the Laneport Hospital."

The laughter went out of Paul Donato's face, like a candle snuffed. "Nola's dead? Alicia's sick?" He looked from face to face, seeking confirmation and enlightenment. He said at last, "But one calamity's got nothing to do with the other, or has it?"

When Kneeland Babcock had led him to the sofa, had told him what had happened at the Rockledge, he covered his face with his hands and sat hunched, elbows on his knees, fingertips digging into his temples. "I can't get it through my mind," he muttered. "I feel so guilty."

"You do, do you? In what way?" Kneeland Babcock asked.

"Why, I sent for Nola. If I hadn't brought her here. . . . Oh, say, you don't think that Alicia had anything to do with it?"

The District Attorney answered with a question. "She was jealous of your model, was she not?"

Paul Donato's reply came quickly, a shade too quickly,

Mary thought: "Alicia was jealous of every woman I ever spoke to."

"Unusually jealous of this one?"

Paul Donato waved a belittling hand. "That was an old story, an old, old story. Over and done with. I assure you she had no grounds. My relations with Nola" (he was obviously pained by his recollections) "were pure as the driven snow. I might have wished them otherwise. But wishing isn't fact. A lad named Martin Pincus was the light of her life and Paul Donato was just the boy who provided the rent money." He seemed both rueful and incredulous as though he himself could scarcely believe that any woman, at any time, might have preferred a Martin Pincus to a Paul Donato.

The sculptor was attractive, no doubt about that at all, Mary decided, albeit a bit flashy. He was tall and brawny and his nose was proud, his hair curly, bold eyes sparkling. She came into the conversation uninvited: "Mr. Donato, can we get down to dates and specific details? When, where and how did you first meet Nola Spain and what do you know about her?"

He smiled, welcoming her. His teeth, she saw, were white and strong, not the least part of his attractions. "Haven't met this lady before but I'm glad to. Nola's life? The little lady wants it in a capsule. I'm afraid Paul can only hand out a small dose. I met her—let's see—at a Beaux Arts Ball, in New York. It must have been back in 1933. She was there with a painter whom I knew, Denny Rodman. (Sorry, but you can't get hold of Denny. D.T.'s got him first. Two years ago.) She was wearing a white tulle fluff around her middle and a crown on her hair. The 'Fairy Princess' costume. Denny introduced us. I made her get her wrap and leave the ball at once. Took her right back to my studio. That very night we began—at two o'clock in the morning, in the costume she wore at the ball."

He got up suddenly, strode to the mantel piece, came

back with the book-end in his hand. "This is it. If I got into it only a fraction of the loveliness that was hers that night."

He balanced the book-end on the palm of his hand, appraised it. "Yes. A little of it's there. She was something to see, then. I'd have given my right arm to have had her. But there was a Martin Pincus. And she was going to marry him. Marry him! He hadn't a cent. An apple-selling engineer. I heard later that he was on one of the WPA projects before he decided to go off and fight with the Loyalists. Nola wasn't married to him when I first met her but she couldn't have been more faithful if she was. That was my tough luck. From what Denny Rodman told me, before that time she hadn't cared particularly under whose bed she parked her shoes. Denny didn't know where she came from or who her people were. All he knew was she'd started posing for classes at the Art League when she was just a kid. When he first knew her she was on her own, free-lancing among the studios and the studio couches. It was my hard luck to come into her life at the same time Martin Pincus did."

"And the child was his?" Mary ventured.

"The child? Oh, yes, now I remember. She did say something about having a kid. Mentioned it last time I saw her. A few weeks ago. I hadn't seen her for years. Alicia'd had words with her. Alicia came into the studio one afternoon when we were working and blew off, announced she was going to Reno. Nola didn't like it. She took her hat and paycheck and walked out."

"How did you come to invite her to Laneport now?"

"Just luck. Accident of fate. I was in New York a few weeks ago. Had to get some things. There's a tool-maker on East 110th. Way over near the river. I was going there. Vile neighborhood. East Harlem, if any of you know what that means. There's where I found her. She was shopping —lettuce and stuff—from a push-cart. She looked dreadfully ill—all crumpled with heat, hair too heavy for her head. But when I saw her, I saw something else. The princess in exile. A weary, refugee sort of thing. I asked her whether she'd come to Laneport and work for me. That was when she told me she'd have to bring a kid along. Said she was a widow and broke. I left her money for the trip. She seemed delighted to come. 'Laneport,' she said. 'I've heard a lot about it. I've always wanted to see it.'"

"Any special reason?" Mary asked.

He shrugged. "No can tell."

"You can't or you won't tell us?" Kneeland Babcock demanded.

"Don't be an ass," Paul Donato said sharply. "I haven't anything to hide."

"Then why," Mary asked, "weren't you home to help your wife greet her guest?"

"Oh, that." A flush crept under Mr. Donato's olive skin. "I had an engagement."

Mr. Babcock took out his little notebook, poised his pencil over a page. "With whom and where?"

Paul Donato flipped the cover down upon the page. He shook his head. "Bad business to name ladies."

The District Attorney opened the notebook again. "You have no choice. One can't protect one lady's reputation when another has been murdered."

"One's got nothing to do with the other," Paul Donato snarled. "I left Saturday morning. Came back this morning. I have been away. I have nothing to do with anything that's happened."

"Save that you brought the victim here," the District Attorney persisted. "That your wife made her hatred of Nola Spain evident to many persons and that the lady was killed with a point of steel that belonged to you."

They could see his jaw muscles tightening, his lips thinning under his black mustache. "This murder has nothing to do with me. I use a point for marble—not for human flesh. I create beauty. I don't destroy it." He got up from the sofa, strode toward the counter. "Cancel my breakfast," he shouted at Miss Dow. He noticed then that he still held the metal book-end in his hand. He banged it down. "Here." He sent it spinning across the wooden surface. "Keep the thing. I've had enough of it." He stalked out and banged the door.

Chapter Eleven

WITCH-TOWN

THE STATE POLICE put it on the teletype. Up and down the Atlantic Seaboard, state troopers on the roads, policemen at terminals of bus-lines, railroads, steamships, watched for *"Eulalie Hendrix, alias Isabel Chalmers, age 46, height 4-10 to 5, weight about 350, hair gray. Mrs. Elmer Watson, alias Mrs. Ramona Heath, age about 50, height about 5-6, weight about 110, hair gray. Wanted for questioning in connection with murder of Nola Spain, Laneport, Mass., July 28."*

The descriptions were sketchy because no one at the Rockledge had actually been intimate enough with the missing women to know the color of their eyes, the shape of their noses, the character of their attire. Two pale wraiths, they had been, fluttering about the Annex, nebulous as the mist that came up from the sea.

Delia, the waitress, said that Miss Chalmers' eyes were blue; Marian, the chambermaid who did their room, insisted they were brown; Mr. and Mrs. Whittaker, who had held brief conversation with her, had vague recollection of dark gray slits in a doughy face. Miss Dow said they had always worn tan covert-cloth traveling suits, with long, old fashioned, braid-trimmed coats, for their arrivals and departures. Miss Moffett reminded her that whenever the strange sisters went walking late at night they put on white sport coats, quite like the other Laneport ladies. Then the chambermaid entered the argument and sent it nowhere, by maintaining politely but stoutly that she had seen them as much as anybody had and she for one had never seen them wearing anything but black.

No one in the Annex had heard their departure. No one had met them on the streets of Laneport, at bus terminal or railroad station. It seemed as if the sea had swallowed them, bag and baggage.

"And not a bad idea at that," Chris Whittaker declared. "When the tide goes out, we can pick 'em off the rocks."

But as he leaned across the porch rail, spying the secretive sea, he heard the drone of motors, saw a bright red seaplane dropping out of the sky. He took a second look at the plane, read a name on its fuselage, and leaped up two flights of steps. "Let's get out of here fast," he warned his wife. "Locusts. Buzzards. Tabloids."

Before the noon gong had sounded, Miss Dow and Miss Moffett had a full house again. By air, by motor car, by rail, cameramen, reporters, feature writers, radio special-events men swarmed into Laneport, laid siege to the Rockledge. They rolled dice for choice rooms in the Annex, clambered through the windows of the room in which Nola Spain had died, commandeered the porch rockers, jammed the lobby, pre-empted the telephone, photographed Miss Dow and Miss Moffett, talked with Miss Templeton, Miss Hays, Miss Godwin, Miss Bean, dropped a windfall of dollar bills on Delia, the waitress, and Marian, the chambermaid, made passes at Mr. Parsons, clamored for picture and speech with Mrs. Whittaker, who had discovered the crime, and the child who had witnessed it. Mary and Chris, clutching Baby Doll by the hand, had fled before the invaders.

"Nix on photographers," Chris had declared, passionately. "Ruin our business. Let every thief in the United States know what we look like! Not a chance!"

He backed his car out of the Rockledge parking space. An incoming roadster, *Press* sticker on its windshield, scraped his rear fender. He swore. A head popped out of a car window, yelled, "Rockledge?"

"Wrong address," Mr. Whittaker answered hospitably. "Beat it."

The head yelled back, "Wise guy," and the car under it took Mr. Whittaker's front fender.

"Serves Johnny Reese right," Chris said. "Where to, beautiful?"

"Laneport Hospital. Fast. Before the mob finds out," Mary answered. She turned to the child, said with calculated casualness, "Baby Doll, we're going to say hello to a sick lady. She's in a hospital." They drove through the winding, precipitous streets of the town, and Chris pulled the brakes up before the square, new, pink brick building of the Laneport Hospital. Three pair of heels clacked down the linoleum-covered, iodoform-reeking corridors to the corner where a trooper paced back and forth before a closed door.

A white face lay on the pillows of a high bed, framed by the figures of the District Attorney, a stenographer, and a nurse. Mr. Babcock got up. "We were expecting you," he said quietly. He leaned back against the wall where he could simultaneously watch the child and the woman she had been brought to see.

The face pivoted on the pillow. Lusterless eyes shifted toward Mary and Baby Doll. A dispirited voice asked, "What do they want?"

Mr. Babcock answered, "This is Mrs. Whittaker. She was with me when we found you."

"Very good of her." The faint voice was dipped in gall. "Why didn't you leave me alone? Why didn't you let me die?"

Baby Doll's fingers dug into the flesh of Mary's palm. Mary looked down at her quickly. The child's face was curious, sympathetic, sad, but in it was not the slightest trace of recognition or of fear.

The woman spoke again: "Why do they bring the little one here? This is no sight for a child to see."

Kneeland Babcock answered, "This is Nola Spain's child."

The mauve lips of the sick woman twisted, as if in pain. She said slowly, with a hint of dismay, "I never knew she had a child."

Baby Doll stepped toward the bed. "Did you know my mommy, too?" she asked eagerly.

Alicia Donato closed her eyes. She groaned. "Ask them to go away."

The District Attorney motioned them toward the door. Baby Doll paused on the threshold and waved her hand. "I hope you get better soon," she said politely. "My mommy didn't get better. A bad witch stabbed her dead."

Alicia Donato's gasp followed them into the hall.

"Chris, did that sick lady do something bad?" Baby Doll demanded shrilly. "Why have they got that policeman?"

Mr. Babcock closed the door and came out to join them. "Mrs. Whittaker. Please," he said.

Mary dropped back with him.

"Either the child actually saw no one," the District Attorney began, "or it was not Mrs. Donato whom she saw."

"I don't know how good an actress Mrs. Donato is," Mary replied. "But she did give a very good imitation of amazement at discovering that there was a child. Whoever entered Nola Spain's room must certainly have seen that youngster."

"Mrs. Donato is no actress." Mr. Babcock's tone was positive. "She's a bitter woman. She detested Mrs. Spain or whatever her name was. Makes no bones about that. Calls her a loose woman, a home wrecker, Jezebel, Delilah. But she insists that she did not leave her house after her last guest departed Saturday night, and we have no evidence to refute her. And so, I am more certain than ever that as soon as we find Miss Chalmers—"

"No word? No trace?"

"Not yet. But they must turn up. Sooner or later. Unless

they have done away with themselves. The State never objects to that." He smiled wryly. "Justice is served and the taxpayers economize."

She changed the subject quickly. "Has Paul Donato been to see his wife?"

The District Attorney shook his head. "He has not left his house. Sitting in sackcloth. Over a broken statue. When you saw him this morning, he seemed to have had enough of the 'Fairy Princess.' But now he insists that the smashing of a statue has broken his heart. 'I don't want to see that woman,' he raves. 'The stupid beast! The vandal!' Ah well," the District Attorney mopped his brow, "the future relations of the Donatos need not concern us. Dr. Sulloway is performing the autopsy today. We have scheduled the inquest for eleven o'clock tomorrow. After that you will be free to pursue your holiday, with the gratitude, I may add, of the District Attorney's office for your kind co-operation."

She said, "Very well," but she felt a twinge of pique. Mr. Babcock was so sure of his case that he could say, "You've been a good little girl, Mrs. Whittaker, now run along and play." It was dismissal. Cold, business-like. A few errands, a few questions. That was all the Commonwealth of Massachusetts required of the famous Mary Carner. The lady's vanity smarted.

She was frowning when she got into the car.

Chris asked, "Where to now, modom?"

She answered crossly, "Let's ride around. Any place."

"Whatever you say, modom. Modom looks annoyed. Anybody hurt modom's feelings?"

"Drive on."

Chris drove up the street. At the end of the block, the concrete ended and the road became macadam. "Want to keep going this way?" he asked.

"What difference does it make?" she said petulantly.

Sun-baked fields, splotched with the garish blooms of

devil's-paintbrush, spaced the houses. The road led sharply uphill, became a dirt path, thorny with stones, wide enough for only a single car. Low hanging branches swished against the windshield, dusted the roof.

Chris shifted into second speed. "Tough traveling," he complained. "Sure this is where you want to go?"

She shrugged. "It doesn't matter where we go. As long as we stay away from the wolves."

Ahead of them stretched a vast, gray, boulder-strewn plain, divided by the dusty road. In the center of the plain, a towering rock loomed like Gibraltar. On it, some pious hand had painted in foot-high yellow letters: *Prepare to meet thy God.*

The sides of the road alone knew the fresh green of living things. There were low gnarled trees, poison-ivy twined; berry bushes, sprawling thick and wild over rotting wooden fences—the lush magenta fruit of blueberry, blackberry and elderberry, the narrow shiny leaf and gray spike of bay. Beyond the road, the foliage was sparse —huddled clumps of scrub pine, scanty-leafed trees, grotesquely twisted by a hundred winter winds. Against the horizon stood the unfallen, unburied skeletons of half a dozen tall, dead pines.

The grass itself was sere, baked by the relentless summer sun until it seemed as gray as the rocks. The rocks, they saw, as they jounced up the miserable road, made a sort of pattern. Small stones lay together around hollows in the turf. Near each one, on a larger boulder, a numeral was carved into stone.

Mary said, "These must be the moors. Lane Common. The deserted village of Lane. Mr. Parsons' witch-town."

Chris stopped the car. "Cheerful dump," he observed. "Perfect spot for a murder."

It was a weird place. Thus, they realized, the world must have looked after the great glaciers had melted, before man or beast had risen from the primordial slime. A place of the dead or the not-yet-born.

Mary opened the car door. "Nothing to do till tomorrow," she suggested. "Shall we explore?"

Chris answered, "Anything you say. Let's go, Baby Doll."

The child drew back against the seat cushions. She was pale, her eyes seemed strained and miserable.

"Baby Doll, don't you feel well?" Chris asked.

"I don't like it here," the little girl whimpered.

Chris settled back into the seat. "You go ahead, Mary. I don't feel like hiking. I'll stay here with the kid."

She climbed a low stile, pushed aside the bushes, came out upon the plain. There were people on the moors, she saw. Up ahead, a troop of khaki-clad Boy Scouts were clambering over the rocks, hallooing to one another. On the crest of the plateau, a figure was silhouetted against the sky, a painter seated before his easel. A few yards from him a woman sat on a campstool, her face shaded by a broad-brimmed hat, her head bowed over a book. Boys hiking, artists painting, woman reading—casual human activity on the weird, forbidding moors. There was nothing to be afraid of here. Why, it was actually pleasant—picturesque, at any rate.

Mary strolled across the dry turf, stopped, diffidently, a little way off from the painter and surveyed the landscape which he was evidently trying to transfer to his canvas. Far below, where the gray rocks and stubble ended, she could see a stretch of white beach and turquoise ocean meeting azure sky.

She stepped behind the artist to look at his painting. His shoulders twitched. She said, "Do you mind?"

He glanced at her apathetically. His was a hollow face, weak, ineffectual, with a beaten look about it—a symphony in drab browns—ochre skin, faded hazel eyes, pointed brown beard.

He moved his palette upward till it covered half the

canvas. He said, "This isn't finished. You can't judge it yet." His voice had an agreeable pitch, but like his face it was hollow—an echo of a voice rather than its reality.

The little beard seemed vaguely familiar. She frowned over it until she was sure. The wilted lily in the garden. Mrs. Lyndall's garden. *Why, this,* she said to herself, *must be the good-time Charlie who woke up half the town!* She wondered where he'd found the gumption to get drunk. When she looked at the painting, Fern Godwin's words came back to her: "He gets things on canvas fairly well, in an academic sort of way. But his work is so drab, so spiritless." That was over-praise, she decided. The canvas was dead as the moors—dull grays and greens, a lifeless smear of blue where the sea and sky commingled. She squinted at the painting. It had a curious unbalance. On the right hand side of the canvas, the artist had improved upon nature, had rolled into the scene a huge square boulder, had overlaid it thickly with pigment. The gray rock dominated the landscape, and she felt, though she assured herself that she knew nothing at all about these things, that it was wrong.

The artist daubed a few tentative smears of white, then held his brush immobile as if waiting for her to fill the pause. She murmured. "It's a depressing vista, isn't it? So little color. Rather difficult to do, I should think."

He raised one shoulder half-heartedly. "I find it interesting," he answered. "It doesn't matter whether other people do."

The statement had an air of finality, of dismissal. She backed away, muttering, 'Thank you for letting me see it."

The artist did not answer.

Out on the road, Chris honked the horn imperatively. She scurried across the fields and got into the car.

Chris asked, "Seen enough? Let's get going. . . . How does anybody turn in this road?"

The car jounced in first speed up the path until it came

to a fork. Chris swung into reverse, backed toward a brambled fence. As he turned, the thick, low-hanging bushes parted. For a fragment of a second—between the winkings of an eyelid—it seemed to Mary that she saw the furtive movement of a human form, the flash of fingers, white teeth, sharp between parted, purple lips, dark eyes gleaming.

Whatever she had seen, the child had seen. Baby Doll screamed. She trembled from head to toe. Her breath came fast. "Take me back. Take me home. This is where the witches live."

The car teetered perilously over a ditch.

"I'm scared. I'm scared," Baby Doll cried.

"Take it easy, Baby," Chris swung the steering wheel; the tires gripped the road at last, held it. The car bumped triumphantly down the narrow lane. "Nothing to it. Everything's under control. Nothing to be scared of, Baby."

Baby Doll slumped in the seat, her head burrowing into Mary's side.

Mary ground her teeth. "That Parsons man. He's made this child crazy with his fool talk. He told you there were witches up here, didn't he, Baby Doll?"

The child shuddered. "But you saw them, didn't you, Mary? Didn't you see them too?"

Mary answered thoughtfully, "I really don't know what I saw."

When the car reached the macadam at last, it met a stream of automobiles coming up. In the front seat of the first car rode the silver hair and pointed ears of Mr. Parsons.

Mr. Parsons had had quite a morning. At first he had watched the Press from afar, had listened with bashful disdain while Miss Templeton told them *her* story and Miss Godwin told them *hers*, but as he listened, his aloofness became envy and when Miss Hays cried finally to the reporters, "Why don't you talk to Mr. Parsons? *He* knows a great deal about it," he had come forward, shyly at first, and then expanding in the warmth of their evident interest.

These young men and women weren't impatient, weren't scornful. They listened eagerly, wrote down every word he said. They urged him to speculate, to theorize. And so, grateful for their encouragement, he told them all about the white fox and the white woman and the "Fairy Princess," going out and coming home, and the footsteps in the fog and the swan boat, *Cynisca*, and Prince Charming and the witch whom Baby Doll had seen. That was where he had them.

They fairly shouted with glee, "Shades of Gallows Hill! A natural! What else, Mr. Parsons? Tell us more. Were there Laneport witches too?"

"Of course there were. This entire coast had witches. I am an authority on Laneport witchcraft. No one knows more about it than I do. Shall I tell you? Shall I show you?"

He told them and he showed them. He rode like a coxswain in the cavalcade of Press cars, ordering them to turn up this street for the Donato House, that way, down the Neck, to find the *Cynisca*, where state troopers guarded a distracted young man on his yacht, and then he took them up Lane Common to see the cellars of the houses in which Abigail Drake and Nancy Loveran, the witches of Lane, had lived. He stood among the loose gray rocks that marked the vanished dwellings, proudly pointing with his cane, while cameras clicked around him. It was a triumphant morning.

He hoped Ryon Lyndall didn't mind too much when the Press streamed over the moors. "Be as quiet as you can," Mr. Parsons admonished the newspaper people. "There's an artist painting up there. He's the one," he lowered his voice, fearful that the wind might carry it and bring offense, "who sang about the fox."

Flushed with excitement, he waved at Mrs. Lyndall. To his amazement, she got up from the camp stool and stalked over to them, cold, slightly angry curiosity in her eyes, and asked, "May I know what this is, Mr. Parsons?"

"The Press," he stammered. "I am informing them on Laneport history."

"Oh, that!" Her granite nose cracked into little wrinkles of disdain. "Please be quiet. My son does not wish to be disturbed."

"Can we peek?" a girl reporter asked.

Mrs. Lyndall raised her chin. "Of course not. If you are seriously interested in art, this painting will be exhibited at the Laneport Art Society's gallery. You may see it then."

"Tut-tut-tut." A brash young man thumbed his nose after Mrs. Lyndall's retreating spine. "Who the hell does she think she is—Mrs. Laneport?"

"Marvelous atmosphere!" a young lady of the press twittered. "Perfect. The hiding place of the witch who murdered the artist's model."

Mr. Parsons hedged. "I wouldn't quite say that. Please don't misunderstand me. A witch is spirit. Personality. Not supernatural being. Now these two ladies of whom I spoke before were—"

"I've got enough of this." The girl reporter opened her car door. "Let's find the D.A. and get a quote."

Miss Dow spread a round table for the new arrivals in the center of the dining-room. Mr. Parsons moved from his seat by the window and sat at the head of the festal board. Chris Whittaker found him there when he came into the dining-room to ask that Delia bring a tray up to the balcony of their suite where, he and Mary had decided, it was wisest to feed Baby Doll while the omnivorous Press was in the house.

Mr. Parsons saw Mr. Whittaker. He nudged the man next to him and cried, "There he is. The one who has the little girl."

The reporters pushed back their chairs. Chris clutched his throat. "Can't talk," he croaked. "Lost my voice. Damp air." He wriggled away.

"It's a hoax," Mr. Parsons said tartly. "He can talk as well as you and I."

Mr. Whittaker paused in mid-flight, whirled around on the door sill. "You!" He pointed at Mr. Parsons. "*You talk too much!* Mind your own business, if you know what's good for you." He fled up the steps and barricaded his door.

The siege lasted half an hour. Mr. Babcock rescued them. His office telephoned to the Rockledge that the District Attorney would see the Press if it came immediately, and so, reluctantly, the reporters abandoned the steps and the hall. The Whittakers fled to the beach and lay on the sand, anonymous among the bathing infants and their mothers and nursemaids. They built castles, moats, and tunnels, assembled mounds of shells, dipped into the surf until the descending sun and evening chill drove them back to the Rockledge.

The coast was still clear. The newspaper people were at the Donato House, interviewing Paul, Miss Moffett whispered to them, but the Boston evening papers had arrived and would they just take a look and see what those dreadful, dreadful people had done. Chris took a sheaf of papers upstairs. While they dressed, they scanned the headlines.

The Laneport murder cut across the front page rules in headlines eight columns wide: "WITCH KILLS ARTIST'S MODEL" . . . "WITCHES HOLD SABBATH ON LANEPORT MOORS."

"Cotton Mather rides again! Listen to this: *The outraged specter of New England Puritanism,*" Chris read, "*returned to take a bloody vengeance for the moral derelictions of the North Shore's Bohemian artists' colony. . . .* Here's another lulu: *A witch, re-incarnation of the weird sisters who once inhabited the moors of the fishing town and artists' colony of Laneport, killed beautiful model Nola Spain, according to Gorham Parsons, antiquarian, and authority on New England witchcraft. . . . Mr. Parsons declared in an exclusive statement to this paper that he has no doubt of his ability to identify the witch and bring her into custody."*

"The man's crazy," Mary cried indignantly. "He talks too much! He'll get into trouble!"

Chris laughed. "Let him have his fun. What do you care? It's not your murder."

That was correct, too. The responsibility was no longer hers. Mr. Babcock had given her notice. Suppose Mr. Parsons did make a joke of the whole macabre business. It no longer concerned them. One more statement at the inquest and her part in the Laneport tragedy was ended. Of course, there was Baby Doll. Well, they could take her along to Maine and if some next of kin turned up—

Baby Doll flounced into the room. She held a sheet of paper up. "Look, Mary. I drew a picture. I made a picture of the big bad witch that killed my mommy."

Mary looked down at the crude penciled lines on the page. "Very nice, darling," she said. "Save it for Halloween."

Chapter Twelve

A Philosophy of Murder

THEY FILED INTO the old courthouse at the county seat, rustled into hard, polished, folding seats in a small, musty, high-ceilinged, diamond-paned courtroom.

The Rockledge ladies—Miss Dow and Miss Moffett—their guests—Miss Godwin, Miss Templeton, Miss Hays, Miss Bean and Mrs. Bean, Mrs. Merrill, Mrs. Prentiss, Mrs. McAlistir—sat demurely in the front rows behind the press table, gloved fingers playing with clasps of handbags, white straw hats bobbing stiffly, as they assured one another in sibilant whispers that this wasn't anything to be afraid of. This wasn't real court. Just friends and neighbors gathered to talk over a matter that interested them all. There wasn't any judge. That man in the big chair on the dais was just the County Coroner, a man named Ferris, an electrical contractor, the fellow who had wired the lights on the Rockledge porch. And there were Kneeland Babcock and Doctor Sulloway, sitting alongside him, and Sam Dolliver and Jacob Haskell standing guard over a pasteboard suit box. Familiar faces. The whole thing was a family affair. Intimate. Casual.

"They're just after facts, my dears," Miss Templeton explained to them. "Plain, straight facts. So they can be sure she didn't die a natural death of some awful, contagious disease. If they call on you, tell them what you actually know. That's all they want to hear. I shall tell them what *I* know—if they ask me."

"But do you know?" her friend, Miss Hays, ventured. "Do you really know anything at all?"

Behind them, next to Dr. McAlistir, Mr. Parsons sat very straight, trying to look tall, his pointed ears cocked, his eyes shining, anxious anticipation written over every inch of his face.

The Whittakers were in the back of the room with Baby Doll between them. The District Attorney had urged them to come up front, inside the lawyers' rail, but Mary had begged off. At the rear, most of the testifying voices were wordless drones, and the less Baby Doll heard, the better.

Todd Amroe came in with a state trooper at five to eleven. He had on a white and gold yachtsman's cap and blue flannel jacket over a striped basque shirt. He saw Mary and Chris and the child, slid into the row behind them, ruffled Baby Doll's hair, saying, "How's my little girl today?"

Paul Donato, red-eyed, walking unsteadily as though he had been drinking, came in right after Todd Amroe and sat down alone in the opposite corner of the room. His head was bowed, his fists clenched. A court attendant had to yell at him three times before he realized that he had his hat on and finally removed this affront to the dignity of the courtroom.

As the hands of the clock behind the dais swung around to eleven, Mr. Ferris asked, "Ready?" The District Attorney said, "Quite", and Sam Dolliver climbed up into the witness chair and told them when and where and what. He reported on the phone call to the headquarters of the Laneport police at five minutes after three on the morning of July 28, his own response to the call, his discovery of the body, his preliminary examination of witnesses, his observations of the premises, his notification of his Chief. Mr. Haskell followed him and sheepishly offered an edited version of what he had seen and done. Thus the fact was established beyond peradventure by two trustworthy eyewitnesses that on the misty morning of July 28, a female cadaver had reposed in the A suite on the first floor of the

Rockledge Annex in the town of Laneport, the Commonwealth of Massachusetts.

They had, of course, heard all this before, had told these
things to one another over breakfast and dinner and on the
piazza while the waves lapped the rocks and the seagulls
screeched. But in this musty room, the facts about the
death of Nola Spain were no longer merely gossip. They
had become due process of law.

Mr. Ferris nodded to Doctor Sulloway. The doctor
cleared his throat, carried a typewritten sheet to the stand.
He read from it in a gallop, his voice pitched just above a
mumble. In the back rows, it was possible to catch only a
word here, a word there—"*called at 3:20 . . . arrived at
. . no rigor . . . penetration of right ventricle . . . hemorrhage . . . indications of chronic . . . alcohol content of
brain*"—

"Would you say, then," Mr. Babcock asked when the
doctor had put down his paper, "that the deceased was in
an alcoholic stupor when she met her death?"

"Decidedly." Dr. Sulloway's inflection was as much
moral judgment as medical opinion. The front rows
creaked and hissed.

Then the coroner called Miss Dow's name, and the
plump, pansy-faced inn-keeper swished forward, her chin
wobbling nervously, to tell how Nola Spain's reservation
had been made by Paul Donato and what he had said
about his wife when he had made it. "I don't usually take
people of that sort," she explained. Her eyes, roving over
the benches, caught Paul Donato's sullen glare. "But I've
known Paul for a long time," she added quickly. "His
recommendation—oh, I don't blame him—or Alicia either."

After her, Miss Moffett made considerable narrative of
the arrival of Nola Spain and her child, of what they had
done on Saturday, what Mrs. Spain had said in the lobby
before she left for Paul Donato's. "We never thought—we
never dreamed it would be the last time any one of us

would see her alive."

Then Miss Godwin, jangling her silver chains, speaking with obvious relish, went through the details of the domestic drama at Alicia Donato's—Nola Spain waving the steel point as though it were the "Fairy Princess's" wand, swaggering out of the house on the arm of the young man, taunting her hostess with, "I'm still interested in my contemporaries."

When Miss Godwin came to the feverish tête-à-tête between Alicia Donato and Nola Spain, she had to pitch her voice higher because of loud noises behind the closed courtroom doors and she had to stop altogether for a few minutes when the doors swung open and a tall, bald, florid, impeccably tailored man in blue and a shorter, spectacled man in gray came in.

Heads pivoted; chairs creaked; the press table scribbled excitedly: *Industrialist Carson Amroe made a dramatic appearance at the inquest.*

The florid man surveyed the courtroom with a proprietary air, found what he searched for, said loudly, "There he is," commanded the state trooper, "Your seat, please." The trooper moved two places over. The tall man slid into his chair. Todd Amroe whispered, "Dad!" The greeting was half in fear, half relief.

Carson Amroe extended his hand. His son's face mirrored a child's indecision—longing for the comfort of a parent and yet stubbornly repelling it.

"I brought Geyer," Carson Amroe said. "Thought you might need him."

Todd Amroe nodded at the man in gray, but he shook his head. "No, thanks."

Mr. Ferris banged the gavel. Miss Godwin began again: "That was when the young man came in. . . ."

Mr. Babcock came down from the dais. He opened the suit box, took out the metal pencil. "Miss Godwin," he held it gingerly by the wider end, "do you recognize this?"

Miss Godwin saw that the point was brown, as if with rust. She felt sickish. "I do," she whispered.

"Is this the object you saw in Mrs. Spain's hand as she left Mrs. Donato's house?"

Miss Godwin wrinkled her brows. "I couldn't exactly say that. Mr. Donato had several."

Mr. Babcock put it back into the suit box. "What time was it when Mrs. Spain left the studio?"

"About ten, I should say. Possibly ten minutes or so before or after. I know it was half past ten when we got home. We left shortly after she did."

"That will be all. Thank you." Mr. Babcock passed a slip of paper up to Mr. Ferris and the coroner called the name of Paul Donato.

Paul Donato made the District Attorney work. Whatever Mr. Babcock wanted to know Mr. Babcock had to ask for, detail by detail.

First there was the matter of his whereabouts on Saturday night. Mr. Donato flatly declined to answer that. "I cannot see why anyone else's name should be dragged into this mess." Then there was the matter of why he had pledged Miss Dow to secrecy about his reservation for Nola Spain. That was his private, personal affair, he insisted.

"Your wife disliked this woman?"

"Ask her."

"But you knew she was jealous of Mrs. Spain?"

"That's the general assumption."

"Had she reason to be?"

"She had not."

"Was there friction in your household over your interest in this woman?"

"I was not aware of it."

"Come, come, Mr. Donato, didn't you yourself tell Miss Dow that your wife was not well disposed toward your model?"

"What if I did?"

Mr. Babcock smiled his slow, stingy smile. "Yet, knowing that her presence here was likely to cause difficulties you urged Nola Spain to come to Laneport?"

"I've told you why I brought her here. I had a piece of work in mind."

"Oh, yes; yes, indeed." Mr. Babcock hesitated. Then without preliminaries, he hurled a question. "Is it possible that you hoped to bring about domestic peace by eliminating a cause of friction?"

Paul Donato's body jerked sharply as though a hangman had sprung a trap. He glared at the District Attorney. He said, incredulously, "Are you trying to insinuate that I killed Nola Spain or had her killed *to please my wife?*"

The spectators blinked, let their breaths out in slow horrified gasps. Mr. Babcock went to the suit box again. He lifted out the newspaper bundle. He unwrapped it slowly, held up the shards of marble. "Do you recognize this?"

Paul Donato's mouth tightened. "Must you drag corpses into the courtroom?" he asked frigidly.

"Was this your statue? Your portrait of the murdered woman?"

The muscles of Paul Donato's face were working. He clenched his fists but he did not answer.

"You were fond of this work—proud of it, I might say?"

"You know damn well how I felt about it."

The coroner leaned over to the witness. "I'll ask you to remember that there are ladies present, Mr. Donato," he said.

Mr. Babcock smiled grimly. "Would you consider this—the smashing of this marble statue—an indication of your wife's state of mind, of her attitude toward the model?"

"You be the psychologist, Babcock. I'm only a sculptor."

Mr. Babcock put the bundle back into the box. He took out the steel pencil again. "Do you recognize this, Mr

Donato?"

"I do."

"What is its name?"

"It's a point."

"You use this in your work?"

"I do."

"Can you tell us how it is employed?"

"I use it for delicate work on stone, usually on marble. For fine detail on face or hands."

"Do you recall having used it on the work you call the 'Fairy Princess'?"

"That or something like it."

"Is exceptional strength required to manipulate it?"

"No."

"Will you show us exactly how it is handled?"

Paul Donato's heavy eyebrows shot up quizzically but he accepted the weapon from Mr. Babcock's hand. He balanced it delicately on his palm, studying the brown, clotted blood at the tip. He gripped the stubby end, closed his fingers over it, held it for an instant, like a dagger, pointing at the District Attorney. Then he whirled in the chair, plunged the point into the soft leather cover of the Bible on the coroner's desk. The tip clicked against the wood below the book.

The courtroom held its breath.

"Sacrilege!" Mrs. McAlistir wheezed. "He'll be struck down dead!"

Mr. Ferris picked up the steel-pierced Bible, examined it with interest, passed it to Dr. Sulloway. The doctor smirked. "Human flesh," he observed, "offers less resistance than wadded paper."

Mr. Babcock bowed. "Thank you, Mr. Donato. An excellent demonstration!" He took the Bible from the doctor, gave it to Jacob Haskell. The police chief, clucking ominously, pulled the point out of the book, put it back in the box.

Mr. Donato got up. The District Attorney put a restraining hand on his arm. "Oh, no, please don't go yet. We have not finished." He took the coat out of the box, held it up. Paul Donato said, yes, it had belonged to his wife. Then Mr. Babcock showed him the wedding ring and Mr. Donato said yes that too had been his wife's, adding caustically, "Do you rob the patients in your hospitals?" Then he identified the dagger pin as his own and after that Mr. Babcock gave him Alicia's note. His olive skin flushed and he gnawed the middle of his mustache, admitted grimly, "It's my wife's handwriting," but he seemed only half attentive while the District Attorney explained for the benefit of the coroner and the stenographer where and how these things had been obtained.

Then he was excused and the coroner looked down at his list again and called the name of Todd Amroe.

The whispers swelled to a hiss of excitement as Todd Amroe walked swiftly down the aisle.

The back rows could see no more than a bright red forehead, crimson ears and the golden crown of his hair, heard only the murmur of his troubled voice. The front rows cupped their hands around their ears.

"You maintain that Nola Spain threw away the steel point before she reached your boat?"

"I do."

"Where did she drop it?"

"I don't know."

"Near Mrs. Donato's house?"

"I don't remember."

"On Central Road?"

"I don't remember."

"On Johnson's Neck?"

"Why do you keep pestering me? I tell you I don't know where she dropped it. I just remember we were walking along and she said suddenly, 'How silly of me,' and threw it away."

"You are certain, are willing to swear, that that weapon was discarded?"

"I am."

"Is it not barely possible she may have carried it aboard the *Cynisca?*"

"She didn't. I tell you she didn't."

"And she did not give it to you?"

"She did not."

Kneeland Babcock went to the box again. He took out the point, extended it, dagger-end first, to the young man. "Please take this, Mr. Amroe. Take it. It won't bite you. . . . Tell us whether this is the object you saw in Mrs. Spain's hand." He laid it across Todd Amroe's palm. The young man's face blanched. He began to tremble. The point fell from his shaking hand, clanged to the floor.

The Chief of Police stooped and picked it up.

"Thank you," Mr. Babcock said. "It is not a pleasant object to handle. . . . Now tell us, Mr. Amroe, whether you met any persons on your way from Donato's studio to the yacht—any persons who might have picked up the object which you insist was discarded?"

"I've told you before, I didn't notice anyone on the street. There might have been, but I didn't notice."

The District Attorney shook his head. "Singular," he said. "You are clear and positive on one point. Only one. That this object was discarded by Mrs. Spain before she reached your boat. I find your vagueness on other matters a trifle—inconsistent. . . . Well, let us go on. You have heard the Medical Examiner's report that Mrs. Spain was intoxicated. She got that liquor aboard your ship, did she not?"

"We drank champagne."

"Was the lady conceivably affected by the alcohol when she left the *Cynisca?*"

"She wasn't drunk, if that's what you mean."

"She didn't require assistance?"

"Not especially."

"What was your own condition? Were you, possibly, somewhat under the weather yourself—not quite aware of what you were doing?"

Todd Amroe raised his head. His eyes were blazing. "We weren't drunk, I've told you. I don't care what the medical report says. We knew perfectly well what we were doing and saying."

The District Attorney shrugged. "The party terminated early," he observed. "Was Mrs. Spain aware that the doors of the Rockledge were locked at midnight?"

"She didn't mention it."

"Yet she left the ship in time to return before midnight?"

"She was worried about her little girl. Leaving her alone in a strange place."

"I see. Was Mrs. Spain, to your knowledge, concerned over any other person or events in Laneport?"

"I've told you that. She was unhappy about someone who'd said or done something to her."

"On your return to the Rockledge, you met no one on the streets?"

"Nobody. It was a pea-soup fog. People don't go walking in that kind of weather."

"You found the doors of the Rockledge open when you brought Mrs. Spain there?"

"I believe so."

The District Attorney drew himself up to his full height, let out his full voice. "Now, when you came to the Rockledge, Mr. Amroe, did the lady, by any chance, invite you to enter her room?"

Todd Amroe's ears flamed again. "She did not."

"And you did not later decide to enter it, uninvited, through the window?"

Todd Amroe got up, his face working. "I won't answer any more questions. You're insulting me—insulting Nola's memory."

"Please be seated, Mr. Amroe. We are merely trying to get at the truth. . . . If you decline to assist us—"

Todd Amroe said stonily, "I am not under arrest. I won't submit to this inquisition. I stand on my constitutional rights."

A chair seat slammed up in the back of the room. "I am Mr. Amroe's attorney," a voice boomed. "I advise him not to answer any further questions."

Mr. Babcock bowed. "Excused," he said.

Todd Amroe stalked down the aisle. Behind his retreating back, Lorna Bean hissed, "Communist!"

"Let's take the next," Mr. Ferris said. "It's getting late." He called Mary's name.

She began at the beginning and told them how the touch of the child's hand had awakened her to hear the foghorn and the weird tapping in the walls and the frightened voice at her side, how she had stumbled out of bed to find a woman pierced through the heart. Remembering it, putting it into words now, she felt once more the chill of her original fear. The open window, the open eyes of the dead woman, the hand still warm. "It had just happened. I felt she might still be alive." The panicky concern for a person she had never seen before, driving her out into the hall. "The tapping had stopped. My first thought was to get a doctor and police. Mr. Parsons—I didn't know it was Mr. Parsons then—opened his door and asked, 'Who is dead?' Not 'What's happened?' but 'Who is dead?' I thought it was strange at the time."

Necks craned toward Mr. Parsons. He seemed to be oblivious of the attention but rather to be absorbed with some preoccupation that made it necessary for him to move his lips, nod his head vigorously.

"Mr. Parsons told me there was a doctor on the second floor. I ran upstairs. In the hall, I saw what seemed to be a ghostly white shape. It tried to talk but a hand came out of a door and dragged it away." This was like an old-fashioned melodrama. Clutching hands in the dark. "I heard a voice call, 'Isabel! What are you doing there?' I know now that the white shape was Isabel Chalmers and the voice which called to her was her sister, Mrs. Heath."

"That was the Isabel Chalmers whom we now know as Eulalie Hendrix?"

"It was."

"Miss Chalmers was also responsible for the mysterious tapping noise?"

"I found that out next day, when I heard it again. My husband realized it must be some sort of code. We investigated together, went to Miss Chalmers' room. Miss Chalmers told us she was trying to attract someone's attention. She told us she had tapped 'I saw her' in Morse code." The details were so many that her head began to ache. She was beginning to tire of the sound of her own voice.

"Mrs. Heath found you in her sister's room and ejected you? Is that correct?"

"It is."

"Do you believe that the woman whom you knew as Isabel Chalmers was telling you the truth? Could she conceivably have been inventing the story to conceal some actions on the part of herself or her sister?"

"Everything's possible."

"You found their conduct peculiar?"

"Decidedly."

"What prompted you to assist the authorities in obtaining fingerprints of these two women? Was there any specific reason?"

"No." She considered the question carefully. "Merely that the ladies seemed to be protesting overmuch against being searched. People who have nothing to hide don't mind." People who have nothing to hide. Nola Spain's murder had been an unveiling. It had rolled a curtain from so many dark lives. She began to think of that and she became so preoccupied with her own thoughts that Mr.

Babcock had to repeat his question.

"I have asked that you tell us about the footprint you and Officer Dolliver saw."

"Oh, that!" She sighed with boredom. "A hoof-print. A cloven hoof." And then she had to tell them about Baby Doll's witch. "You mustn't take it too seriously," she added. "The child's very imaginative. Shapes or sounds in the night might suggest a witch to her." She could hear Mr. Parsons clearing his throat, truculently.

"I quite understand," Mr. Babcock said. He asked if she would mind bringing the little girl to the stand.

Chris led the child up the aisle. Baby Doll settled back in the armchair, perfectly self-possessed, her Titian curls a flaming aureole around her face, her sturdy legs straight out under her diminutive skirt. Her glance shifted from Mary to Chris, strayed over the audience. She saw Mr. Parsons and waved to him. He nodded back encouragingly.

Mr. Babcock began, very gently, to question her and she answered that her name was Baby Doll and her mother's name was Nola and she didn't have any daddy and she didn't go to school but she could read and write and spell and she knew that it was bad to tell lies and so she never did and her mommy had brought her to Laneport to play in the sand.

Then Mr. Babcock said, "Todd Amroe, please, stand up." Todd Amroe stood up in the back of the room. "Do you know this man, Baby Doll?"

The child smiled brightly. "He's Todd. He's Mommy's friend."

"Please be seated, Mr. Amroe. . . . Paul Donato, stand up. . . . Do you know this man, Baby Doll?"

The little girl looked curiously at Paul Donato. Her smile was shy but friendly. "Mommy told me about you," she said. "I'm pleased to meet you."

"Baby Doll,"—the absurd name stuck in the District Attorney's craw—"did your mother tell you why she came to Laneport?"

"Uh-huh." The curls swung up and down. "She came to work for Paul."

"Did she ever tell you (try to think, Baby Doll) that she was afraid of anything or anybody?"

Baby Doll's eyes widened. "Oh, no," she answered. "Mommy wasn't afraid of anybody—excepting maybe the landlady, when she hollered because Mommy didn't have any money for the rent."

The front rows tittered. Mr. Babcock scowled. He took the child's hand. "Little girl," he said, "I want you to tell us just what you saw in the room when your mother was—"

Baby Doll did not let him end the sentence. "I saw a witch." She marked the slow, dubious shake of Mary's head. Temper flared in her. She kicked the top rung of her chair, beat the arm with her little fist. "I did. I did too."

"Of course you did," Mr. Babcock said soothingly.

"A big, big witch," the child repeated.

"Fat? Like this?" Mr. Babcock puffed out his thin cheeks.

Baby Doll giggled. "No," she said. "Witches aren't fat like that. They couldn't ride on their broomsticks if they were fat."

Mr. Babcock said abruptly, "That will do." He helped the child down.

The clock hands pointed to half past one. Mr. Ferris asked, "Any more, Babcock? I've got to get back to the shop."

"One more." He wrote the name on the coroner's list.

Mr. Parsons straightened his necktie, pulled down his coat sleeves, shifted forward in his chair.

The coroner called the name of Dr. McAlistir.

It was Dr. McAlistir, tugging thoughtfully at his white mustache, who set off the bomb. He had finished his testimony, had told them with meticulous detail how he had been awakened that early morning by voices calling his name, fists pounding his door, how he had gone into the death chamber and having made certain that death had been there before him, had waked Miss Dow and Miss Moffett who had summoned the police. Mr. Babcock had already said, "Thank you, Doctor," when Dr. McAlistir settled back in the chair.

"There's one thing more." He took second wind. "In the light of what has been said and implied here about the women whom we know as Miss Chalmers and Mrs. Heath and in the light, too, of the fact that these two women left the Rockledge so precipitously, I believe that another fact in my knowledge is worthy of mention. As I entered the Rockledge at approximately eleven o'clock on Saturday night, I saw Miss Chalmers and Mrs. Heath moving furtively along the wall of the building and entering the door of the Annex. It was their custom, I understand, to go out for a stroll each evening at a time when they might be unobserved by the other guests. It has occurred to me that, if Mr. Amroe's story is true, one of these women may have, in the course of their peregrinations, picked up the discarded weapon. . . ."

The courtroom buzzed. A veteran murderess had dwelt under the Rockledge roof, had been abroad while the murder weapon lay in the streets, had known where Nola Spain resided, had been awake, about, during the hour of death. The faces in the front row said plainly, *Well, what are you waiting for?*

Doctor McAlistir stepped down, and then Miss Dow and Miss Moffett were called back to the stand to tell all they knew about the missing, mysterious ladies and the District Attorney read into the record the Reformatory report on Eulalie Hendrix and Dr. Sulloway sagaciously made comment on the fact that Eulalie Hendrix's original crime had occurred during what presumably was her adolescence and that at the present she was in the mid-forties, a time of the female cycle which was also conceivably subject to emotional aberrations. Someone snickered in the front rows. An attack of self-consciousness overwhelmed the coroner. He blushed, banged his gavel much more emphatically than was necessary, and when the room was silent, he read a formal statement of the time and cause of death: *"Hemorrhage due to puncture of the right ventricle of the heart, caused by an instrument known as a sculptor's point, in the hands of persons unknown. . . ."* And that was all.

Mr. Babcock climbed back to his chair beside Dr. Sulloway and Mr. Ferris, and the trio went into low-voiced conference. Seats banged up, skirts swished, feet shuffled in the aisles. But Mr. Parsons remained in his place, his chin sagging on his chest, pink fever spots burning his cheeks. Dr. McAlistir nudged him. "Come, come, Gorham. It's all over. Don't you want any lunch?

Mr. Parsons shook his head but he got up and moved reluctantly toward the aisle. There he stood, looking one way and the other. Finally, he made up his mind. He went up to the dais and tugged at the District Attorney's sleeve. "If you'd like me to explain about the witches," he began timidly.

Mr. Babcock glared at him. "I believe you have done enough explaining," he said coldly, "to the Press."

Dr. Sulloway leaned on his elbows, folded his hands, one over the other, and laughed raucously.

The room swirled around Mr. Parsons. His knees were jelly. Without another word, he turned and crept up the aisle. Mr. Babcock's nasal voice lashed his back: "I wish he'd keep his nose out of this. Did you see his interviews? An infallible scheme for tracking down a witch!"

"Ha, ha," Dr. Sulloway cackled. "That's exactly what we need. This county's had enough witch hunts to last a thousand years."

Mr. Babcock brought the Whittakers home to lunch off

wafer-thin china and venerable mahogany behind the graceful fanlights of a historic doorway, in a fine old house, crowded with carved ivories, embroideries, teak wood, ancient treasures and trinkets, looted from the Orient by clipper captains who had sailed round the Horn. He presented Mary to his wife as one of the family. "Caroline, this is Mrs. Whittaker, Mary Carner that was, the friend of Aunt Martha's cousin, Phyllis Knight. (You remember about poor Phyllis?) And her husband and the little girl I told you about."

Mrs. Babcock stroked the child's head. "Oh, yes, Mrs. Whittaker is the detective, isn't she? Kneeland tells me you've been such a help to him."

"I'm afraid I haven't done very much. As a matter of fact, I never do much." Mary laughed. "My severest critics tell me that I just sit and wait for clues to drop into my lap. They feel I should go chasing around like Perry Mason or pontificate about little gray cells like Monsieur Poirot. But I'm not a story-book detective. I'm a thief spotter. That's all."

"It isn't true," her husband protested loyally. "Mary's wonderful. She's practically a—"

"I'm sure she is," Mrs. Babcock helped him. "Kneeland has been so pleased to have her on the scene. It's been a comfort, he says, to have one investigator who isn't muddle-headed. Poor Kneeland, he works so very hard. Do let's sit down. . . . You took longer than you expected, Kneeland. Anything interesting turn up?"

Mr. Babcock shook out his napkin. "Dr. McAlistir's last statement was important, don't you think, Mrs. Whittaker?"

Mary said, "I'd be more impressed if he had supplied a motive too."

Mr. Babcock agreed. "But when we find those women we shall learn it. I may say, of course, that I have by no means discarded my suspicions of Mrs. Donato. Dr. Sulloway is inclined to be rather interested in Mr. Donato, too —that little exhibition in the courtroom . . . Caroline, he drove that weapon all the way through a King James Bible."

Baby Doll looked up from her plate. "I didn't see Paul. I saw a witch," she said firmly.

"L-i-t-t-l-e p-i-t-c-h-e-r-s h-a-v-e b-i-g e-a-r-s," Mrs. Babcock reminded them.

"Little pitchers have big ears," Baby Doll translated promptly. "That's a funny thing to say. What's it mean, Mary?"

Mrs. Babcock said hastily, "Dear, if you'd rather have a chop instead of that lobster. You don't mind her having lobster, do you, Mrs. Whittaker? Of course, our children are raised on seafood."

After that, until the blueberry pie was served and eaten, they talked about New England seafood and diets for the young. Then Mrs. Babcock tactfully took Baby Doll away to make the acquaintance of the scotties of the household, and Mary asked the District Attorney, "Are you going after an indictment?"

"Of Miss Chalmers or Mrs. Donato?" he countered.

"Six of one, half dozen of the other," she replied. "Mrs. Donato certainly had motive, access to the weapon. But the child didn't seem to recognize her."

"Look here," Chris interrupted. "Be fair to the kid. One minute you insist that she doesn't know what she's talking about. The next minute you're banking on her identification. Make up your mind. Either the kid's an eye-witness or she isn't."

"We've listened to her much more than we realize," Kneeland Babcock said thoughtfully. "On the basis of her statement, we've assumed that a woman killed Nola Spain. When it might well have been a man. Todd Amroe. Paul Donato. Or a person unknown to us at present."

"Isabel Chalmers spoke about a woman, too," Chris

said. "Described a woman, definitely."

"Possibly describing herself," Mary suggested. "In an attempt to make us believe it was someone else." She shook her head. "It's hard to see Isabel Chalmers in this. Not one of all the people we've spoken to has given any hint that Nola Spain might have had any past or immediate acquaintance with Miss Chalmers."

"Unless," Mr. Babcock ventured, "some irrational antagonism developed between them in the few hours Mrs. Spain occupied her room at the Rockledge. Haven't you ever heard of homicidal maniacs, Mrs. Whittaker?"

"Sure," Chris put in. "I knew a guy once who bashed in his boss's head because he said the devil was sitting on it and he had to kill the devil before it got him. Died in the nut house. So batty he couldn't even tell his right name."

"This is different, Chris. This was planned execution. No mad impulse of the moment. It was all too neat, too deliberate. . . . You see, I have a—a philosophy of murder." She blushed with the instinctive embarrassment of those who suddenly become aware that their conversation has gone beneath the superficialities of social intercourse. "I see murder as a struggle for possession. Just like war. Have and have not. You've got something I want. I'll get it from you even if I have to kill you for it. Or I have something which you want—something precious to me—something on which my life and happiness depends—and you threaten my ownership of it. I've got to put you out of the way before you grab it from me. . . . What did Nola Spain have that someone else wanted? What did she want that she'll never be able to have? Somewhere in this crime is a primitive struggle for possession. Find that and you'll have all your answers."

"But in any case," Mr. Whittaker got up, "it's nice that Mary doesn't have to worry about it any more. It's your headache, Mr. Babcock. Have fun."

Chapter Thirteen

FROM THE MOORS

MR. PARSONS RODE HOME in silence with the McAlisters. When they got to the Rockledge he announced that his dyspepsia was troublesome and he guessed he'd be better off without food.

The late-lunching guests saw him through the dining-room windows, going toward the Annex, leaning heavily on his cane.

"I wonder what's gotten into Gorham," Dr. McAlistir commented. "He's become so disagreeable."

"Jealous probably," Mrs. McAlistir replied. "They called on you to testify and they didn't call on him."

"Conceited little cuss, Lucy. Delusions of grandeur. Thinks nobody's as smart as he."

When the McAlistirs came out of the dining-room, they saw Mr. Parsons walking slowly up Central Road in the direction of the town. They watched his bowed, lonely figure pass the red sail loft and move out of sight around the bend in the road.

Mr. Parsons climbed Lane Common hill.

Two pairs of eyes watched him from the underbrush. A voice whispered, as softly as the hiss of wind through leaves, "There's Mr. Parsons again." Another answered, "Get down. Don't let him see us."

A young man in shirtsleeves, guide book in hand, saw him sitting on top of the heap of loose stones in the wide shallow rectangle which marked the cellar of the long vanished dwelling of Abigail Drake. He wondered why the old man was talking to himself so vociferously.

Mr. Parsons sat on the rim of the cellar, swinging his heels over the edge, speaking loudly, earnestly, as though a listener sat opposite him. "You understand, Abby. I don't mean to insinuate that you or Nancy came back in the flesh and killed that woman. I've better sense than that. I understand quite clearly just what a witch actually is."

It was then that he heard the soft footsteps behind him on the grass. He was so startled that he nearly slid down into the pit.

"Is that you, Abby?" he gasped.

The woman pulled him back. She said, "Be careful, Mr. Parsons."

"Oh!" His breath came fast. "I thought—I thought I was alone."

"You were," the woman said. "Till I saw you."

He whisked a smudge of loose earth from his trouser leg, said politely, "Won't you sit down," and motioned to the grassy bank beside him.

She answered, "Thank you." She remained standing.

"You don't mind if I don't rise. I'm—I'm rather tired. . . . I was at the inquest."

She said, "That's why I came. To ask about it. What does Mr. Babcock say now?"

"Mr. Babcock!" he answered with bitter scorn. "Don't talk to me about Mr. Babcock!"

"Stupid, eh?" The woman chuckled softly.

Mr. Parsons was surprised. He realized he had never heard her laugh before. "Stupid!" he echoed. "All of them. All they can think of is how to make fun of their betters. Those who know more than they." The heat of remembered humiliation rose in his cheeks. He lowered his head so that she might not see his face.

"Why, Mr. Parsons," she asked slyly, "do you know more than they?"

His head came up sharply. "Of course I do. I know perfectly well—if they listened to me, they'd have the murderer in their toils already."

"Mr. Parsons!" Her accents were of thorough, complete surprise. "Did you see the—," she stumbled over the words "—the killing?"

"Not with my eyes," he answered reluctantly. "With my mind. I've thought it out. I've reasoned it completely. I know exactly how to find the murderer of Nola Spain."

"How, Mr. Parsons?" The woman's voice seemed importunate now.

He clambered to his feet, stood unsteadily in front of her on the edge of the ruined cellar, balancing himself with his cane. "The little girl told us her mother was killed by a witch," he explained patiently. "Now, I know exactly what a witch is. An incarnation of mischief, of evil. A ruthless creature. One who will use any means to gain her ends. Not just a flying fool on a broomstick. . . ."

He raised his head, shyly delighted with his own humor, looked at her for approval. But she was not smiling. She was watching him, as a snake watches the mouse it is about to devour. The glitter in her eyes, the set of her jaw, terrified him. His heart thumped his ribs.

"Yes, go on, Mr. Parsons," she said impatiently.

His mouth opened. "Why, you! Why, you're the witch!"

He felt the pressure of a knee against his own. His heels slid backward on the dry, slippery grass. He felt himself falling. He flung out his arm to clutch her garment and save himself. His fingers grappled the empty air. The stones of Abby Drake's cellar cracked his spine and then the world dissolved in pain and darkness.

The young man with the guide book found Mr. Parsons when he came down the hill just before sunset. The young man was very happy and very much excited. He was a teacher of geology and it had been his privilege that afternoon to see a superlative example of the terminal moraine

—the boulder-studded girdle across the belly of the moors. As he passed the cellar of Abby Drake's house, his mind was fashioning the lecture that he would deliver about it in the third week of Geology I. It occurred to him then that it might not be too bad a notion to have some specimens of the glacial deposits on the Massachusetts shore and he bent down to scoop up a few stones.

He noticed that there was loose dirt around the edge of the old foundation, as though someone else, before him, had removed the stones. Then he saw a shoe. And another shoe. After that he saw a flung-out hand and the bashed face of a human skull and silver hair matted with blood. He ran, hell-bent for leather, down the hill, screaming for police.

In the gathering dusk, Jacob Haskell's car and Doctor Sulloway's car and Judkins' coach and two vehicles jammed with reporters and cameras climbed Lane Common hill. Flash bulbs bit the murk. Hurrying hands raised the stones from the battered shell of Mr. Parsons. He was a shocking sight. Even Dr. Sulloway, inured to the gruesome aspects of mortal flesh, was moved. "Cruelest death I've ever seen," he said. "Every bone in his body's probably broken."

"Couldn't 'a' been an accident, Doc?" Mr. Haskell asked.

Dr. Sulloway shrugged. "Sure could. He could have slipped and loosed a—what do they call those things?—an avalanche. But look at that ground, Jake. It's all trampled. As if somebody stamped around. Look at these marks. As if somebody pried up the stones with a stick or something and threw them down on the old man."

"Pressed to death!" a reporter suggested. "Good old New England custom, pressing to death."

"Let me find the guy that kicked these stones on the old man," Jacob Haskell growled. "And I'll do some pressing myself."

Kneeland Babcock closeted himself in the Laneport police headquarters with the young geologist who told him, with understandable incoherence, how he had seen the old man sitting on the cellar's rim, apparently talking to himself, when he went up on the moors.

"Did you see anyone else? Any other person or creature?"

The young man reflected. "Yes," he said slowly. "There was an artist. An artist with a little pointed beard, painting a picture. There was an elderly woman sitting alongside him."

"That sounds like Esther Lyndall and Ryon," Mr. Haskell said. He got into the District Attorney's car and together they drove out to Esther Lyndall's house on Johnson's Neck.

Ryon opened the door for them. His pale eyes brightened with mild surprise when he saw Mr. Haskell's badge and the grave visage of Kneeland Babcock. "What is it?" he asked. "Anything wrong?"

The Chief of Police said gruffly, "Evenin', Lyndall. Can we come in?"

"Why, I think so." Ryon Lyndall looked over his shoulder, as if uncertain of his invitation.

They shuffled into the studio. The Chief said, "Lyndall, I understand you were painting up on Lane Common this afternoon."

"Why, yes. Finishing my picture." He waved toward a canvas which stood against the wall. "I'm bringing it down tomorrow. For the—"

His mother's voice, out in back, cut across his halting words. "Who's there, Ryon?"

"Mr. Haskell. Mr. Babcock." The artist looked over his shoulder again.

"Oh! Bring them out here."

Ryon Lyndall led them through the dim studio to the dining porch at the rear of the house.

Candles flickered on a dinner table, set for two, over the half-eaten chop congealing on Ryon Lyndall's plate, over the tufted mole on Esther Lyndall's champing jaw. Beyond the window screens, harbor lights gleamed on the water and the sea splashed gently against the slimy piles. In the cozy, intimate domestic scene, the District Attorney felt the timidity of the intruder.

Mrs. Lyndall made no effort to put him at his ease. She said brusquely, "Well, gentlemen! To what do we owe this invasion? . . . Ryon, your food's getting cold. Go ahead and eat."

Obediently, Ryon Lyndall picked up his fork.

"There's been an accident," Mr. Haskell announced. "Up on the moors. We've been told you and Ryon were up there today."

"We were," Mrs. Lyndall answered. "Ryon was finishing his picture. What sort of accident?"

"Mr. Parsons. An elderly gentleman stopping at the Rockledge." Mr. Babcock sat down uninvited, twirled his hat in his hands. "Mr. Parsons was killed. Possibly accidentally, possibly murdered."

Ryon Lyndall's fork clattered to the floor. His mother looked quickly at him. He reddened, reached down for the silver. She said, "Don't pick it up, Ryon. Here's another. . . . Murdered, did you say, Mr. Babcock? Why and by whom?"

Ryon Lyndall's beard quivered. "But when?" His eyes were as bewildered as his words. "We were there. We were there all the time. We didn't see anyone."

Mrs. Lyndall said crisply, "I'll tell about it, Ryon, if you don't mind. . . . We saw Mr. Parsons. Both Ryon and I."

"You saw him, eh? What time was it when you saw him?"

"I had no watch. As I recall, it was early in the afternoon."

"You knew Mr. Parsons? You were a friend of his?"

"I should scarcely call it friendship. Acquaintance. We had played cards together. Ryon, dear, you're not eating. Do stop daydreaming. . . . These artists!" Her face softened. "His mind is always on his work. If I weren't after him continually, I daresay he'd go without food altogether."

Mr. Babcock was sympathetic. "You have your problems; we have ours. Ours is to find out how Mr. Parsons met his death. . . . Hence this visit. You noticed Mr. Parsons, then? What was he doing when you saw him?"

"Nothing in particular."

"He was alone?"

"I believe so."

"You saw him, recognized him, but you paid no attention to what he was doing?"

"My dear Mr. Babcock." Mrs. Lyndall waved her fork. "Mr. Parsons comes to the moors frequently. So do we. We do not interfere with one another."

The District Attorney sighed. He had anticipated that Esther Lyndall would be difficult, but her cold indifference was more than he had reckoned on. It was like drilling granite to get anything out of her.

"Was there anyone else on the moors today?"

"I saw no one."

"Not even a geologist? A young man in shirtsleeves?"

She shook her head. "I cannot say that I noticed him. Ryon and I—" her lips folded, curled in what might pass for a smile—"have a habit of minding our own affairs. And wishing that other people would do the same."

Mr. Haskell slid toward the door.

Mr. Babcock stood up, bowed stiffly. "Thank you for your kind assistance," he said, his tone ironic. "Good night."

Mrs. Lyndall answered. "Get on with your dinner, Ryon. They'll find the way out."

Mr. Babcock turned his car, ran slowly down to the

corner, drove into the Rockledge parking space. He met the Whittakers on the front steps.

Mary greeted him gaily. "How nice to see you! Gives us a chance to say good-bye."

"You're not leaving?" Mr. Babcock asked quickly.

"Check," Chris answered. "Tomorrow morning. Sending a telegram tonight. Mary asked a pal of hers in New York—the guy we stole the car from, Chief—to look something up for her. On Nola Spain. Just had a wire from him. Seems he's having a tough time with it and do we really need it?"

"I asked Detective Reese," Mary supplemented, "for data on the woman's marriage, if any. We didn't know when or to whom. It appears that some sixty-five thousand couples get married in New York every year. That's a lot of names to go through. Poor Johnny's only worked his way back to 1934."

"And no dice," Chris finished. "We decided no use us waiting for it."

The District Attorney looked crestfallen. "I have no right to impose on you," he agreed miserably.

"But you said you didn't need us any more. Has anything happened?"

Mr. Haskell answered for him, "There's been another one."

"Another what?"

"Murder."

"Who?"

"Mr. Parsons. On Lane Common. This afternoon. In the cellar of the witch's house. Stoned—pressed to death."

Mary sat down abruptly on the top step.

Chris whistled. "I knew it. . . . He talked too much. . . . I'll swear he talked himself to death."

"Lane Common." Mary shuddered. "We were there yesterday. A ghastly place. Baby Doll was terrified. I was frightened myself." Across her mind a scene darted—the fork in the road, the flash of white that seemed like a human hand, a human face.

Chris said, "That was where you talked to the painter, Mary."

"Ryon Lyndall?" the Chief of Police asked. "They were there today too. But they didn't see a thing."

Chris scowled deeply. "Golly," he said. "Those people do get around. I'm getting so I'd hate to have a Lyndall cross my path. Bad luck. Like a black cat or walking under a ladder."

Mr. Babcock smiled wearily. "Where's your philosophy of murder now, Mrs. Whittaker? The struggle for possession. What could Mr. Parsons have had? Or wanted to get?"

She answered, "That's too easy! He had the murderer's name!"

They went into Mr. Parsons' room in the Annex. They searched his things and found his diary. Mr. Babcock read aloud what Gorham Parsons had written on Sunday night: "*It is my conviction that she will recognize not Mrs. Donato, as the authorities seem to believe, but Mrs. Heath. . . .*"

Mary said somberly, "The blame is ours. If we had listened to him, we might have saved his life."

The door opened suddenly. Miss Moffett's pompadour popped in. "Oh. . . . What's this? I didn't know you were all here. . . . Miss Templeton thought she saw Mr. Haskell going this way. . . . There's a call for you, Jacob. The Laneport Hospital's been phoning all over town for you. I don't know why they thought you might be here."

"You've got another room to let, Olive," the Chief said grimly. "Mr. Parsons won't be back." He followed Miss Moffett to the lobby. In two minutes, he was back, running, breathless with excitement. "They've got Isabel Chalmers at the Hospital and they've just gone up the Common to get Ramona Heath."

The switchboard attendant at the Hospital had heard a noise, like a mewing cat. He looked up from the board. There in the hall a woman had stood—a short, fat woman, with gray hair and tears streaming down a blotched, purple-stained face, a black dress that hung in shreds, daggled with burrs, brambles, dirt; hands scratched, bleeding, swollen. At first the woman had wept so violently, so ceaselessly that he could hardly understand what she was trying to say. He had called the Night Superintendent, the house doctor, and after they had washed the woman's wounds and forced a sedative upon her, she had calmed a bit and her words were plain at last: "Please get my sister. She's dying."

Up the Common hill, just beyond the fork in the road, where the bushes grew thick and low, the ambulance driver found a rude, foul cave, made of boulders with luggage piled across the wide bramble-veiled mouth to bar the entrance. There, on a bed of coats, with a valise for a pillow, lay Ramona Heath.

The stretcher had just carried her upstairs. The doctor was with her now. The telephone operator didn't think they could talk to her yet. Yes, he thought they might be able to see Miss Chalmers. He'd ask the Night Superintendent. He plugged in a cord. "Miss Craig, the Chief's here with some other people. About those women. . . . All right. Miss Craig says you can go up to Miss Chalmers."

Wisely, kindly, since all sick people were alike to them and all were suffering humans who needed their ministrations, the nurses had taken off Miss Chalmers' tattered garments, had bathed her, helped her into a clean, comfortable bed, had brought her warm milk and broth. A nurse sat at her bedside, feeding her, when they came into the room. The nurse said sympathetically, "She's starved. They've been living on berries since Sunday night."

Kneeland Babcock approached the bed. "Good evening, Miss Hendrix," he said.

Every trace of color drained from Isabel Chalmers' lips. Her face grew white as the pillows behind it, quivered like aspic. "So you know," she said. She lay still and without speaking for a long minute. Then she motioned weakly for the nurse to leave. "No more. Go to my sister. Take care of her. . . . Please, please, take care of her. . . . She'll be all right, won't she?" Anxiety tightened her face. "She won't die? Oh, please, please, please, my sister won't die? My poor, dear sister." Great sobs shook her. She moaned and rolled as if with prodigious pain. "My poor, dear sister, my darling Ramona, what have I done to you?"

Mary touched her shoulder. "You won't help your sister," she said gently. "You won't help yourself if you carry on like this."

Isabel Chalmers stared at Mary. She gulped. "You're the one who came to my room?" A shadow of a smile flickered on her lips. "You believed me. Ramona didn't. My sister didn't. She was sure that I had—she made me run away and hide." Her eyes filled with tears again. "And now I've killed her. I've killed my darling sister."

Slowly they drew the story from her—in faltering words, low-spoken—of two and a half decades of shame and concealment and two days and nights of terror on the moors.

"There were just the two of us. Mother and father died the year after Ramona was married. Ramona took me to live with them. Elmer's cousin—Elmer was Ramona's husband—his cousin Ella came to visit. She was so pretty. All the boys in town used to call on her. Sit on the porch with her. Serenade her on their mandolins. She made me stay in my room whenever her beaux came. But I could hear her telling them about me, laughing about me. She tormented me. She teased me about my size. 'The boys won't look at you when you're so fat,' she used to say. She'd snatch food out of my mouth. 'You eat too much. You can get along without food.' She made me wait on her, shine her shoes, iron her dresses, run up and down stairs all day, fetching and carrying for her. 'You're lazy. You need the exercise.' She kept at me and at me and one day I couldn't stand it any more and I picked up the kitchen knife. . . . Ramona defended me. She stood up for me in court. Elmer didn't. Elmer, her husband. He divorced her, he went away from her, because she defended me. . . . When I came out of the reformatory, Ramona took me home. 'I'll take care of you. We'll change our names,' she said. 'Nobody will ever know.' . . . She didn't trust me. I knew she didn't. She always felt I might do something terrible again. She didn't believe I had learned my lesson. . . . You don't do that twice. You see, the first time, it happens because you don't think. Because you don't realize you're so strong. You want to frighten, to hurt, to get even. And when you realize what you've done, you know that as long as you live—if they let you live—you'll never again raise a hand to any living thing. . . . Ramona didn't believe me. She watched me. Like a hawk. She wouldn't let people see me, come near me, for fear somebody'd say something and it would happen again. That's why she—why, do you know—?" Miss Chalmers' soft voice rose and sharpened with surprise, "I believe she thought I'd done that other too."

"And did you?" the Chief of Police asked.

"Of course not. . . . Why, you can't believe—why, I told them what I saw."

Kneeland Babcock came to the bedside. "Miss Hendrix." (The woman shuddered away from the name which had once been hers. Each time the District Attorney spoke it, she blanched and trembled.) "Miss Hendrix, while you were on the moors today, did you see a small, gray-haired man?"

"Mr. Parsons?"

"You know him?"

"Of course. I've seen him every summer. For years. Not to speak to. Ramona knows him to speak to. But I don't.

I don't know anybody at the Rockledge to speak to, except
Marian and Delia. And Miss Dow and Miss Moffett, of
course. But I know who he is. . . . That's how it happened,
you see. That's how it happened today. We saw him coming up the road. We saw him sitting all by himself. We
were so hungry. We were so tired. We couldn't sleep at
night. When you're out like that, when you're not used to
being out in the fields at night, everything frightens you—
the dark, the noises in the trees, things scampering over the
ground. Ramona would put her arm around me and say
'Don't be afraid, sister.' But her teeth were chattering and
I knew she was more afraid than I. Not having anything to
eat makes you sleepy too. . . . We'd sleep in the daytime.
One would sleep while the other watched. When we saw
Mr. Parsons we talked it over. Ramona said finally she'd
go and speak to him and see if he would help us—bring us
some food. There were some other people on the moors,
too, an artist and a woman. We didn't know them, so we
couldn't trust them. The day before there had been many
people. We saw you." She nodded at Mary. "But we were
afraid to speak to you. We couldn't trust anyone. We
talked about Mr. Parsons. Sister said he always seemed
like a very kind person. She thought we could trust him.
Well, we went back in the cave and Ramona tried to comb
her hair and smooth her dress, so she wouldn't look so—
so frightening. And then she went out. I must have fallen
asleep. When I opened my eyes, Ramona was there in the
cave with me, lying on the ground, writhing, vomiting. I
didn't know what to do.   I heard the cars come up the
hill. I saw the lights. I wanted to call out to them for help.
Ramona stopped me. She could hardly talk but she got
her hand over my mouth and begged me, 'For God's sake,
sister, don't let them find us now. . . . It got dark. I
couldn't see Ramona at all. The cars went away. Ramona
was groaning. And then she began to pray. . . . I couldn't
let her die."

The house physician met them in the hall. "Mrs. Heath will recover," he said. "We pumped her stomach. Washed it out. Not much more than a handful of blueberries there. Combination of hysteria, belly-ache and a tricky heart. But please don't try to talk to her now. Too weak."

Kneeland Babcock said, "Tomorrow will do. . . . This time we get an indictment. Ramona Heath for the murder of Gorham Parsons."

"And Nola Spain?" Mary asked.

"That too. Mr. Parsons thought so. Mr. Parsons named Ramona Heath. And Mr. Parsons died."

Chapter Fourteen

WITH BROOMSTICK

MISS GODWIN INSISTED. Everybody who was anybody
would be there. She had gone to all the trouble of getting
them cards. And don't think for a moment that that was
easy. Varnishing Day wasn't free for all. The Gallery tried
so hard to keep invitations down to people who really mat-
tered. Especially since the members had to pay for the tea
and cookies and the rent of Judkins' chairs. The little girl?
Oh, she was no problem at all. The Rockledge maids went
to the beach every afternoon. They'd be delighted to take
care of the child. Besides, the Whittakers wouldn't have to
stay at the Gallery all afternoon—unless they were having
a good time, which wasn't altogether beyond possibility. A
swim? Miss Godwin appreciated how they felt about that
too. It was hot and the beach was tempting. But why not
do both? Practically everyone did. Plenty of time for a
swim after the exhibition. And so, their excuses cut from
under them, the Whittakers went to Varnishing Day at
the Laneport Art Society, although, definitely, their hearts
were not in it.

Chris had groused as he squirmed into his white flannels.
"On your own responsibility, woman. This is fair warning. If no good comes of it—"

She had answered lightly, "This is culture, my sweet.
Not smallpox. Never killed anyone yet. After what we've
been through it'll be a picnic."

"Now you're talking. Don't ever give me another day
like yesterday."

Wednesday had begun at a hospital and ended in a

graveyard. The morning had been drenched in the tears of Ramona Heath and Isabel Chalmers.

Weak and wan, Mrs. Heath had found the strength to cry out, to Mr. Babcock's bald insinuations, "But I didn't touch him. I didn't even speak to him. I saw him lying there under the stones. It made me sick. That's what made me sick."

"Did you see the artist painting? And his mother?"

"Of course. They were a good way off."

"Did you see a young man crossing the Common?"

"A young man? Oh, yes. But he went past."

"You didn't see anyone approach Mr. Parsons?"

Ramona Heath's eyes had gone blank. "Nobody. . . . Oh, of course, somebody might have come up. We didn't watch every single second."

Mr. Babcock had changed his line. "You fled the Rockledge, hid on the moors because you thought your sister had killed Nola Spain?"

Mrs. Heath had gripped the counterpane then, twisting it in her writhing hands. Her answer had come through clenched teeth—flat, definite, with weary hopelessness. "But she did. Isabel killed her."

"She did, did she?" Mr. Babcock pelted her with his questions. "Why? Did she know Mrs. Spain? Had she had words with her?"

"I don't know. She won't tell me. She insists she didn't but I know she did. She did that once before. She killed a beautiful woman who taunted her. Before. And now again. . . . Oh, I've watched her, guarded her for so many years. I've tried to help her. I've given up my life for her. I've done all I could. But I've failed." She started up from the bed. "They won't hang her. They won't. She's crazy. I'll prove she's crazy. I'll save her. They don't execute people who don't know what they're doing."

But when they had stood beside Isabel Chalmers, she had given no sign of madness. Faint color in her pasty cheeks, her hair neatly brushed, she had been poised, calm, and her voice was steady, as she maintained, "I never saw Nola Spain, living or dead. Ramona may have seen her. But I didn't. No, Ramona wasn't out of her bed that night. She was fast asleep. Yes, I think Ramona killed Mr. Parsons. I think she must have killed him to protect me. He must have found out something. About that other. He must have said he'd tell the police who I was. Ramona said she'd protect me with her life. . . . Oh, but I'll save her. I've got to save her. There's some way. There must be some way to save her now."

"I'll be goddamned," Chris had summed up as they stood on the hospital steps. "Each one thinks the other's done a murder. I love my sister but she's a killer. From me to the electric chair—with love and kisses."

"They were both in this," the District Attorney had answered. "In both crimes. We'll have a full confession before we're done."

"Like Mrs. Donato's?" Mary asked. "The wish, the intent, but not the deed?"

Chris said, "We really ought to pay our respects to Alicia, too. She'll feel neglected. Nice and handy, Mr. Babcock, all your suspects tucked away in one little hospital. Why don't you move Todd Amroe in—and Paul Donato? Get 'em all under one roof."

In the afternoon there had been a solemn half hour in the stuffy chapel of Judkins' Funeral Home, where they had huddled—a handful of them—Baby Doll, Paul Donato, Todd Amroe, Fern Godwin, who had known Nola Spain in life, and the Whittakers, the District Attorney, the police who had seen her only in death—and they had looked for the last time on the chiseled marble of her face, white and small, under a blanket of golden gladiolus. There were no speeches, no eulogies, not even a prayer, for none of them knew what sort of God Nola Spain might have beseeched to receive and cleanse her soul. A last look and good-bye.

And then they had toiled after Judkins' coach to a willow-shaded country graveyard where Todd Amroe had bought his beloved a final gift of six feet of gentle earth.

In the evening there had been a grief-stricken child to comfort and console.

To Mary, at any rate, the artists' tea was a change and welcome from the days and nights of tragedy and horror. She came gratefully out of the glare of afternoon sun into the cool shade of the gallery of the Laneport Art Society. She stood in the doorway, holding her husband's arm, surveying a long room, cream-tinted, bright with the gilt of picture frames, the glow of pigment, the kaleidoscopic print of summer dresses.

The dowagers had laid aside their tweeds and bouclés, had blossomed out in swirling, swishing chiffon and broad-brimmed, garden-party hats. The shanks of their aging gallants were swathed in pin-striped flannel, and here and there a morning coat made gala doubly festive.

Sedately, by twos and threes, they paraded the long room, pausing before each canvas, bending forward, with the connoisseur's stately tilt of the rump, venturing meager, undiscriminating praise in the awe-stricken gargle which issues from the human larynx only in church or in a picture gallery. Pairs and trios flowed together into swarms along the middle of the floor, drifted back toward the table where a thin ribbon of steam floated over the polished brass of a Russian samovar, over stacked teacups, platters of grocery-store cookies.

Mrs. Lyndall stood beside the samovar. Black and white chiffon softened her cliff-like figure; a broad-brimmed hat shaded her granite face. She turned the samovar spigot, measuring hot water into the cups with the practised grace of the lady of the manor, conversing with mannerly affability with the clucking, fluttering ladies who had charge of lemon, cream and sugar.

But, even as she poured, Mrs. Lyndall gave evidence

that her mind was elsewhere. Her eyes darted over the room; came to rest when they found Ryon, followed him down the gallery. Ryon Lyndall was in a group of four—Mrs. Bean and her daughter, and a stout, blond man in a morning coat. Mr. Lyndall seemed cheerful, almost animated.

Fern Godwin swept up to Mary and Chris. "Mrs. Whittaker! My dear Mr. Whittaker! Have you been around? Have you met everyone? . . . Do let me show you my Delphine. It's on the line. On the line, of course." She linked her arm through Mary's, drew her into the gallery.

Miss Godwin's painting hung in the exact center of the left wall, a position attesting as plainly as a sworn affidavit her eminence in the art colony of Laneport. It was the portrait of a doll-faced woman in white evening dress, with cornflower eyes matching a blue drapery flung across her lap, posed woodenly in a high-backed crewel chair.

"She's Delphine Quigley. The New Haven Quigleys. Northern Tobacco. She sat for me early in July." Miss Godwin's voice pretended nonchalance but her eyes devoured their faces, avid for admiration. "Oh, I didn't care too much about that white gown myself. But she insisted. It was all I could do to get her to leave off her silver fox. I added that lovely blue scarf. It gives us the dramatic color we need. Matches her eyes. They're precious, don't you think? And her hands and that beautiful line of her throat?"

Miss Templeton rustled behind them. "It's perfectly exquisite, Miss Godwin. Like a china doll," she babbled.

Miss Godwin slanted her bosom toward Mr. Whittaker. "I especially wanted you to see it, Mr. Whittaker. Your wife said she wouldn't think of sitting for her portrait unless you—"

Christopher glared at his wife.

"Of course," Miss Godwin went on, "Mrs. Whittaker has much more personality. I'd do her with a rose background.

A soft rose, so flattering to her eyes and hair. We could start on it right away. Tomorrow morning."

Mr. Whittaker squirmed. He decided that his collar was a size too small. He looked around desperately for escape, but he saw Miss Hays advancing with Mrs. McAlistir, towing the Doctor between them. Dr. McAlistir looked as bored and miserable as Mr. Whittaker felt.

"Oh, Mr. Whittaker," Miss Hays began. "Fancy meeting you here! I never imagined detectives were interested in art."

"You forget, dear," Miss Templeton suggested helpfully, "the Mona Lisa was stolen. I always think it's so comforting to have detectives about. At least you're certain nothing will be stolen."

"We were talking about portraits," Miss Godwin interrupted. "Mr. Whittaker is thinking of having his wife's done."

"Are you really?" Mrs. McAlistir chirped. "I do wish I could persuade Alpheus to take some interest in art. He's so Philistine. Who is your favorite artist, Mr. Whittaker?"

Mr. Whittaker scratched the side of his nose. His lower lip came forward as though he were giving the question his earnest consideration. He said finally, "Frank Willard."

"Willard, did you say? *Frank* Willard? I don't believe I ever heard the name."

"That's fame for you." Mr. Whittaker sighed. "But of course you know his work?"

Mrs. McAlistir pursed her mouth. "I don't think I've ever seen it. Is he in the Academy?"

"Search me," Mr. Whittaker said blandly.

Miss Godwin said warily, "I do believe Mr. Whittaker's pulling our leg. Or else he's made a private discovery."

"Discovery? I should say not. Millions of people know Frank Willard's work."

"Really!" Miss Godwin sniffed. "What sort of things does he do?"

"Moon Mullins."

Dr. McAlistir's face brightened. But his wife said, vaguely, "Moon Mullins? Mullins, did you say? Not moonbeams, or moon-magic by any chance? . . . Have you ever head of Moon Mullins by a Frank Willard, Miss Godwin?"

Mr. Whittaker shrugged. "Can't see how you missed him. He's the tops. Moon's only part of the strip. He's the one with the banjo eyes, you know. There's Kayo, the little fellow who sleeps in a dresser drawer, and Uncle Willie and Mamie. You'd like Mamie, Mrs. McAlistir. A very strong-minded woman. Or maybe you'd find more in common with Emmy Shmaltz. She's the one that used to run a boarding house before she married Lord Plushbottom. Thin as a slat. And what a schnozzola!"

Dr. McAlistir seemed to be strangling but his wife was occupied far more with her own distress than his. "You aren't talking about one of those awful Surrealists, are you, Mr. Whittaker?"

"Surrealists? You mean the guy that paints melted watches? I should say not. I'm talking about a *real* artist. Of course, it's been pointed out to me that the drawing's better in Terry and the Pirates. Some of those women are lulus. Burma. Normandie. The Dragon Lady. But I don't know much about art. All I know is what I like. And give me Moon Mullins any time."

Dr. McAlistir found his voice at last. "Moon's not bad," he agreed, enthusiastically. "But I'm a Bungle man myself."

Mr. Whittaker thought that over. "Not bad at all, Doctor. Especially when Zooie was in the strip. Remember that, Doctor? When he ran around putting the squitch on everybody? I could use a squitch in my own business. Bet you could too, Doc. And say, how about the time Bungle got the ball club? Caught his nose in the knothole and sued the ball park. And Doodle and the Z ball and McGonigle, the mouse, and Tootsie, the elephant, who got full of wind and floated off." He chuckled deep in his abdomen. The Doctor giggled.

The ladies stared at them as though they had lapsed into madness or Jabberwocky.

Lightning struck. It all became clear to Miss Templeton. She drew a long breath. "You aren't by any chance talking about the comics, are you, Mr. Whittaker?"

"You bet your life I am," he answered.

"Oh!" Miss Templeton and Miss Hays receded. "Oh!" Miss Godwin's was a profound sigh of despair. "Oh! Such people!" Mrs. McAlistir's face was scarlet. She backed away. "Come, Alpheus."

Dr. McAlistir bent his mustache to Mr. Whittaker's ear. "I misjudged you, sir." He shook Mr. Whittaker's hand. "I apologize."

Mr. Whittaker's face was as innocent as a babe's. "What's that for? What did I do?"

"Do?" Dr. McAlistir slapped his shoulder blade. "I wish I had your courage. Thank you, thank you, my boy. . . . Er, by the way, what is your personal opinion of Dick Tracy?"

"Nix," said Mr. Whittaker. "He's too good. Too perfect for my taste."

"My point of view, exactly." Dr. McAlistir beamed again. Then he corrected his face and scuttled off to join the ladies.

Mr. Whittaker dusted his hands. "That takes care of art. I've done my duty. Now, let's go swimming, Mary."

Mrs. Whittaker shook her head stubbornly. "Oh, no, my pet. You've had your fun, now you do your penance." She put her arm through his and led him toward the pictures.

In the farthest corner of the gallery, Ryon Lyndall stood with Lorna Bean and Mrs. Bean, contemplating a painting high up the wall. As Mary and Chris drew near them, they heard Miss Bean shrilling, "But it's wonderful. Per-

fectly, perfectly wonderful. I don't see how you did it."
Her eyes were on Mr. Lyndall and not on the picture.

Praise seemed to discomfit the artist. He shifted from
one foot to the other, said uneasily, "Won't you have some
tea? Mother'll pour for you." He touched her elbow.

"Oh, no. Not tea. Let's just walk out on that lovely little
balcony."

"Enjoy yourselves, children," Mrs. Bean twittered. "I'll
run over and have my tea."

Mary and Chris moved into their place and stared at
the drab landscape above the line. Chris wrinkled his
nose. "Let's go swimming."

"What's wrong with this picture?" Mary answered.

"Everything. It's putrid."

"I didn't ask for art criticism. What's wrong with the
paint. Doesn't one side—the right hand side—look out of
balance—as though it had been padded?"

Mr. Whittaker squinted obligingly. "One side's as bad
as the other. . . . Sweetheart, the sun's shining. It's wonderful at the beach. Baby Doll misses us. We're neglect-
ing her. Let's go."

Mary moved nearer to the painting. Tentatively she
pecked at the heavy pigment with her thumb nail. Chris
slapped her hand. "Mustn't touch. Even I know better
than that."

She drew away reluctantly, looking back at the painting
with a serious, puzzled frown. She allowed Chris to lead
her to the door, but there she said, "Wait for me, darling.
I've got something to do." She came back and sought out
Fern Godwin.

"Miss Godwin, are these paintings for sale?"

"Certainly, dear." Miss Godwin's face lit up like a dollar's worth of matches. "Of course, I wouldn't want to sell
Delphine until I was sure that her husband isn't going to
buy it. He hasn't told me positively, one way or the other.
But I can wire him that somebody else is perfectly crazy

about it and to make up his mind at once. Of course it's Mrs. Quigley's portrait," she simpered. "But it's such a decorative thing, isn't it? It doesn't matter who the subject is, as long as it's a work of art."

"I'm sorry." Mary hardened her heart. "I'm interested in Ryon Lyndall's picture. Who do I speak to about that?"

Miss Godwin's mouth snapped shut. Her cheeks puffed out with indignation. "Mr. Van Alstyne is the gallery manager." She pointed at the man in the morning coat and as Mary hurried toward him, she muttered, "Pearls before swine."

Mr. Van Alstyne beamed when Mary said, "I want to buy a picture," but he arched his thin eyebrows when she told him which one. "Oh, that!" he exploded. He recovered his aplomb at once. "It's a very unusual painting. Marvelous *chiaroscuro*. A bit somber but it's caught the spirit of the moors, don't you think? Do you know Mr. Lyndall? One of our coming men. Not very widely recognized yet, except by a small circle of discriminating connoisseurs. Now, if you'll excuse me, I'll have a conference with the artist. He's around somewhere. I saw him just a moment ago. . . . Ah, there he is, out on the balcony with a young lady. One of his admirers. If you'll excuse me. . . . Wouldn't you like to talk with Mrs. Lyndall, his dear mother, while I discuss mundane matters with Mr. Lyndall?"

"I'd love to," Mary said. "If she'll talk to me."

"Of course, she will." Mr. Van Alstyne beamed again. "Mrs. Lyndall is a bit reserved about meeting strangers. One of our patrician families, you know. But when you're properly introduced. . . . That's the nice thing about Varnishing day. Gives people a chance to get acquainted in a dignified, but intimate atmosphere. Helps so much to a proper *rapport* between the artist and the collector. . . . Oh, Mrs. Lyndall—"

"Yes, Mr. Van Alstyne." Mrs. Lyndall handed a teacup to Mrs. Bean. Her face stiffened as she saw Mary.

"Mrs. Lyndall, I'd like you to meet Mrs.—I didn't quite catch the name."

"Mrs. Whittaker," Mrs. Bean assisted. "The famous Mrs. Whittaker."

The gallery manager bent toward the granite *grande dame*, whispered, "She's interested in buying Ryon's painting."

"Really!" Suspicion tinctured Mrs. Lyndall's delight.

"Suppose you give her a cup of tea while I talk to Ryon. He's out on the balcony with a young lady."

Mrs. Lyndall's glance followed his gesturing arm. "So that's where he is. Tell him I'd like to see him, please."

Mrs. Bean put down her teacup. "He's in excellent company," she said. "He's with my little girl."

"Indeed!" Mrs. Lyndall drained a cup of hot water for Mary, whisked a tea bag through it. "Lemon or cream?"

Mary answered, "Lemon and one lump, please."

Mrs. Lyndall studied Mary's face as she put in the lemon and sugar. "I didn't know you were interested in Ryon's work," she said.

"Yes, indeed." Mary smiled brightly. "Especially in this picture. . . . Of course, I don't pretend to know much about art but, as my husband says, I know what I like. You see, I watched him doing it—painting it, I mean—on the moors. And I thought then that I'd like to have that picture —well, as a reminder of the scenes of our honeymoon as much as anything else. Of course, it's a perfectly lovely picture. Such," she gulped, "such *chiaroscuro*."

Mrs. Lyndall said coldly, "I hope your art appreciation is superior to your pronunciation."

"We don't expect her to know too much about art. She has other interests," Mrs. Bean bent over the teacups. "She brought back my little girl after she was kidnaped on a yacht. She's been helping Mr. Babcock. She's very modest but I understand she's been a great help to him. She's a detective, you know. . . . Why, Mrs. Lyndall. Oh, dear you must be tired, standing so long."

A flicker, a grimace, a shadow—of pain, surprise, dismay —had passed over Mrs. Lyndall's face. A sudden thing, as though she had sat on a pin. But she recovered instantly. She said firmly, "I am not tired."

Mr. Van Alstyne came slowly across the room, the corners of his mouth sagging with disappointment. "I've bad news, Mrs. Whittaker. Mr. Lyndall doesn't want to sell. . . . Perhaps you can influence him, Mrs. Lyndall. . . . It's unusual. I know it's unusual but sometimes an artist gets attached to his work. Won't let it go for any price. He was quite adamant about it. . . . I'll tell you what I'll do, Mrs. Whittaker. Grace Hartman—she's one of our better known artists—she's done a lovely thing of the moors. I'll talk to her. Perhaps she'll let you have it for the same price—or not much more than a Lyndall."

"Don't trouble." Mrs. Whittaker rose. "I'd quite set my heart on Mr. Lyndall's painting." She nodded at Mrs. Bean and Mrs. Lyndall, scurried across the room to join her husband. "Can't do any business here," she said. "Let's go swimming."

The afternoon shadows lengthened as they lay in the warm, powdery sands of Hadley's Beach, watching the lazy sails and the floating white rags of cloud while Baby Doll heaped mountains over their bare legs and dug tunnels to their toes.

"This is the life," Chris said. "What'd you want to hang around that gallery for? And what was that nonsense about buying that dopey picture?"

"But I want it," Mary answered.

"No, ma'am. Not in my apartment. Anything but that."

"Darling." She sat up, put her hand on his arm, cajolingly. "Darling, Mary wants picture. Mary won't be happy without picture. Chris is going to get picture for Mary."

"Don't try that baby talk on me," he growled. "Besides, how'm I going to get it? The dope won't sell it. Doesn't know a sucker when he sees one."

"Steal it, darling. Don't be afraid. I know the Chief of Police."

"But the guy can't paint for sour apples," he protested. "He knows he's no good. That's why he won't sell his stuff. . . . All right, all right, don't get dramatic. I'll get it for you, even if I have to spend the rest of my life in jail. But Lyndall's work stinks, I tell you."

"Not so loud." She gripped his arm. "There's his mother."

Mr. Whittaker sat up too. "Well! Well! Her majesty goes to the bath."

A regal procession plodded across the strand, advancing on the turquoise sea—three majestic ladies, pushing their shapeless shadows before: Miss Templeton, Miss Hays and Mrs. Lyndall, pock-marking the sand with her cane. Flowing beach robes swathed them from neck to ankle; wide beach hats flapped over their faces. They looked neither to left nor right.

A foot from the water's edge, they squatted down together, pulled off their shoes, slipped back their bathrobes. They rose together, three water nymphs out of the fashion books of that dear, dead day before the Annette Kellerman —bathing dresses well below the knee, above the clavicle, liver-spotted arms alone nude to sun and sky and ogling glance.

Shuddering coyly with each advancing step, they tripped toward the sea. Across the wet sand lay the tracks of their discreetly stockinged feet. Two pairs of tracks were long and slender but the prints of the woman who walked between them were wide, grotesque, distorted. Swollen knuckle joint and big toe together left a mark like a cloven hoof.

Thus Mary saw it again, in the wet sands at the rim of the sea. But why, she asked herself? And how? . . . In stocking feet, of course. Footsteps in the fog are soft. What was that line? *"The fog comes on little cat feet."*

Her eyes saw the footprints in the sand; her mind, the murderer stealing through the fog, squatting down to take off shoes—to make no noise, to rouse no one—balancing herself on tiptoe outside the window, open to the room where a woman and a child—

She said, "Baby Doll, come here." She held the child tightly against her side.

The ladies dipped, once, twice, three times; up to their hips, to their bosoms, to their collarbones. They shivered. They looked reproachfully at the declining sun. They dipped again. Then they splashed heavily through the surf. They wrung their skirt hems. They swathed themselves in flannel and terry cloth. Baby Doll stared at them.

Esther Lyndall came up from the sea, her beach wrap belling around her, her gray hair straggling under her peaked beach hat, her cane before her.

Baby Doll stiffened. She buried her head in Mary's shoulder and wept into her neck. "Don't make me look at her, Mary. Don't make me see that witch again."

Chapter Fifteen

EXORCISED AT LAST

THE NIGHT WAS fragrant with clethra. The sea, gold-dappled out of shore front windows, rocked gently against the piers. The Cape Point beacon winked at the spangled heavens, swept them with a milky broom, raked the dark ocean, picked out the white hull of the *Cynisca,* the figures of a man and girl strolling down a pier. The clock in a church steeple bonged the strokes of ten.

It was a still night. Moonless. Secretive. Perfect for romance and for second-story work.

Mary stood listening, wrapped in her long coat and the deep shadows of the balcony of the Laneport Art Gallery. She heard the tinkle of glass and then the loud, pervasive clang of a burglar alarm. Chris slid down a pillar, thudded to the turf. He thrust the picture at her. "Under your coat, baby. Run like hell."

They slunk along the building wall, muffled in its shadow. The siren clanged above their heads. Running feet slapped urgently on Johnson's Neck. They crept across a strip of damp grass, huddled in the lee of a darkened building. Before them stretched the harbor; behind them the road full of burglar-hunters. Under Mary's sport coat was three feet by two of stiff, unyielding, framed canvas.

"No use. We can't make it." Mary put the picture on the ground. "Turn on your light, Chris," she commanded.

Crouching, she shaded the flashbeam with her coat, took out a hairpin. While Chris played the light above the canvas, she dug into the paint which had formed the square, heavy boulder, scraped it ruthlessly. The thick pigment came away easily. Beneath it, she saw, not the coarse mesh of canvas, but the smooth surface of a folded sheet of paper, held firmly under a film of shellac. She plucked at the varnish and held a thin sheet of paper in her hand. She unfolded it, glanced quickly at a salutation and a signature. A scream—a piercing, terrified outcry—bit the darkness, dissolved into the shouts and clamor on Johnson's Neck.

Chris snapped off the flashlight. "What's that? Where'd it come from?"

They heard the sharp syllables of anger—a woman's voice and a man's. The voices came from the water's edge.

Chris gripped Mary's hand and they ran, wading through garden plots, stumbling over back-yard debris, in the direction from which the scream had come. They saw as they ran, out on a dock, over the water, a man struggling in the arms of a tall woman.

The voices were words now, the man crying despairingly, "Let me go. Let me go. She'll drown." The woman: "I won't let you. I won't lose you now." They saw the man wrench himself free, fling himself into the water, the woman dash to the end of the string-piece, stand there a moment, wailing, "Ryon! Ryon!" The splash of swimming limbs answered her.

Chris Whittaker threw off his coat. He turned on his flashbeam, gave it to Mary, saying flippantly, "Keep a light in the window for me, darling."

The woman on the string-piece heard him, saw the light. She began to run. Chris shot past her, going the other way, shouting, "Hold on. I'm coming," as he dived into the dark tides of Laneport harbor.

The woman ran heavily, clumsily. The cane in her hand hooked into the soft, rotten planking of the dock. She stumbled. Mary caught her as she fell. The flashlight dropped to the pier, rolled into the water.

Mary's arms closed like a vise. The huge woman sagged

against them, dazed, done in, and she gasped, "Oh, God! Oh, God, help me!"

Mary said softly, "The show's over. Take it easy now. There's nothing you can do."

"Eh?" Slackness dropped away like a discarded garment. Esther Lyndall's frame grew taut. She raised her head. Her eyes glistened in the darkness. Hoarse with fury, she breathed, "Let me go, you little fool. Let me go." She struggled, squirming desperately. She was strong, Mary realized. Frenzy gave her the strength of ten. But her arms were pinned across her chest. She could not free them.

Suddenly, Esther Lyndall's jaw crashed against Mary's skull. She butted the smaller woman's face like a goat. Mary's nose spurted blood. Mrs. Lyndall bobbed her head again. Her teeth sank into Mary's wrist. The sharp pain brought a scream of anguish but Mary's arms did not relax. The woman's knees pressed upward against her abdomen, kicking, prodding savagely, working rhythmically, like hammers, pounding, forcing Mary back, inch by inch. Her breath was the staccato puff of an engine—hot, foul.

"Stop that, you devil! Stop that!" The agony was unbearable. *A minute more. One minute more. If I can just hang on. Oh, Chris, where are you? Why doesn't someone come?* . . . "Help!" Mary screamed with ebbing strength. "Help! Help! Murder!" Her arms grew limp at last. The stars swirled.

Chris looked so funny. His wet hair was plastered in a Hitler forelock against his brow; a rivulet trickled down his long sharp nose; a green ribbon of seaweed lay across his chest; the Atlantic Ocean oozed from him. In the pale crisscrossing light of flashbeams, he seemed a weird creature—something fished from the bottom of the sea. But his voice was warm and real and deep with emotion as he asked, "You're all right, darling?"

Mary struggled to sit up. The pain across her middle was excruciating. She fought back faintness. "Did they get her?"

Chris knelt in a pool beside her, propped her with his arm. "Got both of them," he said. "The old lady's in the hoosegow. The girl's back in mama's arms. Imagine trying to get away with that! Pushing a kid into the water!"

"Who?" she asked sharply.

He laughed sourly. "You'll never guess. Little string Bean. Lorna Doone. Old Lady Lyndall dumped her in the harbor. That'll teach her not to fool around with mama's boy."

Mary closed her eyes to shut out the image of the monstrous gray woman. When she opened them again, Jake Haskell was circling a ring of curious faces, pushing people back, repeating, "The lady's all right. Stand back. Stand back." And then she heard Ryon Lyndall's voice, complaining through chattering teeth, "I don't know what got into mother. How could she do a thing like that? Where have they taken her?" She put her hand into her pocket and she felt the reassuring crackle of the letter.

Chris asked, "Think you can walk, honey? Got to get some dry clothes. Night bathing isn't what it's cracked up to be."

Though it was past closing time, Miss Moffett made a fresh fire in the lobby and Mary sprawled gratefully on a sofa before it while Chris changed his clothes. He had telephoned to Kneeland Babcock at her behest, had asked the District Attorney to come at once and bring young Lyndall with him.

Miss Moffett had shooed Miss Godwin, Miss Templeton away. "Let Mrs. Whittaker rest. Run over to the Annex, won't you, and see if poor Lorna Bean needs anything. . . . I'll make some hot coffee for you, Mrs. Whittaker."

When Miss Moffett had trotted off to fetch the coffee,

Mary took Ryon Lyndall's letter from her pocket and at long last she read:

Dear Ryon,—It's years since you've heard from me but a lady in distress may surely turn to the man whom she once called husband. A great deal of water has gone under the bridge since we had our two brief weeks. I have kept my word to your mother. I have never tried to communicate with you. Not even when things seemed most difficult. And they have been very hard. I know you would have helped if I had told you—out of simple, human generosity—if not out of any love for me. I know only too well that what is undying passion at sixteen—or your nineteen—seems idiotic when one looks back with the sober eyes of maturity. I will not task you with the memory.

Even now, I do not ask you to help me. I only mean to suggest a way in which you may, if you wish, be of service to one who is dear to me. My little girl. My child has no father. When I am gone there is no next of kin to care for her. I may not live much longer. My heart has been doing tricks. I'm not concerned for myself. Whatever is ahead cannot be worse than what has already been. I have had my hell on earth—and only a glimpse of heaven. So that I do not fear the one and hope for the other. But it worries me a great deal to think that I may have to leave my Baby Doll to strangers.

I don't know what your circumstances are—perhaps you have a wife and children of your own by this time. But if it is at all possible, I should like you to take an interest in my little girl. Am I asking too much?

I thought of you because I ran into my old friend, Paul Donato, the other day and he asked me to come to Laneport to pose for him. We'll leave any day—as soon as I can sub-let my room. I hadn't seen Paul since we did the "Fairy Princess." Perhaps you have seen it. It was a nice thing but I got sick of it. It caused me too much trouble. When Paul said Laneport, I remembered that was where your family had a summer place and it occurred to me that, if you still lived there, a letter would reach you. The post office might know where to forward it, anyway.

If we could meet, quite casually, perhaps at Paul's, while I am in Laneport and you got to know my Baby Doll, I think you might be willing to do something—for her sake, if not for mine. In any case, I don't intend to bother you or to make any claim upon you. I have forgiven everything. . . . Nola.

The letter dropped into Mary's lap and she turned her face toward the leaping fire. So this was the struggle for possession—for a mother-ridden man called Ryon Lyndall. A struggle between two women for a timid, ineffectual man who lived like a boy. But was it a struggle? Nola Spain no longer claimed him. She asked so little. Not the renewal of love. Not the fulfillment of duty or the payment of debt. Merely a modicum of interest, protection for a child. If Esther Lyndall had read this letter, she surely must have realized that Nola Spain claimed neither the body nor the soul of the man who had been her husband. But had she read it? And why had Ryon Lyndall hidden the paper, buried it under layers of paint? What a strange person he was! Queer. Driven to peculiar ways by the possessiveness of his mother. Esther Lyndall was a demon. But, surely, Ryon Lyndall must have known that Nola Spain had come and died. He must have known that she was murdered. Was he trying to shield his mother? Perhaps he had even conspired with her. Helped her without knowing what he was doing. While he was drunk. Drunk in the fog. "Nya, nya, said the little fox." The little fox, jeering at the hunters. . . . So Esther Lyndall was the hunter, holding the desperate little fox at bay.

Chris came in and sat down on the sofa with her. "Are you all right, darling?"

She answered him with her own solicitude. "Are you?" She gave him the letter.

He was reading it when the front door opened and Kneeland Babcock led Ryon Lyndall into the Rockledge.

Mr. Lyndall's damp beard glistened; he was pale but he bore himself with a sprightliness that was new and becoming and his hazel eyes seemed fully awake. He looked around the Rockledge lobby with a sort of timid eagerness. Miss Moffett, entering with Mary's coffee, saw him, gasped, "You, Ryon! Why, you've never been here before!"

"Miss Bean?" he faltered to her. "I came to see her. Is she all right?"

Mr. Babcock spoke before Miss Moffet answered, "Not just yet, Lyndall. Save Miss Bean. We want to talk to you first." He took Ryon Lyndall's arm, propelled him toward the sofa. The small man darted from his clutch, swooped down on Chris. "My letter. How did you get my letter?"

Mary said, "So Nola Spain was your wife?"

"Spain?" His eyes clouded. "My wife was Nola Andrews."

Mary scrambled to her feet and went, wincing with pain, around the sofa, lifted the bronze image of the murdered woman from the mantel shelf. She gave it to Ryon Lyndall. He caressed the flowing metal hair, the sleek chocolate-smooth arms. His eyes filled.

"There's the motive," Mary said. She took the statue back from Ryon. "Tell us about yourself and Nola."

"Why?" he asked. "What has that to do with the way mother acted tonight?" His eyes were frightened now. They fluttered, echoing his question, from Miss Moffett's familiar countenance to the inquisitive faces of Mary and Chris and back to the stern visage of the District Attorney.

Mary said, "It has everything to do with it. Mr. Babcock needs to know."

Ryon began, slowly, fearfully, crouching in a deep arm chair, his hands clasped over his crossed knees, dragging his words as though the thoughts they spoke came a long distance, "I married Nola Andrews back in 1925. I was studying at the Art League. She was a model there. It was one of those things that blaze up like a skyrocket. I was nineteen and she was only sixteen. She swore she was older. And the clerk at City Hall married us. We went to a little place in the country. Two weeks of paradise."

A soft glow warmed the man's yellow face. "I wrote to mother. I thought she would welcome Nola—love her as I loved her. Nola had no family, you see. She was an orphan. I was sure my mother would be glad to be a mother to her. Mother didn't answer my letter. I needed money. You see, I had only my allowance from mother. . . . Mother's always given me an allowance—even now."

He reddened, paused to dam up the flood of embarrassment. Then he went on, "Our money had given out. We couldn't leave the Inn because we couldn't pay the bill. I called mother on the phone. Finally she came. With a lawyer. She had learned somewhere, somehow, that Nola had lied about her age. They threatened us both—with all sorts of horrible things. The lawyer said I could be sent to jail for twenty years. Nola to a reformatory. They made it all seem so horribly foul. I didn't know what to do. I guess I didn't stand up awfully well. Nineteen's so young. Younger than it realizes. Nola finally agreed. She let mother annul our marriage. She let mother take me away. I don't know whether mother gave her any money. I don't think so. Mother said she paid her off. But I think it was threatening to send us to prison that did it. Nola took her things and went away and mother brought me back to Laneport. When I got here I was dreadfully sick. Nervous breakdown, they told me afterward. Mother was so good to me while I was sick. So very kind. And she would sit by my bed and tell me how lucky I was to have escaped from the clutches of an adventuress. Nola was just after our money, she assured me. Nola had heard we were rich. She had no money, no family, nothing. Was just out for what she could get. That sort of thing, mother told me, often happened to artists. They were unworldly, and designing women got hold of them and dragged them down. I must concentrate on my painting now, live for my art, and mother would help me become a great artist—be so proud of me." His voice broke. He sat with his head in his hands.

"You never saw Nola again? Never heard from her?" Mary prompted.

He shook his head sadly. "Not till this letter came. I got it Saturday morning. Picked it up at the post office on my way to Lane Common. Mother never knew about it. I'm quite sure she didn't. I hid it. I couldn't let her see it. . . . But you can't imagine what that letter did to me. You think something's dead and forgotten and suddenly it's alive. You think you, yourself, are dead. You've got used to just dragging along from day to day, doing what somebody plans for you, orders you to do. And suddenly you're a person again. That's what Nola's letter did to me. She was coming back. I was going to see her again. She wanted me to help her. But if mother knew that, she'd try to stop me from seeing her. I had to tear up the letter. But when I tried to I found I couldn't. It was Nola's. That was her handwriting. Those were her words. It was something real, something tangible, to tie me to her. I hadn't anything of hers—nothing except a memory. But how could I keep the letter? Mother took care of my things. Mother'd find it in my pockets. But I was lucky that day. Mother'd let me go up on the moors alone. And that's where I got the idea."

Fox-like cunning sharpened his eyes, his expression. "There was one way to hide the letter where mother wouldn't find it and it would be mine forever. In my painting. That was why I wouldn't sell it. Any other, I'd have been delighted. But not that one. But that was why you wanted it, wasn't it? For the letter? Not for the picture? I can't imagine how you ever saw it."

Mary smiled. "It was plain as the nose on my husband's face. Even an amateur knows that paint should be put on canvas evenly."

Ryon Lyndall's face fell. "I was sure no one would see it. And if they did, it wouldn't matter. Pigment thicker on one side than the other. Sloppy work, nothing more. . . . I stayed late on the moors that day and when I came down, I didn't feel like going home. I wanted to do something I had never done before. Something to celebrate—because I —because I—"

"Because you were a man again and not a mouse," Chris suggested.

"N-Not exactly," Ryon Lyndall stammered. "Well, all right, yes. Because I had stopped being a mouse. A sort of declaration of independence. I went into a bar on Main Street and bought a drink. Rye whiskey. First whiskey I'd ever had. And then I said what the hell and had another. And then Manuel Silva walked in. He'd been one of my models. I bought him a drink and then he made me come home with him. He had some home-made wine. He taught me some songs. One about a fox. We had a wonderful time, drinking and singing. It was the best time I'd ever had. I remember I went home feeling like a king. . . . Mother was waiting up for me. She was terribly angry. I remember she had a little steel point that she kept waving at me as though she was going to run it through me. It made me nervous. And I said, 'For godsake, put that down, you old witch, you'll kill somebody with that.'" He blushed deeply. "That was how far gone I was. Forgot myself completely. . . . What's the matter with you all? Why do you stare at me like that?"

Kneeland Babcock said huskily, "Go on, Lyndall. What did your mother say when you said that?"

Ryon Lyndall shrugged. "I don't remember. I remember she said some things about Nola. She asked me about Nola. But I was too sleepy. The next morning, she was perfectly wonderful about it all. I remembered how I'd talked to her but she never said a word about it. . . . I had the rottenest headache. My stomach. Seasick as the very devil. She was so good to me. She knows just how to make you comfortable. She's a wonderful nurse. Used to be one years ago, before she married dad."

"Knows her anatomy, eh?" Mary asked quickly.

"I guess so. Why do you ask?"

Mary passed his question by. She asked, "On Sunday, did your mother make any comment on Nola Spain—ask you any questions?"

He furrowed his brow. "I remembered her asking me whether I had seen Nola lately. I wondered if she had found out about the letter. But the canvas hadn't been touched and I knew she hadn't. I remember that I said to her, 'You know I haven't seen Nola in fifteen years,' and she answered, 'You won't see her in a good many more.' I smiled to myself when she said that because she didn't know what I know—that Nola's coming here. . . . Why, what's the matter? What *is* the matter? . . ."

Amazement blanketed their faces. Could it be that he had not heard—that he knew nothing of the murder?

"What makes you look at me like that? What did I say that's so strange? I've been waiting to see her—any day now. I meant to ask Paul Donato when she's coming. Thought I'd have a chance to speak to him at the gallery today. But he wasn't there. Or else I missed him. I was busy talking. . . . Miss Bean—" He stalled. "She's a very sympathetic young woman, isn't she?"

Mary sniffed.

"Well, she's not much for looks," Ryon Lyndall defended stoutly. "But she has character and understanding. Mother had no right to take that attitude. Mother was a perfect fiend. We were just standing out on a string-piece, looking at the water and talking. Miss Bean thought the scene would make a fine painting. And I was trying to explain to her some of the technical difficulties of painting night scenes, when there was mother behind us. She must have followed us, trailed us. I'd never seen her so furious. She was quite out of her head. She shrieked at Miss Bean, 'You adventuress!' She yelled something about not letting any adventuress get me after she had done so much to keep me."

"And so she had," Mary said solemnly. "She had killed two people to keep you for herself."

"Are you crazy?" Ryon Lyndall asked.

"She murdered two people," Mary said again. "And one of them was Nola."

They left him alone after that, to sit with head bowed, tears running through his fingers, wailing, "I wasn't worth it," sobbing his pity for himself, for his mother, for Nola.

Kneeland Babcock said, "I have to thank you, Mrs. Whittaker, for clearing this matter up for us."

"Not me," Mary answered. "Thank Chris."

"Don't be a dope. I only stole a picture."

She shook her head. "That came after. You broke the case, Chris, night before last. After Mr. Parsons' body was found, when Mr. Babcock told us the Lyndalls had been sitting nearby. You said, 'Those Lyndalls. They get around. I'd hate to have a Lyndall cross my path. Bad luck. Like a black cat.' "

"Wonderful. Wonderful," Chris jeered. "Great brain makes chance remark. Everything becomes clear as mud."

His wife patted his shoulder affectionately. "One little thought leads to another. Your idea gave me one. At every turn in this case, there were the Lyndalls. Mrs. Lyndall had been in the lobby when Nola Spain had passed through. She had gone to Paul Donato's—to hunt for Ryon. Expecting to find him there with Nola probably. She had had a chance to pick up the weapon, in the studio or in the street. Where, you'll have to find out from her. But we've just heard from Ryon that she had it. She knew the Rockledge. Possibly someone there had told her what room Mrs. Spain occupied. Did you, Miss Moffett?"

"I?" Miss Moffet's face turned green. "I?" she gasped.
. . . But the scene in the lobby came back to her clearly:
the women and Mr. Parsons gossiping about Nola Spain.
She heard their words once more. She said, "I didn't but
one of the girls did. Miss Templeton, I think it was. She
had the room under Miss Templeton. Miss Templeton
mentioned that."

"Thank you," Mary said. "That was perfect. Blueprint
for a murderess. Where to find the victim. And the weapon
handy. And mama's boy suddenly gone wild. What other
surmise than that he had met his former wife, had come
under her evil influence again, had taken to strong drink in
her loose company? You'll have to ask Mrs. Lyndall to
verify that, too. It's just my guess. But as far as we knew,
the Lyndalls were only bystanders—background for murder. Nobody gave them more than casual thought, casual
gossip. Everybody knew about them, talked about them,
but considered them part of the landscape, like the rocks,
like the sea. Well, you can't go around suspecting every
passerby of murder. It was just coincidence that their
shadows lay across both murder pictures. But coincidence
is always phony even when it's true. And when Chris called
the coincidence to my attention, I began to think seriously
about the devoted mother and her son. And the padded
paint on the picture annoyed me. If my friend, Detective
Reese, had come through, we wouldn't have had to steal
the picture. But he didn't. So we had to take the hard way
to find out why Esther Lyndall wished the artist's model
dead."

"See here, Mrs. Whittaker," the District Attorney interrupted, cracking his knuckles thoughtfully. "Your cart's
ahead of your horse. How could you have suspected that
Esther Lyndall might have had reason to kill Nola Spain
before you knew about the marriage?"

"Not suspect. Know," she corrected. "I knew that Esther
Lyndall had killed Nola Spain before I knew why. Do you

remember the cloven hoof? The strange print which Sam Dolliver and I both saw on the damp floor outside the window? I saw that print again this afternoon when Esther Lyndall walked across the sand in stocking feet."

"Now, Mrs. Whittaker," Mr. Babcock reproved her. "What do you think a jury would do, if I should be fool-hardy enough to offer a lady's pedal extremities in evidence?"

"Laugh their heads off," Mary answered promptly. "But it won't be necessary. We had an eye-witness to the murder of Nola Spain, and Mr. Parsons had a theory. A witch, he said, will always be a witch to a person who once saw her thus. Baby Doll looked at Esther Lyndall today, her cape swirling around her shoulders, her cane before her like a broomstick, and recognized the witch."

The front door creaked. A man came in—a young man, in dusty city clothes, with curly hair, a long scar down one cheek.

Chris Whittaker greeted him cordially: "Go away. I hate you."

The young man grinned. "That's no news. H'ya, Mary, darling." He glanced at Mary's bruised face. He said belligerently, "Has he been beating you again?"

Mary kissed the young man's cheek. She said, "Mr. Babcock, meet Detective Reese of the New York Police. And what, may I ask, are you doing here, Johnny?"

"An errand. You asked me for something, didn't you?" Detective Reese fished in the lining of his coat, grumbling, "Spent a whole damn week on it." He drew out a notebook, flipped its pages. "Reese always delivers. Here it is: Nola Andrews—Ryon Lyndall, married June 14, 1925."

"We know it," Mary said. "There's the bridegroom in the corner."

"You had to come three hundred miles to deliver it in person," Chris growled. "Western Union isn't efficient enough for Detective Reese?"

"Now listen, now listen, Whittaker—"

"Nice business," Chris went on. "If you had half the sense you were born with, if you'd have sent a wire, Mary wouldn't have had to take a beating."

"Aha," Detective Reese swung on his heel, shook his fist under Mr. Whittaker's chin. "I knew you wouldn't treat her right. Goldarn shame to waste a girl like that on you."

Mr. Whittaker yawned. "Give him a room in the Annex, Miss Moffett," he said. "That's where the customers get killed. He deserves it. The nerve of him, busting in on my nice, peaceful honeymoon."